COPYRIGHT

This is a work of fiction. Names, characters, organizations, places, events, and incidents are either products of the author's imagination or are used fictitiously. Any resemblance to actual persons, living or dead, or actual events is purely coincidental.

However, the cities and sites described in the Dominican Republic, Mexico, the United States of America, and Europe are very real.

Text copyright © 2021. All rights reserved.

No part of this book may be reproduced, or stored in a retrieval system, or transmitted in any form or by any means, electronic, mechanical, photocopying, recording, or otherwise without express written permission of the publisher.

First edition

www.vincentjwallace.com

DEDICATION

To my wife ... for all her support, her many recommendations as I was writing this novel, and her unconditional love. Love you "woman", for the rest of our lives.

To my daughters, my parents, brother and sister, brothers and sisters-in-law, nephews, and the five adorable children in our family. Thank you for your love and for always being there.

To my editor Hugh Cook. Your invaluable, constructive, detailed, and thoughtful recommendations helped me polish my manuscript and finish with a better book. I appreciate your kindness, patience, and the encouraging comments as well.

CHAPTER 1

Alexander Stern had agreed to leave his job. He wouldn't continue inside a toxic bubble. Immediately, he felt some anxiety; tuition needed to be paid, as well as rent and groceries. He was concerned about his loans, including his mortgage, a substantial one. But most of all, he was worried about his dreams.

Many important milestones had dissipated, at least temporarily. The next anniversary trip was canceled in his mind.

He expected to get another job soon but getting there was another story. A Saturday meeting in July with the President and general manager of the company was definitely not to have drinks.

After feeling anxious, he felt sad. His team, his friends, his business partners–the real ones. Almost seven years working there. He felt thinking of them a loss of time, an effort thrown into the garbage. Politics. More than in government. He did not know then that afternoon was preparing him for significant success months ahead.

After a minute of conversation with both executives, he felt somehow relieved. Everyone was expecting that agreement soon, and he had made plans accordingly. A negotiation with another company might start soon, and he had bet on that.

Anyway, nostalgia invaded him. That decision crystalized before it should, he thought. But actually, it was the perfect timing for him. He would get much more cash than he expected to receive when leaving the bank. He had to agree with both gentlemen the details, although confirmation would come days after their meeting. Some approvals were needed, but both executives would make sure to get them. It was better for all. Too many secrets were a precious asset. Notwithstanding, his loyalty would be rewarded.

Alexander had been tempted to leave the bank before. Several opportunities had come years back. He was too loyal. Stupidly and naively loyal. He had confirmed that gut speaks wise, not loud, not clear, but regularly smart and right. It speaks from our unconscious mind, although we prefer senses to decide. He meditated deeply for a minute in silence while the President was in the bathroom and the general manager was scrolling down his phone, not willing to talk and avoiding eye contact. An awkward moment, but it was better that way.

The last day of August was agreed for him to leave the company. Controversial thoughts were spinning inside his head, and his heart felt pressed. After a deep breath, he felt a breeze of peacefulness.
This is what I really wanted, time to move forward, he thought.
The conversation shifted topics as if no one wanted to talk extensively about his resignation. Neither he nor both men wanted. After the preliminary agreement and ten minutes of casual conversation, Alexander excused himself. All shook hands and then walked out of the office.

The elevator was his choice, not willing to walk the stairs three floors down to his office as he usually did.
"No regrets," he said aloud inside that silver-plated box. Nonetheless, there are always some regrets; we are humans. We learn to live with them. He remembered the nice words one of the owners of his previous employer said at his farewell party: "Alexander, you're leaving as a Repo. We'll bring you back home." It would result in a quasi-seven-year bond, but he would be back.

Both men continued discussing the details. What to include in the package? What would be approved? After half an hour, they reached an agreement.

"This would need the approval of the board," the President said.

"We need to get it," the general manager added while both calculated some numbers and agreed on them.

It was fair, but most of all, they had to play it safe. It was safer for everyone. Both men agreed to ask Alexander for a list of requests to ensure all were aligned.

After passing the glass door outside the elevator, he turned left. His office was steps away. The whole floor was quiet. Nobody was expected to be there ten minutes before 2:00 p.m. on the weekend. It was different than the long weekdays or weekends when budget meetings were scheduled.

He came into his office and walked around his bamboo-color manufactured-wood desk; between it and the window lay a view of the south parking lot. He pulled back his graphite ergonomic chair and sat on the comfortable mesh while resting his arms in the pads. After shifting his body to get more comfortable, he looked to the wall at his right. He knew Gabrielle didn't like his Alberto Ulloa painting, but he would have to take it home before it could be hung at a new office.

A text appeared on his phone.

"????," Gabrielle typed.

He'd been expecting that message anytime. The meeting with the President and the general manager was scheduled at noon, but it started five minutes after one. The President arrived late. Alexander preferred to pick up the phone and dialed Gabrielle.

"Hi, I just came out from the meeting. I'm closing the office and driving home."

"How was it?"

"As we expected."

"OK. I'll wait for you for lunch. I'll see you here."

He grabbed his car key, security tag, and walked out of his office. Standing at the door, he saw inside for a few seconds. He would miss it for some time. He got into his SUV and fifteen minutes later he was driving into his apartment building. He felt a mix of emotions on his quiet way back home. The electric gate started opening when a new text arrived. The general manager asked him to send an email detailing what he wanted to submit for approval.

Gabrielle hugged him when he walked into the kitchen. Lunch was ready, so he and Gabrielle agreed to discuss his meeting later. They didn't want to have that conversation in front of Andrea or Brenda. No one else had to get worried unnecessarily.

Brenda has cooked one of his favorite meals. A grilled salmon with Chinola sauce and Integral rice. Once a week, she prepared it for the family. Alexander and Andrea loved it. Gabrielle knew he would be feeling down somehow after the meeting, so she wanted to motivate him. Food was always an effective resource for such a purpose. If she had added ice cream for dessert, he would feel even better. No one would ever think this homemade sauce recipe would be massively produced by Gabrielle's business and be sold locally and overseas.

After lunch, he went to the studio and Gabrielle followed him two minutes later. Alexander made a summary of the meeting. She looked down at the floor when he finished. Her face showed an uncommon somberness.

"We'll be fine, Alex. This decision would be for a good reason, and God had always protected us," she said more loudly than usual and added, "A toxic ambiance is not worthy."

Alexander nodded. He could feel her mix of worriedness and deception. The same one he'd experienced about an hour ago but knowing it would be for the best.

A couple of days back, he had been contacted by his previous boss and friend, William Braxon. A job was vacant, but he still needed final approval to move forward and hire someone. Alexander was at the top of his list.

Without news from him yet, he decided to start contacting headhunters. Then he made some forecasts to understand how many months they could make it until he found a new income source, or after one of his previous businesses was reactivated. Maybe both. Sixteen months, if his vehicle was sold, they would have to keep their current lifestyle and pay their debts.

Gabrielle spent two hours with her two sisters and her mother drinking coffee and playing Parchís, a custom to keep the eighty-five-year-old woman entertained. She enjoyed it. Her older sister noticed something different about her.

"You're kind of quiet today, Gabrielle."

"I'm just tired," she said while preparing to leave. She didn't want to talk about it. She and Alexander had agreed on discretion until they had a plan.

She was somewhat distracted on her way back home, thinking about Alexander's meeting.

"Shiiiit," she yelled while the tires screeched when a sudden stop halfway home. She was only three feet away from the red sedan in front of her. She got out once the car stopped and smelled the tires burn.

"The hell with them," she said.

She accelerated again, completely focused and driving more slowly now. Once at home, she went to the studio. Alexander was still there. She gave him a kiss and a hug.

"We'll be fine. We've always been."

They didn't talk about leaving the bank for the rest of the weekend.

His scheduled Monday meeting with his directors started on time. A team he respected and had become his friends.

After his speech, a long silence followed. It looked like a funeral. Well, funerals were noisier. Some nodded side to side, disapproving of his decision to resign. He had to speak with them before sending an email to everyone in less than an hour.

The following five weeks were busier than many others. He wanted to leave all pending items closed. Not much time to think about anything else than work.

On Thursday, his assistant brought some brown carton boxes he had requested. He saw them after lunch and somehow felt relieved. That didn't happen with part of his staff.

"This is actually true," a credit analyst told him before leaving his office.

On Friday, he arrived early and assembled two boxes. He filled it with books and personal files. He left them on the meeting table in front of his desk. One of his more loyal friends saw them and later came back accompanied by another team member.

"Alex, please give me your vehicle's key."

"What for?"

"We'll put these boxes inside it. We can't see them here for three more weeks," she answered quietly.

***

Next Tuesday, Alexander's mother called him early in the morning. It was a strange call; they never used to talk at such time.

"Hi, Mom, how are you?"

"Hello, Alex. Please don't worry. Your father is not feeling well. He's kind of tired. We're taking him to the hospital for a check-up."

"But what's the problem? Did you call his doctor?"

"Dad stayed by our bed the whole day yesterday. He didn't go up to take any of his meals and ate them in bed.

Alex, the driver arrived. I'll put Dad on for you to say hello."

Several seconds of silence worried him more.

"Hi, son, how are you?" his father said slowly.

"Fine, dad. Worried. How are you?"

"Don't be. I'm just feeling tired. I'd better go to the hospital. We'll call you later."

"OK, dad, let me know how you're feeling later."

"Sure, son. Bye."

"Bye, Daddy."

After hanging up, Alexander remained concerned. His father didn't sound very bad, but it was strange to go to the hospital just for feeling tired. He called his brother right away.

"Hi, Matt, how are you?"

"Ey, I guess Mom already called you?"

"Yes, she left me worried. What's going on?"

"I'm not sure, Alex. I'm in Mexico City now, but I'm driving immediately to Acapulco. I'll call you later when I arrive."

"Perfect, Matt. Drive safe, and please call me as soon as you have any information."

"I'll do that."

Alexander called her mother several times in the following hours, the first one before his father was admitted at the hospital, other calls until his brother arrived. He was waiting for more news about his father. Alexander's mother sounded concerned. When Matt arrived at the hospital, he dialed Alexander.

"Alex. Dad is in a coma."

"What?" he said, almost whispering.

"Yes. I was able to speak with him for two minutes. The doctor let me get inside the ICU."

"Where?"

"The Intensive Care Unit. I'm out now. He's been tubed."

"What's the doctor saying?"

"He's not doing well. His lungs are not working properly due to the EPOC."

Alexander remained silent for some seconds, then his brother finally spoke.

"Alex, I'll call you later. Mom's crying. We'll call you back."

"OK, please call soon."

Gabrielle came into the bedroom. When she saw Alexander's face, she noticed him distraught.

"What's going on?" she asked, concerned.

After a deep breath, Alexander detailed his conversation with Matt. Both remained silent.

The next two hours were a mix of concern and sadness. They were expecting the worst, and his mother was not taking it well.

His sister Paula arrived forty-five minutes later. Everyone was waiting for an update from the doctor. All were hoping that his father showed a miraculous improvement. Ten minutes before 4:00 p.m., the doctor approached them.

"Look, Mr. Stern is not doing well. I'm letting you come and see him inside the ICU. Just to be prepared, if you wish, I can call the chaplain."

Her sister nodded, and the four of them started walking.

Once inside, his mother came closer to her husband, at the right side of his bed. Matt stayed beside her, and Paula stood on the other side. She asked the doctor if they could get a phone to call Alexander. He had to speak to him.

"Sorry, phones are not allowed inside the ICU for patients or relatives," the doctor answered.

When he saw her face, he said, "I can lend you mine."

"But it's a long-distance call, doctor. Alex lives in the Dominican Republic. I can use mine."

"Don't worry. Please use mine," the doctor insisted while passing his phone to Paula.

Without hesitation, she grabbed her notepad where she had Alexander's number and dialed him.

"Hello?" Alexander said, not recognizing the phone number, but he knew the area code well.

"Alex, this is Paula. I am calling you from the doctor's phone. Dad isn't looking well. Do you want to say some words to him?"

"Yes, thank you."

She put the phone gently by his ear and said slightly more loudly, "Speak now, Alex."

Alexander, not prepared for that moment, waited some seconds while thinking about what to say. He wanted to say something that mattered.

"Daddy, you've been the best dad ever. I am thankful for all your love, your lessons. You've been an example for all of us. And for many. You will always live in my heart. I'll love you forever."

Alexander had to stop talking. Plenty of tears came out of his eyes as his voice quivered.

Seconds later, Paula asked, "Are you done, Alex?"
"Yes."
"We have to go now. We'll call you later, brother."
"OK."

Sadly, that day was the last time he would speak with his father.

At 4:35 p.m., his father passed away. After a long disease, he was finally resting in peace. His brother called him, crying. He spoke to her mother, too; she was crying.

A long five-year deterioration of his health, and now his father was gone. His mother was now alone, without her forty-nine-year companion. She had a whole family that would watch for her, but she would feel incredibly lonely.

After hanging up, Alexander called Gabrielle. She was inside the walk-in closet.

"Gabrielle, my father ... just died."

"I'm so sorry, Alex," she said, crying. She came to him and hugged him.

Both pulled apart kindly after several seconds.

"He should have been very tired of this disease. Too many years suffering it. Finally, he's resting," he said, then added, "We need to get there fast."

He called his daughter Rachel and explained everything. She cried after hearing the news.

"My grandpa is gone?" she asked.

"Yes, Rachel."

After some minutes of speaking about him, Alexander told her he would make all arrangements to get there on Wednesday. He would be calling her later with the final itineraries.

He spent the next half an hour making all reservations. He called the President and the bank's general manager to inform them. All plans to deliver his duties to someone else had to be postponed until his return, on the last week of August.

He canceled an important dinner he had scheduled later that night. They had planned it for some weeks with his friends. Neither Alexander nor Pablo knew their lives would be crossing again professionally in the following weeks.

CHAPTER 2

Alexander was born at the Spaniel hospital. His father, a respected civil engineer, had no words to describe his feelings. He contributed to building several projects during his long professional career, which started during his last year at university, a year before his first child arrived. He worked building hotels, ports, commercial centers, the Mexico City subway. Watching his children come to life was incomparable to any project he had worked on.

Alexander's mother dedicated practically her whole life to her family. She had a small fabrics business sold months before Alexander was born. She opted for the priceless, but demanding, career path of being a mother.

Life granted them only three kids; they wanted at least five. A happy childhood marked Alexander's characteristic joy for life. He was a mirror of his mother and inherited discipline and work ethics from his father.

His parents' values ran inside his veins, honesty and loyalty at the top. Life would test him continuously to keep these virtues, and indeed, he would be tested soon.

When he was eleven, his father lost his job due to an economic downturn. It was ten months until he was able to get the next one. This marked and drove him when choosing a major at the university.

At fourteen, he recursed eighth grade, another impactful event in his life. "Never again," he said to Matt on his first day at the new school.

Experiencing failure and overcoming became his life story—a catalyzer to achieve his goals and the Stern Group's foundation many years ahead.

He had to fulfill six months of military service. He learned the severe impact of procrastination when he was late to sign some documents at the military central post. Having been out drinking the previous night with his friends sent him to march and other punishment every Saturday from seven to twelve, a painful but valuable lesson.

Industrial engineering was his choice at university. Since his first semester, he made new friends, some for life, and some became his partners. All had similar family values.

MBAs followed. Some were paid by their companies or their parents. Alexander paid for the first six months of the two-year program with a loan from his grandmother. He repaid her with his income as a credit analyst and profits of two entrepreneurial endeavors. His first employer, an international bank, paid the remaining eighteen months.

One of his business activities was selling trademark apparel bought at San Antonio and Austin's outlets. The other was framing lithographs of famous artists and musicians. Both paid for debts and entertainment.

"Alex, why don't you take an airplane instead of a bus?" his mother asked one day.

"Mom, a flight to Texas is too expensive."

He had to take a fifteen-hour bus ride on Friday afternoons, arriving twelve hours later at his uncle's home in Laredo. He shopped all Saturday and on Sunday afternoons, and he was back on the bus, arriving before six on Monday morning to be at his 7:00 a.m. class. It was exhausting, but it was the only feasible option for him to make a decent profit.

Being successful with his micro-business didn't diminish his strong hope to enter a large corporation. Brokerage firms were his first choice. He soon realized that he was not theirs when he was rejected twice. Paradoxically, he would achieve his dream many years later. After several intents, he finally entered the bank and rose quickly by accepting challenging assignments.

He met his first wife (the first administration) a month after getting his first job. They got married a year later, and after four months, they moved to Monterrey, where the bank offered him a new position. Stephen, his new boss, was a distinguished American banker, a true gentleman who, twelve months later, would help him to make one of his dreams true.

His daughter Rachel was born seven months after they moved to Monterrey. He would never forget the moment at the hospital when the doctor told him that she was healthy. He went to the bathroom of their assigned room and cried several minutes, unloading all the tension accumulated in the last twenty-four hours. More relaxed, he felt happy as never before.

***

A year later, Stephen called him to his office.

"Hi, Alex. I've just received a call from the regional office. They're requesting candidates for a new vacant position in a Caribbean island. We have a business there."

"What position?"

"Risk manager for the consumer business. Would you be interested?"

"Of course."

"Don't you want to check at home first?"

"Yes, but it's something we've discussed previously. I'm interested."

"OK. I think it would be a good fit for you. You'll need to travel for an interview."

"Not a problem, Steve. Thank you for your recommendation."

The following week he was on an airplane reviewing his notes and preparing for his interviews. He researched the business and realized that the position had not been filled the last eighteen months, but he didn't pay much attention to this fact.

Interviews were held as planned, and he felt great about them. He would not realize that he was not the chosen one until he returned home. It was demoralizing as he was so enthusiastic about the position.

On Friday of the following week, he received a call from the recruiter.

"Alexander, would you still be interested in the position?"

He was surprised to be called again.

"What happened to the other candidate?"

"He just advised us that he's leaving the bank. Do you want to continue with the process?"

"Yes."

He didn't believe the job was being offered to him. He had even bought a car during the week, but he didn't care about it. When he received the offer, there was little to discuss it. It was a generous one. He accepted it on Monday.

During next week, he settled everything, and in seven weeks, he was transferred to his new hometown. A new chapter in his life, an important one, was about to start.

***

The Dominican Republic shared about two-thirds of Hispaniola island with Haiti. The eight million habitants, when he arrived, had increased to more than ten.

The country was blessed with some of the best beaches in the world, many still inhabited and hidden. The country had beautiful landscapes in the north, south, and east regions.

The most valued asset of the country was its people. Dominicans were naturally kind and helpful, especially with foreigners.

Santo Domingo de Guzman. On the afternoon of September 27th, 1999, Alexander arrived with his family.

The following day, Alexander hired a driver. They drove through the main neighborhoods, including the bank's main office.

Ninety minutes later, they were on their way to the oldest neighborhood of Santo Domingo, founded in 1498 and home of the first European settlement in the continent, namely the Spanish monarchy.

The vicinities they had just visited with buildings, malls, and modern avenues contrasted with the Colonial Zone. The Cathedral, museums, the old fortress, and the brick streets were emblematic of the zone. It boasted more than five hundred years of history and was visited not only by tourists but was loved by locals.

After visiting both museums, the Alcazar de Colon and the Royal Houses, they sat down in a restaurant right across the street. Pat'e Palo was impregnated with many years of history; the main dining room's interior felt like a medieval tavern. Maybe five hundred years ago it had been.

The first week at the bank was a reality check. Some tough decisions had to be made. In just two weeks, he gained his boss's trust despite making difficult decisions that could affect him, but were necessary. That year, the company registered a financial impact, but the following year would make record profits.

He enjoyed the four years working there, and the last year he won a major worldwide recognition, his most valued achievement at the corporation. As a risk officer, Alexander was responsible for leading all matters related to granting loans, preventing frauds, and collecting past due accounts in pro of healthy and profitable credit portfolios.

In contrast, Alexander's personal life was crashing. A mutual agreement with his wife to separate ended with a divorce. His vision to have a life-long marriage, following his parents' example, vanished.

This situation marked his last twelve months at the bank. His productivity diminished, and finally, in June of 2003, he resigned and went to a new microfinance bank in the country, where he would spend the next three years.

The last four months in that new job would be stressful. He unmasked some fraudulent activities that created a financial impact. The main executive was ousted, and months later, he left the company, which would change Alexander's life and set him on track to achieve many successes.

After his divorce and a two-year chaotic relationship with a girlfriend, he'd decided to focus on himself and avoid any formal attachment with someone for a while. He wanted to stay single for at least two years.

His plan lasted for only five months. Back from a Christmas vacation with his parents, he started dating a fellow executive at the microfinance bank. This was against his own rules, but his rules in such matters hadn't worked so far, so he trusted his gut this time.

Alexander invited her for dinner at his favorite restaurant, Peperoni. She accepted for next Sunday when she would be back with her daughter Andrea from a resort. Alexander and Gabrielle realized the commonalities in their lives, but mainly in their shared values. Their relationship started just there.

In four months, their relationship became closer every day. He asked Gabrielle to go on a trip together. Twenty days later, they arrived in New York City. They had reservations at Le Cirque, and after ordering some drinks, he removed a little box from his jacket's right pocket. He left it discreetly on the table. After a few seconds, she saw it and covered her lips with her right hand. She was not able to say a word.

"Do you want to marry me?"

"Yes, of course," she said.

"Are you completely sure, Alex? We've dated only four months."

"I'm sure," he said. "We're meant for each other. We both know that by now."

Later that year, Alexander spent Christmas with his parents, when he told them about his plans with Gabrielle. He was able to see her daughter the whole week. His ex-wife was in a good mood, or she wanted something from him. He didn't care.

After two years that she kept Rachel hidden from Alexander without even knowing where they were, he was hoping to see her as much as he could.

Alexander and Gabrielle got married in May, one year after their engagement trip. A modest reception for family and close friends. There was not too much drinking and not too much partying, but everyone enjoyed the warm and elegant ceremony.

Days later, Alexander found himself with no job, no business, and various debts, but full of hope. He had more experience now and would take advantage of it.

He founded his own company. With no news from headhunters or companies, he decided it was stupid to wait until a job opportunity came up. Their cash reserves wouldn't last long, only four months.

They started a business, a silver jewelry store importing products from Mexico. This allowed them to go there for a week after getting married and would serve as an uncommon honeymoon. Both would spend some days with Alexander's parents and Gabrielle would meet his daughter for the first time.

Rachel and Gabrielle had liked each other since the first moment. With her eight years, she didn't understand many things about his parents' relationship, but with

Gabrielle, it was another story. It was hard for them to say goodbye to Rachel. Months had passed since they'd seen her, and months would pass until the next time.

Minutes after leaving her, they were on their way to Taxco. The ninety minutes' drive passed, and before entering the city, the highway curved to surround the slopes and limited their speed, allowing them time to admire the sunlight hitting edifices enclaved in the mountain ahead. The combination of vast white walls and red roofs shining appeared to be a painting more than a real city, worthy of a talented artist.

They spent the day reviewing products while meeting with vendors, and late that afternoon, they headed for Acapulco. They didn't know their plans would change drastically.

Past midnight, the telephone rang. Alexander heard it and had a bad feeling about it. Unfortunately, he was right. His grandmother had passed away minutes before. After years of being sick and in bed, she didn't resist anymore. Alexander felt grateful to have seen her days before when they arrived.

His mother cried and then calmed down and started getting dressed. In forty-five minutes, all were inside Mr. Stern's SUV on the highway to drive four and half hours to arrive as early as possible to the Mexico City funeral.

The day after the funeral, he and Gabrielle went back home. Walking through the duty-free section before their gate, Alexander stared at Gabrielle.

"What a honeymoon. I owe you a real one," Alexander said, and she smiled softly.

"It helped to meet your family all at once, and I loved to meet Rachel."

In November of 2006, he received an unexpected email from a headhunter. He had a vacancy for a senior-risk vice-president position at the headquarters of the same international corporation Alexander had been contacted by from Europe for two different jobs months ago. He held some interviews in Stamford, near Greenwich, where his good friend Louis lived.

In early December, they offered him a job, but on the 17th, the headhunter told him that some issues came up with the visa to work in the United States. This process was tightened after the events of 9/11 years back, so the offer was finally rescinded.

At the end of March, the same company called again. He didn't believe it. Its branch in Mexico City asked him if he would be interested in a position there. This was the fourth time this company was calling him.

"Gabrielle, this should be some kind of record," he said.

"They must really want you to work for them."

By then, Alexander was completely refocused on his business. He blocked any new disappointment with it, but he would travel anyway to hear them. A week later, he was on an airplane to Mexico City, but he remained skeptical.

When he came back, he received an email from his longtime friend William Braxon. They'd met in Mexico when they worked at the same bank and they'd worked together back at the microfinance bank. William was recently assigned to Santo Domingo, where an international brokerage firm from Jamaica hired him to replicate their business model.

"Hi, Alex," the email stated. "For the brokerage firm I'm working for, I have half the positions covered, but still have others in Sales to fill. I need your help. Can we meet?"

Instead of sending him a reply, Alexander called him back.

"I guess you saw my email," William said.

"Yes, I read it. What positions do you need to cover? Do you need some contacts? I know many in risk."

"Alex, maybe I didn't explain myself well. If you're interested, I would like to offer you a position at the brokerage firm. Would you be interested in staying here instead of going back to Mexico?"

Alexander was surprised; he wasn't expecting this.

"How did you know I was in Mexico for that opportunity?"

William explained that Gabrielle had commented something vague during the week to his wife.

After some days of waiting for the other company's outcome, Alexander finally accepted William's offer.

CHAPTER 3

Alexander and Gabrielle's flight to Mexico City departed on time, at 9:11 a.m. The driver left them at the airport earlier than usual. They wouldn't risk missing their flight and not arrive at his father's funeral. While seated outside the assigned gate, Alexander was quiet. Gabrielle eyed him. Without any words from both, she felt his grief.

He would be able to be out only for the rest of the week, but he decided to help his mother more days in all she needed, so he added one more week. This time he was placing his personal life first before anything else.

Soon after the airplane started to gain altitude, Gabrielle slept. Her pill to avoid flying anxiety had begun to take effect and knocked her out. Alexander reclined his seat, plugged in his earphones to the IPAD, and played his favorite music list. He tried to read a book, but he wasn't able to focus. Thoughts of his father came incessantly back to him.

Alexander finally slept for almost the rest of their flight. He had to. He would have to drive many hours until they arrived at his father's funeral.

He opened his eyes seconds before the captain announced, "Ladies and gentlemen, as we start our descent ..."

He yawned. A three-hour nap. Once the airplane landed and they could unbuckle their seat belts, they hurried out. His father's mass was scheduled at five. They still had to lease a car and drive four and a half hours to Acapulco. It was 12:06 p.m. After waiting fifteen minutes to get their documented suitcase, both left Customs. Rachel was waiting there for them. She hugged them and walked rapidly to the rental car dealer. Minutes later, they started their long trip.

They made a quick stop at Fonda Cuatro Vientos, a place well-known for its famous Cecina (dried meat). They hadn't eaten anything on their respective flights. Twenty minutes later, they were back on the highway.

They were already delayed. Driving faster was the only chance to reduce the gap, but Alexander hadn't counted on the ten-minute loss when the highway patrol stopped them an hour later.

"Here we go again," Gabrielle said.

When both made a full stop, an officer in a blue uniform came out of his patrol car and walked by the driver's left side, his hand on his holstered gun.

"Sir, your documents, please," the officer requested while looking to the vehicle's rear and front seats.

Alexander grabbed his Dominican driver's license from his wallet and the envelope containing the car rental contract.

"Here they are, officer. I'm Mexican. Here's my passport too."

"Sir. Do you realize you were driving at ninety-three miles an hour? Why the hurry?"

"I'm sorry, officer, my father just died. We're trying to get to Acapulco before the mass; it starts at five. We arrived today from our home country."

"Wait here, Sir. I'll be back in a minute."

The officer went back to his vehicle and sat in the driver's seat, headed to the center, and apparently reviewed something on a screen. A minute later, he got out of the vehicle and returned with the documents in his hand.

"Sir, based on your situation, I'm letting you continue your trip, but you have to drive under the speed limit," he said.

Before Alexander could say a word, the officer added, "Sir. Drive carefully. You've already suffered a tragedy in your family. Don't add three more lives to it."

His words shook Alexander. "Yes, officer. Thank you."

The officer came back to his patrol car and passed their vehicle.

"Alex, of all the times a patrol has stopped us, this is the first time you manage to avoid the fine," Gabrielle said.

"How many times have you been stopped by a patrol, Dad?"

"Oh, on every trip," Gabrielle answered.

When they arrived at the funeral home, they walked the aisle until the last chapel. He located his mother and walked until he could stand by her side. They hugged each other. His mother was crying, unable to say a word.

After mass, Alexander approximated his father and touched him. With tears in his eyes, he said some words and prayed for a minute. It was one of the most difficult moments in his life. His father looked serene, as if he was sleeping. Alexander wished he'd been able to arrive one day earlier.

Most of all, Alexander remembered his father's lessons, his values, and his work ethics. His character too. He'd taught Alexander to be independent and pushed him to achieve everything on his own merits and always be a supportive husband. First was his family, without any doubt. He was loved by everyone in the family and by his friends. He was a respected leader, loyal to his people, and people were loyal to him.

On Saturday, Paula left and took Rachel to Mexico City for her flight back to Aguascalientes. Alexander was happy having seen his daughter.

Next Tuesday, while preparing breakfast for his mother, Alexander received an unexpected call. Two weeks back, he'd had a casual conversation with his previous boss, William Braxon, and with the head of human resources. Both contacted him to understand why he was leaving the bank and to know if he would be available to come back to manage one of their companies. It had been almost seven years after his job experience at the brokerage. He told them he had been contacted by another company, but he was open to considering it.

The call surprised him because it was planned with a human resources executive, but she advised him one hour earlier that the owners wanted to speak with him on the same call. He thought their condolences would be the subject, and it was. But after that, the topic changed.

"Alex, we want you to come back," one of the owners said. "We need you here, and everyone loves you, man. Would you consider coming back to us? We know you're leaving your actual job at the end of this month, or early the next one, I'm not sure."

"Of course, Sir," Alexander happily said. "I would love to go back to the company I helped launch years ago. I appreciate you wanting me back."

"Perfect, we'll prepare a formal offer for you. Please contact us as soon as you come back from Mexico to set up everything."

The owner's sister, another one of the shareholders, also had some lovely words for him. She was happy that Alexander considered their offer, and Alexander was highly enthusiastic.

He called Gabrielle to the bedroom they were staying at and told her about the call. They were happy and relieved. Alexander felt this was something he would love to do. Leading a company for them was an honor to him.

CHAPTER 4

They woke up early on Saturday. After a light breakfast, Alexander, Gabrielle, and Mrs. Stern got in the vehicle and started their way to Mexico City.

His mother was happy to be back there, despite the difficult situation. She missed the city in which she was born. Five years were too long. They made plans to visit the beauty salon, one she'd been going to for forty-five years.

After leaving her mother, they went to two nearby libraries as Gabrielle wanted to buy some valuable cookbooks for her new hobby. Alexander waited twenty minutes for her inside the car. Enough time to recall some places they had visited before while they were on a previous trip in Mexico.

***

No doubt San Miguel de Allende was the city they loved most. Some years back, after visiting Alexander's parents in Puebla, they drove their parents' SUV north-west for almost five hours to get there with Rachel.

Before getting there, they made a short driving tour through the center of Queretaro, where they were able to see a section of its famous aqueduct dated from 1738. A stone structure with more than seventy arcs about ninety-two feet high and a total longitude of more than four thousand feet.

Ninety minutes later, they arrived at "San Mike," as many called the magical city. San Miguel de Allende, a UNESCO World Heritage Site, was founded around 1550 and was one of the main tourism attractions in Mexico, admired for its well-preserved Baroque/Neoclassical colonial structures.

The historic zone was well known as it was two hundred and fifty years ago. No parking meters or traffic signals. Streets were lined with colonial houses, inhabited by city residents, or where small businesses were set up. A bohemian ambiance Alexander and Gabrielle appreciated.

Once they arrived, they walked through the center of the city. The central plaza was a beautiful landmark. The carefully maintained Jardin Allende was surrounded by cobblestone streets, as many streets of the city and other historic sites as the Parroquia de San Miguel Arcangel.

They ended up at the bar of Hank's restaurant, with some iron-gated windows. Facades were typically colored in ochre, orange, yellow, and red, and, as in many of the internal courtyards, streets were commonly adorned with bougainvillea.

Next morning, they had breakfast and went to Guanajuato, a beautiful pre-Columbian city where they would spend the day. It was well known for its Mummy museum and the underground roads, with the main one almost two miles long following the original course of the Guanajuato River.

A walk through the main streets continued with a visit to the Basilica Colegiata de Nuestra Señora de Guanajuato. Then they walked to a nearby restaurant, where the food was excellent. Before leaving, they admired the building of the University of Guanajuato, and later on, to the Callejon del Beso, one of the most famous sights to visit.

***

Gabrielle went out of the library and they drove to pick up Alexander's mother, then to the restaurant where they were meeting with some family members.

Mexico City was where all the Sterns were born, lived, grew, studied, partied, and had many life experiences. They loved the city. They regretted at some point having to leave, but they came gladly every time they could.

Twenty minutes after three, they arrived at Cambalache, a nice Argentinean restaurant. Matt was already waiting for them at the main entrance. Paula came from Puebla twenty minutes later. They ordered beverages first, including a shot of tequila Don Julio Reposado to honor Alexander's father. No one would drink Mr. Stern's shot. The same tradition as when Alexander's grandmother died, but with a beer, her preferred choice.

Ten minutes past six, they left for the church. After a small ceremony, now with more friends and family, they said goodbye for the last time to Alexander's father and deposited his ashes in a crypt where his grandmother was too, and where Mrs. Stern would accompany both, hopefully, many years after.

When the ceremony finished, they chatted with some family members, and then they spent time with Alexander's friends from the university. George, Martin, and Frederick were there.

After a twenty-minute conversation, everyone left but George, who talked with Alexander for fifteen minutes. Alexander told George that he would need a partner in a project he was hoping to launch, and he wanted him to be part of it. He agreed to have some conference calls the following week to discuss it.

They had about two hours back at the hotel before leaving for the airport. They spent some time with Mrs. Stern in her hotel room. She was quiet, sad, but looked serene. She didn't want Alexander to go, but he had no option.

Eleven days had passed, and he had to go back. It would be his last week at the bank, and he needed to train the consultant who was taking his place. After goodbyes, they left drove to the airport.

On the airplane, they slept quickly. Neither of them was able to watch the take-off. Either way, Gabrielle never enjoyed it. Getting knocked out by her usual pill was a better solution, ideal for the five-hour flight.

Minutes before landing, he had time to think about his meeting at 10:00 a.m. on Monday. He had planned a quick way to convey all his duties to the consultant.

When he asked for his name, for some reason, the general manager hesitated to disclose it and changed the subject. Alexander didn't care much about it despite it sounding strange. On Monday, he would realize why.

CHAPTER 5

First day of his last week at the bank, Alexander woke up early. Guilty of overeating in the last twelve days, he went to the gym. After a quick shower and breakfast, he went to the office.

The two-mile drive to the same place he'd gone for so long would be ended. His new office, so far, seemed to be just four blocks away from his home.

After parking at the bank, he entered through the east door. He usually used the west one, just steps from his vehicle, that allowed him to pass through all his team's desks and say a quick hello as he walked to the end of the aisle, where his office was. He wanted to prepare some updates for the consultant that were still pending. Anyway, some interruptions had to be allowed for people to give their condolences.

He received a call from the human resources assistant. The consultant was signing some documents and was being photographed for his ID tag. Alexander was advised that he would be at his office before noon.

The day started much as any given Monday. He was given some documents to sign and correspondence to check on, including various invitations for cocktails and conferences. He threw out all to the garbage. He was planning to have a kind of sabbatical just after getting out of there next Friday.

A woman knocked on his door and entered.
"Good morning, Mr. Stern. Here is the consultant."
Alexander was surprised. Someone he knew from his early days at the bank where he started his career in Mexico. Alexander worked as a credit analyst when the consultant was one of the senior managers.
"Uh, John Zent. So, it's you," he said.
"How are you, Alex?"

"Great, what a surprise."

After a hug, they sat down. The human resources woman asked if they needed lunch arrangements, but Alexander said his assistant would take care of it. After she left, both spent the next half an hour updating themselves on their past lives since they'd worked together.

"Making a long story short, your job was offered to someone who couldn't accept for personal reasons," John said. "I've been available for the last ten months as I'm unemployed, so I accepted this assignment for six to nine months."

"Six to nine months?" Alexander asked, curious.

"Yes. I don't want to be away from home for a long time. Accepting this position was challenging for me. My family is my top priority. Your boss wanted more time but not a chance."

"Fair enough," Alexander said.

They were interrupted by his assistant who requested their choices for lunch.

After that, both spent the rest of the day on everything related to the bank and some crucial warnings to help John in the following months.

After almost six hours reviewing and discussing many documents, statistics, and presentations, both agreed to stop until the next day.

Alexander stayed one more hour checking on some pending items and filling a box with some personal belongings remaining at his office. He decided not to leave that difficult task for next Friday.

Then he went back home. Gabrielle wanted to know about his day and who the new guy was. He spoke for some minutes with her, but he was exhausted. He took dinner and went to sleep.

The week passed surprisingly relaxed. He spent part of the day updating John, and the other part with his team, attending meetings and working on administrative matters.

In the last meeting held on Friday morning, a farewell breakfast was served with the main executives. He was asked to say some words. He gave a twenty-seconds speech, not willing to say much more. He didn't expect to have much contact with any of them in the future.

That day, the last one at the bank was awkward. People he was not waiting for passed to say goodbye and show their appreciation. Some were genuine, some false, of course. He was glad at least to know by then who they were. Others he was expecting didn't pass by. Somehow, he was not affected. He was willing to leave the company and start a new phase in his life.

At four, his team planned a reunion outside his office, at the open section in front of his assistant's desk, but aisles were filled too. No way to handle in that small space the one hundred and fifty persons of his business unit that were at the office that Friday. It became extremely emotional for him and many others. They gave him some words of respect, appreciated his friendship, and valued his support through the years.

By the time Alexander was asked to say something, he was deeply touched. Around twenty seconds after he started, he had to stop. His eyes crystallized, and several tears dropped down his face. He finished his speech, and after a moment of applause, everyone walked out while shaking hands with him. A moment he would never forget.

He decided to leave at five. One of the few times he left the bank that early.

Not having anything else to attend to, he recalled an experience from his last day at the bank he worked for when he arrived in the country. Minutes before leaving it, he signed the last required document. He took the seal with his name and position and punched it down on the document. Once the seal was printed, it broke up into three pieces. The director in front of him froze, as if the seal knew it was the final document he would need to print. After some seconds of astonishment, neither Alexander nor she said a word. They just looked at each other shocked.

"This must be some signal," he said.

The same experience didn't happen that Friday. He threw it into the garbage and, with nothing else to do, turned off his MAC, grabbed his portfolio, and walked out of his office.

Rose Carter, his most loyal and valued team member, one of his directors, and one of his most valued friends, accompanied him to his vehicle. He gave her his ID tag, and after a hug, he got into his vehicle and left. He would learn soon that leaving that place was the best that had happened to him so far, professionally.

CHAPTER 6

Alexander planned that September would be a sabbatical month, but his soon-to-be new employer was planning to make him an offer faster than he expected.

Spending at least thirty days or so decompressing was something he was eager to do. Alexander intended to exercise, read, rest, watch movies, and repeat all that many times, avoiding thinking about any job or business initiative. He was able to achieve such a goal for just seven days.

The following Monday, after coming back from the gym, Alexander felt anxious, as if he had missed or lost something. He thought about his previous job, but nothing was pending about it. Alexander discovered the root of his anxiety days later. After receiving hundreds of emails and several texts daily in the past, he founded himself searching for them continuously. They were close to zero. No work emails. No text messages. He realized how powerful customs were and how much time it took to eliminate them from his brain chip. It wasn't until Wednesday afternoon that he was losing that sickness of constantly checking his phone.

On Thursday morning, the human resources executive asked him to have a cup of coffee after lunch to discuss the compensation package they were working on to bring him back. They were pushing to make it similar to the one he had before at the bank.

It was a lower offer but not by much. Alexander requested she consider two minor adjustments, and they could move forward. She would work on getting the approval to issue a formal letter. They hadn't agreed on the entry date yet, but it would be soon.

Once they left, he understood while driving that his sabbatical might not be for the whole month. He had to think about the different options he had. He wanted to avoid dependence on just one source of income. He knew that the best means to continue creating wealth at his age. He had to keep a well-paid job he loved to do and some side business that he could nurture in the following months and years, to dedicate full time to it in the future.

Finally, a job offer came. They thought he would be coming in October, but a two-day meeting was planned with local and group executives to discuss and approve a plan to relaunch the company Alexander was taking care of.

He was achieving a milestone in his professional career, becoming a chief executive officer in a securities market company. Despite the company experiencing challenging times, Alexander was highly motivated to do whatever he needed to make it work.

The meeting day arrived. They spent two days reviewing technical topics, financials, and the market environment, among other considerations to get some conclusions. Alexander had checked everything the day before and had understood better what to do going forward to improve the company's situation.

On Friday, he discussed it with Gabrielle.

"Look, I'm concerned. This business is on a freefall. We reviewed many plans, but it will be challenging to make it work."

After a short silence, she added, "You knew it was not going to be easy. You need to find a way."

What a motivational speech, he thought. But it was true. He had to make it work and improve it fast.

Next Monday, in a conversation with William, he realized that some of the shareholders wanted to get out of the company. By December, a capital injection was needed, and without a sharp improvement, they would sell part or all their shares. He had three months to do something bold, but it was too soon for a huge change.

He remembered two clients he had met several years ago who had invested at the brokerage a year after it had been established. They were part of the list of forty-seven prospects Alexander wrote in a notepad during the weekend.

Two days later, he arranged a call with one of the foreign investors, now Senator Brian Cox, a Republican from Tennessee who had managed to climb the political ladder until getting to Washington. Alexander had met him when he was a candidate for state government. He won, then moved to D.C. when he was elected Senator.

Brian came to the brokerage after a meeting with Alexander in Punta Cana. Serge Arden, then the finance vice-president at a local bank, was ready to play golf on a Saturday morning. Alexander was trying to join any group as he would not be allowed to play alone, and they were three, so he was included in their foursome. He shared the golf cart with Brian, as Serge was in the other cart with Christopher Mattis, a Nashville producer of sauces and other products.

Brian was looking to invest overseas and had already done it at Serge's bank. As he was comfortable investing in the Dominican Republic, he was eager to find new alternatives. While discussing Alexander's business, he was surprised with the high rates they were offering to clients at the brokerage, in a product with government securities that served as collateral. Brian asked him to give him a call during the weekend while researching Alexander's company.

"Not a big one, just starting," Serge said. "It's part of a strong regional financial group and well-known local partners. We're doing business with them."

A day later, Brian and Christopher decided to make a modest investment.

They hadn't been in contact for many years, but Alexander hoped to bring them as investors. He sent a short email updating him with his new assignment and requesting a conference call. He was not investing anymore at the brokerage.

On Thursday morning, he received a call from the Senator's assistant.

"Good morning, Mr. Stern. Senator Cox wants to talk to you. Are you available now?"

"Hello, of course. Thank you."

Seconds later, the Senator was connected.

"Hello, Alex. Bless your heart. How are you doing?"

"Hi Brian, or Senator, how may I call you now?"

"Any way you want, Alex. But everyone calls me Senator. It's been a long and tough road to earn it," he said with a chuckle.

"Perfect, Senator. Thank you for answering my message."

"What's on your mind, Alex?"

"Senator, I'm back with the same group of the brokerage firm you used to invest with, here in Santo Domingo. I was willing if you might be interested in investing back with us. We had excellent investment alternatives in the mutual funds that I manage now."

"Alex, I'm not investing overseas. I have to go now, but I'll text you later today. Thank you. Goodbye."

Alexander was disappointed, especially with the abrupt way the Senator had closed the call. He thought he would not get any results from this short conversation.

Two minutes later, he received a text message from a number he didn't know, but he recalled the area code, 615 – Nashville. That number was not stored in his contacts.

"Hello, Alex. No names, locations, or titles, please. Sorry for hanging up so fast, but I need to be extra careful here. I'm interested to see your investment options."

"Not a problem, Sir. Thank you for calling back so fast. Congratulations, I've heard you're doing well there."

"I'm OK. Swimming with sharks. And some bite hard if you allow them."

"I can imagine, Sir."

"Send me a summary with the details and documentation that would be needed. If rates are decent, money will come from a company I own in Panama. Have to go now, but we'll be in touch."

"Thank you, Sir. You'll receive it today."

He saved the number and prepared everything in less than an hour. He sent him a two-page PDF with the investments' information and requisites to open the corporation's account.

It sounded awkward that the investment could come from a company in Panama. He thought it was not necessarily suspicious; maybe it was a common practice for political reasons.

He spent the rest of the week in meetings and calling previous investors and actual ones. The weekend passed smoothly. He and Gabrielle were thinking about the relaunch of their businesses.

He finally received a text from the Senator on Tuesday.

"Good morning, Alex. The representative of Panama's company will contact you. Let's start with five hundred thousand dollars."

"Hello, Sir. Thank you. Glad to hear that. I'll make all the arrangements."

"Have you called our friend in the south? The bad golfer?" he said, clearly referring to Christopher Mattis.

"Not yet, Sir. But I'll do it today. Next in queue. Are you still in touch?"

"Yes. We're partners now. Call him. I have to go. Take good care of my money."

"I'll do that, Sir. Thank you again."

Alexander asked a team member for Christopher's phone number. Once Alexander got it, he called him.

"Hi, Alex. Long time since our last conversation. How are you?"

"I'm fine, thank you."

"I guess you're calling for the investment options you have there. Our friend in Washington told me everything about it."

"Yes. I'm back with the same group. With other company they owned."

"He explained everything to me. I'm in. We agreed to invest the same amount. Five hundred thousand, right?"

"Yes," Alexander said.

"I'll set everything up. The same person who will contact you on his behalf will call you on mine. Same representative, but different company."

"Perfect."

"Alex, I need to run into the jet. An unexpected trip to Washington, D.C. We'll be in touch."

"OK. Thank you, Christopher. See you soon."

He was surprised to get one million that fast. His gut said it was too good to be true. It has been too easy. Due diligence was still pending, but he didn't expect any problems.

On Thursday, Alexander scheduled a lunch with a client at Trattoria Angiolino, one of his favorite restaurants, a gem two blocks away from his office. A small place with a capacity for around eighty diners, inside and outside, on the small terrace. The food was great. Outstanding service. The classic red and white squares tablecloths reinforced its vast and exquisite Italian menu.

He passed the main door at one and was escorted to his table. His client was not there yet. After answering a text on his phone, he looked up and turned his head to the right to see who was at the restaurant. He saw Serge Arden. Both nodded to each other. Alexander went up and walked seven feet to his table and shook hands with him. The person seated beside him just watched them. After seconds of casual conversation, Serge said, "Congratulations on your new position. I heard about it, back home."

"Thank you. That's right, they brought me back."

"You must have done things right the first time. Glad to hear it."

"I guess so," Alexander said, and both smiled.

"I don't know if you know each other. Let me introduce you. Fred Shultz, our new general manager at the bank."

"Not yet. Hello, how are you," Alexander said and extended his arm to shake hands.

"Hello," Fred answered coldly.

An awkward moment resulted.

"I heard you're now President of the bank, Serge. Congratulations."

"Yes, just one month ago. It's an honor for me."

Alexander saw his client arrive and was walking to their table.

"Gentlemen, I have to go. My lunch invitee just arrived. Have a good meal."

"Bye, Alexander," Serge said, while Fred didn't say a word.

Alexander went back to his table. After greetings with his client, they sat down and started speaking.

Minutes later, Alexander felt he was being observed. When he reacted and glanced at Serge's table, Fred was watching them. They both turned their eyes back to their respective tables.

Alexander and his invitee spoke incessantly during their lunch. Both knew each other, but they didn't have a longtime friendship or a strong business relationship—only some minor investments of his client at the brokerage and in a fund managed by Alexander.

An hour later, Alexander saw Serge and Fred going out of the restaurant. No goodbye ritual. Both took an aisle away from where Alexander's table was, trying to avoid them. He didn't pay much attention until his client said something.

"Alex, you know those guys, right?"

"Just Serge Arden, we played golf together once, and we'd spoken briefly at other events. He just introduced me to the other guy, Fred ... something."

"Alex, take care of that guy, not Serge, the other one, Fred Shultz."

Surprised, Alexander realized that his client knew him more than he did.

"Why is that?" he asked, curious.

"Be careful. He's dangerous."

After perceiving his client didn't want to go any more deeply into that conversation, he just changed the subject and finished with his eighteen-hour-aged ribeye.

Twenty-five minutes later, both men drank their espressos and Alexander paid the check. Outside, while waiting for the client's driver, both agreed to meet a week later to discuss some new investments he could opt for.

Alexander walked the four-hundred-meter path back to his office. He thought about his client's comment about Fred and decided to do some research into him. By then, he was more curious than concerned, something that would shift dramatically months later.

CHAPTER 7

Alexander didn't know much about Fred Shultz, only that he had been finance director reporting to Serge, then finance vice-president, and now recently appointed as general manager of the same bank, when Serge was named President. Nothing else.

A warning like that by a client, but not a close friend, sounded strange. Also, he felt weird when Serge introduced both. He seemed somewhat distant.

At his office, he went online and researched about him. Nothing relevant came on the web. He spoke to William, but he didn't know him. His meeting was about to start, so he paused his Sherlock practice.

That afternoon he went home late. He contacted many of his investors' prospects, and some promised to send some money to the funds. After a quick shower, he told Gabrielle about his lunch. She knew many financial executives but nothing about Fred. Afterward, he decided to forget about him.

Now they had available cash from the bank's handsome farewell package to invest. Alexander would make some personal investments in stocks, too, a practice that could result in a significant profit.

The next three months passed. Alexander had been able to stop the freefall with the issuance of a new tranche of the real estate fund. They hadn't started a growth path, but stopping the bleeding brought hope. He prepared for his board meeting, the last one of that year. The capital injection was the main point on the agenda. They would fail to maintain a regulatory limit if more capital was not approved. Not all shareholders were comfortable with this, but no other option to keep the company afloat.

Discussions were tense that afternoon.

"You're asking us more money now," one of the shareholders said. "And then, next year, you will be doing the same. It's time to invest in a better option."

He refused to invest more capital no matter his ownership would be reduced.

"What a Christmas gift from this gentleman," he told Gabrielle later that day.

"Wouldn't you do the same?" she asked.

After a few seconds' thought, he nodded. He needed to make a drastic improvement and was also crucial to speed up client investments.

Early next year, they would be starting their forecasting process, and if nothing relevant surged, he would have a difficult discussion with the shareholders again.

Rachel, Alexander's daughter, arrived on the fourteenth. Now twenty years old, she traveled alone without the approval of the "first administration," as Alexander called his ex-wife. She would spend fifteen days with them and return on New Year's Eve. Andrea, Gabrielle's daughter, was in Miami with his boyfriend's mother. They were visiting her as she was recovering from a liver transplant.

In the last week of December, Rachel went home. Andrea traveled to Miami and was waiting for her parents to arrive on the thirtieth. They would relax and go shopping and eating out the whole five-day trip. New Year's Eve with Andrea's future mother-in-law was a surprise. It was sort of a spontaneous party for five, with great paella, wine, and excellent music. The day after, Alexander worked for an hour. He didn't want to lose that custom on the first day of a new year, despite his headache. Too much wine from the night before still ran inside.

On January the fifth, they were back in Santo Domingo. Alexander would have to fly again on the eighth for meetings in Kingston. It would be his first time back in Jamaica since 2011, when he worked for the brokerage. He was glad to see again many friends he had made.

Three days later, he was back home. Now he had to deal again with the shareholders' concerns.

Alexander learned that the same concern the local shareholders had was shared at headquarters with the main partner.

By the end of March, the mutual funds were showing considerable improvement. The business was growing. Some shareholders were more comfortable with the new plan, and he gained additional months to deliver even better results. So, he did.

After six tough months at the company, Alexander needed his so-called therapeutic vacations to decompress. He and Gabrielle planned to travel for a week.

The Southern United States or Bogota were their inferred options on the travel bucket list. After checking about both online, he recalled that his parents once made a trip to New Orleans. They went from Puebla to the border, crossed it, and stopped in San Antonio, where they spent the night. A day later, they arrived in New Orleans.

He always liked to hear his mother telling the story of the trip when a highway patrol stopped them near Monterrey. His father was sixty-five, and his mother sixty-six. The officer came closer to their vehicle and requested their documents.

"Mrs. Stern, why were you speeding?"

"I'm sorry, officer. I didn't realize I was going too fast."

"Ninety miles per hour is fast, Mrs. Stern. And above the speed limit."

"I'm sorry, officer. I'll drive more slowly from now on."

"Seventy miles per hour is the speed limit. Mrs. Stern. At your age, reflexes aren't the same. I'll let you continue your journey without a fine, but please drive carefully."

Once the officer was gone, she said to Alexander's father, "Did you hear that? I prefer to get a fine instead of hearing the officer saying I'm old."

She was disturbed, but after some seconds, she smiled while her husband laughed.

In early March, Alexander and Gabrielle took their flight to Hartsfield Airport. Both were excited to enjoy eight days driving through the United States' Southern cities. It was the first time they would be in Atlanta City. They'd been there only to connect with another flight on their way to Mexico City or California.

After a fifty-minute dinner stop, they drove directly to the hotel in downtown Atlanta. Early the next morning, they were on their way to New Orleans. They had breakfast in a place recommended by the concierge, where pancakes were almost like a medium-sized plate and nearly an inch thick. Seven hours later, they arrived.

They liked the city, but the food was terrific. The breakfasts were great and generous. Lunch and dinner were always excellent, sometimes spicy. They were amazed by the huge river oysters, quite grotesque, some almost half the size of a slice of bread, but exquisite. They ordered them at Dickie Brennan's, a restaurant in the French Quarter, with a beer and a shot of single malt scotch whiskey. After spending four days enjoying the city, they went to their next stop, Nashville.

They had not heard much about the city. They had more days left to do something else, so they spent a couple of days there.

After check-in, they took a quick shower and went to a restaurant they knew from another city, The Palm. Excellent place. The ribeye Alexander chose was superb.

Gabrielle's spicy pasta was great too. But drinks at Rippy's bar at the next corner were even better. They were lucky to hear a great country music performer, Kenny P. They would realize later that he had been a finalist in a national talent contest.

After two days of hearing musicians in many bars along Broadway Street, their trip was coming to an end. On Friday morning, they drove back to Atlanta. The next day, they took an early flight back to Santo Domingo.

***

By the end of March, the business enjoyed its best month ever. Alexander had made good money on an online brokerage in the United States. The market was moving upward sharply, and he thought it would be an intelligent decision to bet part of his savings. He never thought this would represent an essential baseline for his future.

After eight months at his job, Alexander was gaining more respect and recognition. It had been a challenging ride, but his company was finally getting to a much better situation. Despite this, Alexander would soon realize that some enemies were flourishing inside and out of the company.

CHAPTER 8

Dedicated to growing his business, Alexander spent the following months struggling to get new customers. New relationships. From any place of the country and other countries, literally. Trips were scheduled to Santiago and Punta Cana periodically. His business was gaining traction. More calls, more visits, more clients, more investments. That was his regular speech to the sales executives. As simple as that.

His company was getting noticed in the market. Not all were fans. Fred Shultz was someone who had been paying close attention to everything they did. They haven't had any conflict, but that would change.

Many skeptics from outside the company and within the group of companies his company belonged to were starting to invest.

A young lady from the sales unit, quite ambitious and an excellent professional, supported his treasury unit. She represented more than thirty percent of the total growth.

All team members were pushing hard. All were motivated and aligned and decided to make the mutual funds business exceed all expectations.

In September, Alexander and Gabrielle joined Rachel in Paris. She would study at a university in Lyon for the rest of the year. Once she finished, she would go back to Mexico, but first to Santo Domingo.

They visited good friends in Amsterdam and Rotterdam, including one of Gabrielle's best friends since both were nine years old. Days before flying back to Santo Domingo, they visited Belgium. Brussels was lovely, but Bruges was the classic fairy tale town you imagine from books. As one friend told Alexander one day, "It's a city built for the sole purpose of enchanting everyone that visits it."

Once back, he didn't have a chance to reincorporate smoothly in the office on Monday. Discussions were held again between shareholders to decide what to do with the company. They agreed that many improvements had been made and important goals had been achieved. However, they were hoping to see better results and faster.

Alexander was able to extend discussions until the year-end board meeting. Now the decision to sell or keep the company was half divided.

On his personal investments, he had done great. The several stocks he chose early that year had increased their value sixty percent, and with the leverage he had used, he was able to double his capital.

Gabrielle's catering business was growing every day. She was becoming an extraordinary chef, specializing in pastries and appetizers, but she cooked other excellent options. The Lubina a la Sal was Alexander's favorite. After coming back from Europe, she replicated a Bruges-style salty oven-cooked chicken.

In December, a few days before year-end, Alexander and his team closed a transaction that would result in a substantial gain for his investors. Everything was set up. They were buying a property from a developer. Due diligence and all the analysis to complete the transaction had been done. Even contracts were made in time by the lawyers. He didn't know the client well, but he knew he was serious, and his projects were well recognized in the market, as was his company.

The meeting was scheduled for the afternoon of the twenty-sixth. One hour before the scheduled time, the seller called and canceled the transaction. Surprised, Alexander called him back, requesting an explanation. A month of hard work to finish all the process to close the deal and he had changed his mind that day. He didn't grant any explanations.

"Let's move forward with the next one," Alexander had to say to his team.

He spent some time thinking about it. It was strange. The developer was excited to close the transaction. He tried to research the property's status; maybe it had some kind of problem, or it had been sold already to someone else at a higher price.

He called the seller back again, but he wasn't able to contact him. He was already on vacation out of the country. He hadn't found any explanation until a good friend from another bank called him to request some information about the property. He knew Alexander was closing it recently, but he didn't know how it had finished.

"Hi Alex, how are you?"

"Fine, thank you.?"

"Great. I want to ask you about a property you were buying. It's located beside the restaurant where we meet every month."

"Yes. What about it?" Alexander asked, surprised.

"Someone is asking me to finance it, but I thought your fund was buying it."

"Not anymore," he answered, trying to show no interest in the property, but he was looking to get as much information as he could.

"You think it's a good property?"

"It depends on the price and what you want to do with it. It has some spaces that the buyer must fix to make it functional. Who's the buyer?"

"Confidentially, it's Fred Shultz and a partner, but not for his bank. It's a personal investment."

Alexander was stunned. Now he understood that Fred had had something to do with his failed transaction.

"Did you approve it already?"

"Not yet. We need to present it to the credit committee."

"OK. I have to leave for a meeting, but may I call you back?"

"Perfect. Thanks, Alex."

He spent some minutes trying to understand why the hell Fred would be willing to have that property. And how he was able to convince the developer to turn down the transaction. It didn't make sense.

I need more information on Fred, his partner, and the developer. What would be the connection between them? He thought.

After thinking about it, he called part of his team to discuss the transaction. Some weeks later, he would realize the truth.

CHAPTER 9

Gabrielle had never been particularly ambitious in the culinary art, neither for cooking for her family nor for business. Notwithstanding, she had acquired all types of kitchen tools and some cooking appliances her whole life.

When they moved to their apartment, she loved to have a complete set of open cabinets inside the kitchen pantry for all her valuable belongings.

On every trip she had made, she had bought something to add to her personal treasure. Every week, mainly on Saturdays, she went to Santo Domingo's cuisine stores.

Three years ago, after looking at all she had accumulated through several years, Gabrielle decided to take a formal culinary course trying to engage in this adventure of becoming a chef.

She started her professional career very young while still studying Marketing, helping to pay for her studies. Her parents were in a phase of their lives when money was limited, very different from when her two older sisters were at college and university.

After some years of working at a marketing agency, she shifted to working for a bank. She rose in higher positions until becoming a seasoned business manager, well recognized.

Two more banking experiences and a consulting entrepreneurship later, she and her sisters bought a couture studio where she used to purchase much of her handmade apparel. After three years of hard work and many experiences, they decided to close the business. She was not enjoying it anymore.

The following three months, Gabrielle decided to relax and wait until next year to do something else. By October, she was again looking for what to do when she saw in a magazine an ad for a culinary school in Santo

Domingo. A new set of courses was starting early next year, so she registered for the next available.

Next January, wearing a modern chef outfit that included a white shirt, black pants, and a hat, she went early on the second Monday of the month to her first cooking class ever.

The first days Gabrielle decided it was what she wanted to do with her life, professionally or not, and she dedicated many hours every day to read books, watch videos and competitions, attend webinars, and review every source of information she could appeal to, in order to learn about this art.

Alexander spent many nights with her watching a TV competition or a chef cooking a recipe while she took notes of anything she was interested in. He thought that after three months into her new hobby, she would lose interest. Maybe six months. But after six months, one more month was added, then one more, and so on.

Three years passed, and no one in the family remembers one day that she had not dedicated some hours to her hobby. Every day she had created something new, replicating a famous chef's recipe or cooking a classic restaurant dish listed on its menu. She had spent valuable hours learning. Alexander now called her "Chef" more often than the traditional "Woman" he had used for many years.

Appetizers had been her main products since her business was launched and were complemented by her innovative decorated pastries and home-produced sauces. This was the baseline of a business that would flourish in the following years, locally and overseas, and would drive them to move to the United States.

***

Jack Dowell came from a wealthy family with businesses in the construction sector. His father started very young, managing a hardware store in Santiago. After a decade, he bought it, and two years later, he opened a branch in Santo Domingo. The family became one of the most important companies in that sector.

The next logical step for the company was to start a construction business. They would be able to buy more significant amounts of materials from vendors and sell them at better prices in the market and their own construction company, resulting in a superior competitive advantage.

In 2001, with a booming industry, they started one project in Santiago, a seven-floor apartment building with twenty-one residences. A year later, they built another one with ten floors. Fourteen months later, they started two more buildings in Santiago and bought land in Santo Domingo to build a fifteen-floor project with thirty-nine apartments and two penthouses.

The father had two sons. Both heirs were in charge of different areas at the hardware store in Santiago and Santo Domingo, closely supervised by him. Jack, the younger brother, was assigned to the vendors' management unit, and his brother to the store's sales and finance operations.

After moving to Santo Domingo to study for an MBA, Jack was assigned to manage all projects in the capital. Once he finished his studies and showed some business ability, his father allowed him to lead the construction business countrywide. Dowell's Associates became one of the leading developers in the Dominican Republic.

The company continued building many projects, except in 2003 when the Dominican financial crisis broke many companies. They were lucky to finish and sell practically all their apartments before the crisis crashed. They had acquired a well-located piece of land for a new project. All architectural designs were completed, and the permits granted, but they would have to put the new project on hold until the uncertainty about what would happen in the country cleared up.

Worldwide, these businesses needed strong banking support to develop the projects and to lend money to the families willing to buy apartments. If banks were in trouble, they didn't have a chance to start construction without having the risk of leaving it halfway due to lack of funding or lack of sales.

In 2005 they started the business again. Fred's bank was the leading financier of his projects. They had met at MBA school, where they became close friends. Fred Shultz was able to finance Jack's business with favorable conditions.

Most important, when construction companies started again, his company was one of the first ones to operate, something that helped Jack to deliver projects faster than the competition. Buyers wanted to buy mainly finished projects, so he was ahead of almost everyone else.

As in the nineties, the recent crisis had hit some developers hard, and many buyers lost substantial amounts they'd paid as down payments. By then, no Trust structures were available in the country that granted more protection to buyers.

Fred's relationship with Jack gained him respect at the bank. He was not in the business unit, but he was part of a committee that granted all big-ticket loans. Many concerns were raised when approval to fund Jack's company was requested, and he struggled to get ahead with it. Once everything moved forward, Fred gained the main executives' trust. Huge loans were granted to build Jack's projects and then were shifted to mortgage loans when families acquired their homes, usually financing a seventy percent average of the property value.

Being first and with fairly good quality and price was Jack's success. Each project was bigger than the previous one: more floors, more apartments, and more square feet per apartment. Buyers of previous projects moved to bigger apartments as their families grew or just to have a better place to live.

Since 2012, as had many other developers, Dowell's Associates started to build low-cost apartments in addition to his medium and high-cost projects. This was the next phase for his business. It would be a business with less margin but a huge opportunity to boost the hardware business, as each project had a minimum of three hundred units. The land needed for these projects was considerably larger than those with ten to twelve floors, as they didn't have elevators for buildings up to four floors. That demanded a bigger piece of land, and in the central zone of Santo Domingo or nearby, options were limited.

Jack had tried to buy one of the last tracts of land available on an important avenue in Santo Domingo, near the subway and various supermarkets. It was perfect for his project. He had pushed the owner to sell, but he didn't want to, as he hoped to be part of a project built on it. Jack was unwilling to go forward with his request and lose part of the gains with a partner.

Alexander was planning to get into this business. With his banking experience, he understood it well. He knew in detail both types of projects, and he managed perfectly the financials, as he had approved many projects at his previous job. He knew the piece of land where Jack wanted to build a project, and he knew the landowner, but he didn't know Jack had intentions to buy it.

***

Alexander dedicated himself and his team to research Fred Shultz. Everything they were able to get would help them know what was going on. He had a strong feeling this was not coincidental.

Until that Wednesday, everything moved smoothly to get the deal closed. It was signed the previous Friday, but some documents from the Chamber of Commerce needing to be signed were not delivered. They waited at the office until six in the afternoon with the seller and his lawyer, and then all had to reschedule the meeting.

The team researched any online site they could to find something about Fred and the seller. Alexander made calls to people in the market who might know both, and, depending on the conversations and openness, he would ask more about them. He called the seller one more time, but his assistant told him he remained on vacation, returning the second week of January. He didn't answer a message Alexander had sent him, and he didn't know if he had read it, but he was sure that he had received it. The seller seemed not to be willing to talk to him.

Next Monday, one of his team members found a photograph of the seller with Fred Shultz. It was a kind of celebration, two years back, somehow related to the seller's company. There were two more men in the photograph, no one they'd met, but it appeared that the seller and Fred were close. The seller had his right arm on Fred's shoulder, and both smiled kindly at each other. It was evident that they knew each other.

Once Alexander saw the photograph, he called a close friend. The kind of guy who knew everything and everyone in Santo Domingo. He asked him for references for both men. His friend was very open and gave him many insights. Fred and the seller were relatives. Fred's brother-in-law was the second cousin of the seller's wife, and they often met with a group of couples from college.

Alexander and his team assumed the seller wanted to sell the property to anyone, no one in particular. It was well located and had a good tenant. They knew the seller had some financial constraints, so the two million dollars net of taxes he would receive from the sale would allow him to pay the eight hundred thousand dollars debt he had at Fred's bank and pocket the rest.

"What the fuck," one of his team members shouted.

Everything made sense. Fred needed to go to another bank, as he wouldn't get funds from his bank for that amount. Maybe their policies or lending limits to related parties didn't allow him. No way to know. But it was clear that he had heard of the transaction and was willing to get in the middle before the seller closed the deal with Alexander's fund.

Apparently, the transaction had not closed yet. His friend at the bank where Fred and his partner requested the loan had told him they were still analyzing it. Due to the amount, a committee would have to grant its final endorsement.

"Who would have a credit committee on Christmas week? Not a chance to be approved these days," Alexander said.

"Well, we were here closing a transaction this week, Alex," a team member said.

"Yes, but chances are few that this bank would have a committee this week. All members must be skiing or drinking wine somewhere else right now."

"Remember the photographs of the seller's wife last Friday on Instagram. They were all at a restaurant in Miami," another team member said.

"Right. Maybe we have a chance to stop Fred, stop the loan from being approved, or convince the seller. How can we do it?"

After a few minutes of discussion, one team member brought an idea. "With cash. Maybe we can offer an additional amount to the seller."

Alexander was reluctant to do this since an agreement with the seller had been made for an agreed amount. But it was also true that even paying a reasonable higher amount, the fund's investment would still be desirable.

After some constructive discussions, all agreed to offer up to one hundred thousand dollars more to the seller immediately after the loan was presented to the other bank committee. In this way, Fred and his partner would not have a chance, at least not soon, to go back and request an additional amount. They would need to wait at least two more weeks for new approval. That would incentivize the seller, and he needed as much cash as possible. Maybe neither Fred and his partner would pay more, nor would they have the money on hand to match the new offer.

Alexander called his friend from the bank. After a casual conversation, he managed to get the next credit committee's date. It would be held on January the eighth at 9:00 a.m. By then, the seller would be back. He decided to send a short text to the seller the night before the committee.

After all the planning, Alexander spent some days out of the office. When he returned in January, he sent the text agreed to the seller.

"Good night. I need to talk to you. If you haven't sold your property, we can make you a much better offer. Please call me."

He knew the seller was back from his trip, and he had agreed with his team to prepare all the documentation dated Wednesday the eighth. The offer would have a deadline to be signed in hours, to put some pressure on the seller and not leaving much time to Fred and his partner to come back with a counteroffer. They agreed that if the seller accepted, they would schedule the meeting that same morning to sign all documents immediately.

That night he didn't receive any response. So far, the plan seemed to have missed its goal. But the day after, early in the morning, the seller called Alexander.

"Hi, Alexander. I apologize for not answering your messages before. I was on vacation. Can you receive me at your office now?"

Alexander agreed to see him half at ten. Once the seller arrived, he received him alone at his office to have a one-on-one conversation. It would be better that way.

The meeting finished in less than twenty minutes. Without saying any names, the seller explained that a relative wanted to buy the property, but he had delayed the payment for some weeks, so he agreed to make the transaction with Alexander's fund. Then he returned the day before he signed with Alexander to move forward. But nothing appeared to be moving, and he didn't want to pay more interest on the loan he had. If Alexander's new offer was attractive enough, he would close immediately.

After agreement on the price, only fifty thousand dollars higher than the original proposal, both men agreed to sign as soon as the documentation was finished. Alexander's team had to make minor changes to the contracts and other documents, so both decided to wait in his office while someone from the seller's office brought his company's seal.

At eleven, the transaction was closed, and by noon Alexander realized that Fred already knew about it; Alexander's assistant told him he was calling and demanded to talk to him. He agreed to take the call, which resulted practically in a monologue.

"Hello," Alexander said.

"Alexander. What the fuck were you thinking about taking me down with this transaction? You don't mind getting an enemy. Now you got one."

Fred hung up without allowing Alexander to reply, but Alexander didn't care.

That afternoon, after celebrating with his team, Alexander remained at his office thinking about Fred's words. He was convinced he would have to deal with him in the future.

CHAPTER 10

In the second week of January, while Alexander watched a news channel, one conversation among two hosts grabbed his attention. A kind of disease was affecting Wuhan, a city in China. No one was clear about what it was or its magnitude. It seemed to be affecting only that city. He didn't pay much attention; it was too far from his side of the world. A reporter compared it with SARS and H1N1, and neither had drastically affected any community as far as he remembered. It sounded to be like strong flu.

The same week, Alexander held conversations with two local shareholders to share the business plan for the rest of the year. With the preliminary 2019 financials, some partners maintained their conviction to sell the business, avoid more capital injections, and accept the company's accumulated losses.

More than being demoralized, Alexander was upset. Despite the growth and constant improvement, they were still hoping to sell their shares to other partners or someone else. He still had to meet with the other local shareholder to discuss it.

A week later, two executives from Jamaica were coming to discuss the financials of all companies of the group in the country. He had seen some signals that concerned him. Information related to the company's value, shareholders, and expenses was recently requested. He was worried that the main shareholder could be shifting to the fence's sell-side.

The company was close to not requiring more capital injections from shareholders. It was a matter of four months, and the capitalization requested for January would be the last one. A new tranche of a fund was being approved, and with the growth it represented, the business would improve considerably. He didn't know how far conversations among them were. He would have to wait until the following week to understand better what was on their agenda. If the main partner decided to sell, he might soon be out of business.

At home, he told Gabrielle his view of the situation. It was not his fault, but trust from shareholders in the mutual funds appeared to be lost.

"We're so close, Gabrielle. It doesn't make sense to sell the business now."

"There must be a way to calm them down," she said.

"If I had the capital needed, I would buy the business tomorrow."

Those words resonated in Gabrielle's mind.

"And why don't you buy it? How much is needed?" she asked.

"Way out of our league. It's too much. We don't have the necessary cash. I estimate it could be up to two million dollars."

"You're right. We don't have that amount of money."

After some thought, she asked, "One of the shareholders would be willing to stay, right?"

"Yes, his shares represent nearly ten percent."

"You need ten percent less. Figure out how to get the remaining ninety," she joked.

"Right, just a ninety percent," Alexander said, and smiled too.

"With our savings and liquidating all our investments, how much can we get?"

"Something around thirty percent if we invest all we have," he said. "We would just keep our apartment and its mortgage out of it."

Then, with more interest in her question, Alexander asked, "Would you be willing to invest all we have in this company?"

"Alex, if you feel it's close to improving in this year, we could take that risk; it would depend on that and on who our partners would be."

"By selling the apartment that Andrea leases we'd be able to add around five percent more. Maybe she would like to be a partner."

"We would have to ask her, but I think she'd be interested."

So far, they had estimated how to get forty-five percent of the company. Both agreed to take the risk if they could get other partners they would feel comfortable with.

That afternoon they thought of a plan to bring more shareholders. Alexander was optimistic that some team members, his closest friends, would be willing to invest with him. He thought they could add ten percent. He thought that maybe he could talk to the shareholders and reduce up to ten percent of the price. If he could achieve that, only thirty-five percent more was needed.

"What about William Braxon, Alex? Maybe he'd be interested in joining us."

"Yes, I can talk to him. He knows the company well and how it's improving. I'll talk to him."

No matter what would happen, they agreed to continue with their personal businesses and accelerate them. In case something unfavorable happened, they would have a safety net prepared.

As soon as he got to the office on Monday morning, Alexander walked to William's office to update him on his plan. He had an excellent relationship with the main owners and could have more information on the partners' thoughts about the company's future.

"You're right, Alex," William said. "They are talking about selling the company. The executives coming tomorrow will talk to you about it."

"I knew it. Too many coincidences. First, the information requested and then these guys."

"It's a matter of focus, Alex. All companies are needing additional capital, and they have to prioritize."

"But capital in this company doesn't help that much to the other big ones."

"They need all the cash they can raise and would sell some smaller companies as fast as possible."

"William, here is the deal. I am thinking of buying the business with other shareholders who would be willing to get in with me."

"Wow. I hadn't thought about that. Are you sure?"

"I roughly estimated a price from the most recent valuation. With a ten percent discount on it, another ten percent from selected team members, and ten percent of one local shareholder that might stay, I just need to find thirty-five percent more. I would invest the rest."

William nodded, surprised. Then he stood up and walked inside his office. After discussing how Alexander could improve the company's sales, reduce expenses, and agreed he wouldn't be collecting any bonus until a specific target in profits was achieved, he said, "Alex, I would invest in it. Based on your estimation, count with twenty-five percent."

"Excellent. We just need to get an additional ten percent. I'll get on it."

"OK. Find it, and we'll continue discussing it."

He went out of his office excited but concerned about selling Andrea's apartment. Alexander recalled that a friend could be interested in it. He would be able to get a loan fast if needed. After Alexander called him, his friend agreed to buy it right away.

He just had to get the new investor. He called two close friends from Mexico, whom he knew would be interested, but neither could invest.

After many thoughts, he recalled the Senator and Christopher Mattis. No doubt they had the cash. Both had already invested much more than the remaining ten percent. He called both that afternoon and they agreed to participate. They wanted, if possible, a higher share of the business. Alexander agreed with them that if needed, he would call them immediately.

He had everything set up. He still had to discuss with the team members, but anyway, he had a chance to get more cash from the Senator and Christopher if needed. As he'd agreed with William, it was important that both jointly held the majority of the company's shares. Otherwise, William would not invest in it. It was too much risk not having complete control of the company.

That night, he discussed it with Gabrielle again. They agreed to move forward with the plan. If the company showed the results he was expecting, it would be a great decision and the base for a bright future. If not, they would be left with no cash, some debts, and no job.

"If it doesn't work, we would be able to dedicate full time to our businesses," he joked nervously.

The meeting with the group executives was at 10:00 a.m. on Tuesday. After some introductions, one of them started with a general discussion of the company.

As expected, they were willing to sell the business and cash out of it. When they said the price, it was ten percent higher than the base price Alexander had thought. He would need twenty percent more cash to close the transaction. He argued that the price was inflated, considering the company's situation and the recent valuation. If they were willing to sell fast, they would have to reduce the price.

After an hour of discussion, the two executives agreed to set the original price, according to the valuation. This would mean getting more cash from the Senator and Christopher, or someone else.

Alexander asked William to participate in the meeting. Both wanted to present them with a potential group of investors. Once William arrived, Alexander explained everything to them.

"Gentlemen, William and I have been discussing buying the company. It's a risky investment due to its actual situation, but we're willing to take that risk."

Both executives were surprised, but as they had a mandate to find an investor soon, and on the first day they had one already, they were very interested in Alexander's proposal.

"We would be able to pay shareholders immediately, as soon as documents are prepared, and we can get a fast approval from the authorities."

"How fast can you pay the actual shareholders?"

"In less than a week," Alexander answered boldly, and added, "We just need your help with something, and William and I can discuss it with the actual owners if necessary."

"What's that, Alexander?"

"We need the base price to reduce ten percent. We don't have a chance to get more, but considering the months it could take to find another buyer, it's a good deal for them."

After ten minutes of negotiating on it, both finally said that such approval had to be granted by the shareholders.

They met again after lunch. William and Alexander had already discussed it with the actual shareholders, but they only accepted five percent less of the price. Alexander called the Senator and Christopher again, and both agreed to invest the necessary five percent. The deal was ready to close. All decided to prepare the documentation and move forward with the transaction.

The details of the new shareholders were promised for next Thursday. They would review the documentation, and by following Monday, and on Wednesday afternoon, a meeting would be held with actual shareholders to sign the deal. The board meeting planned for that day would be the ideal moment to announce it to everyone.

Time had arrived to invite the team members. Alexander sent an email to some of them with a catchy subject.
"Great Investment Opportunity – Confidential."
He sent it to a few. He trusted all of them, and they were working hard for the company.
Everyone arrived right on time the following morning, except for a director who Alexander updated later. In ten minutes, the deal was explained, and all questions about it were answered. Those interested would need to confirm that day and send the cash by next Monday. Of the group of nine invited, eight accepted. The ten percent remaining was allocated.

"Alex, congratulations. With the five percent discount on the valuation, now you own thirty-two and a half percent of this company and your daughter five percent more. You're the main individual shareholder," William said while enjoying his own twenty-seven and a half percent.
"Thanks, and congratulations to you too. But we need to sign first. I'm glad that part of our loyal team members and friends jointly invested ten percent, just as the previous owner who's staying with us."
"Yes. I liked that those eight joined us." After a short thought, he added, "Alex, try that the fifteen percent ownership Christopher and the Senator own represents more investments in the company from them or some of their friends."
"I'm sure it will. I'll press on that."

The details of the new shareholders were sent to the executives from Jamaica. By the end of Friday, they were ready with all the documents, and the new shareholders agreed to review them during the weekend.

Everybody was enthusiastic about the transaction, but Alexander felt a mix of happiness and nervousness. Almost all their family savings would be invested in the company. Of the whole group, he was the one risking more. Soon he would have to accept the outcome of this decision.

After some back and forth with adjustments to the contract's wording, a final draft was printed. Everything was set to sign off.

Alexander met with the regulators to inform them of their intentions, and so far, they were OK to move forward. They had some concerns with the capitalization level, but a plan would be presented for final approval.

The meeting was held on Wednesday with all the owners, the new ones and those leaving, including the representative of the US investors who had signed first and had left the meeting to catch a flight to Panama.

The Chairman started with an emotional speech. Actual owners had to sell, but everyone, including the main owner from Jamaica, was deeply touched that the company would be maintained among various loved team members and an actual shareholder. They committed to supporting the company as much as they could.

A smaller group participated at the board meeting. The shareholders previously acknowledged all members. Alexander appreciated all their support and commented that some adjustments had to be made to the board and committees' structure. It was a needed measure to achieve some goals and improve the company situation. Some grimaced. They knew it would be their last meeting.

After the meeting, Alexander had prepared a cocktail for his team and all the new shareholders.

"Team," he said, "I have an announcement to make. Shareholders have agreed on a change of owners. I'm pleased to tell you that eight team members, William and I are the new owners. Also, one shareholder will remain with us and another two from overseas."

After some toasts, he added, "In the following months, we will invite all of you to be a partner. We want all of you to own part of this company."

After Alexander finished with the first part of his speech, he gave more details of the transaction.

"We have challenging times ahead. We don't have a big brother to back us anymore. But we have more shareholders who will fight for our company, beginning with myself."

The next day he had a meeting with the local shareholders. They agreed to make the proposed adjustments. Many measures were taken to improve the company situation, but future months would be challenging. Nobody counted on the diverse problems to handle.

CHAPTER 11

"The risk we have taken is high. All our savings are invested in this company," Alexander said to Gabrielle that Saturday morning at breakfast.

"Yes, it is. We have to make it work. But we also have to accelerate our plan B in case we need to."

They continued discussing Gabrielle's plans to grow her business, which showed a promising future.

"You have incredible margins in all products," Alexander affirmed when he reviewed sales and costs. "Getting some regular clients would be great. That would allow you to hire someone full-time to help. As soon as the business gains traction, we can lease a retail space."

Gabrielle had everything planned.

In the following months, their kitchen would be a battle zone during the day. Her business, Rachel's macarons entrepreneurship, and daily meals were Brenda's challenge, a sacrifice they were willing to make. They spent the weekend planning it. Both agreed to review their other initiatives until later next week, as Alexander had to work on many other matters.

On Sunday, they decided to do lunch at Pat'e Palo. They loved the Colonial Zone. He was willing to get to the restaurant, sit at the terrace with a beer, and start flying it until it rose two hundred feet above Plaza España. He would make a 360-degree video and nice photographs of the two museums, the restaurant zone, and the Ozama river about three hundred meters away from their table.

After that, they went home to relax and watch a movie. When they turned on the TV, a film both liked was shown, Under the Tuscan Sun. Alexander always joked with Gabrielle about it. In one scene, a character described how rails were built between two cities before the route and the train itself even existed. The train came many years later. He made the analogy with her kitchen gadgets purchased for years. He always said that she was preparing to use them in the future. Her catering, pastries, appetizers, and sauces would be prepared and served with all the treasured objects she had acquired over many years.

Alexander had to think of a way to inform the authorities of the new shareholders' approval. They also had to devise a new name, logo, and many other items. That afternoon, he called the person responsible for the marketing unit, one of the new shareholders. By the end of the week, she would have prepared graphic design options to discuss with all shareholders.

The new company was required to sign the contracts. The previous week, a brainstorming session had produced a list of different names, and then they voted. Many options were excluded, but two of them had divided the new owners. The final decision was made concerning the legal name required by regulators, which had to be added to the chosen one. One option had three words; it would be too long. Finally, they voted for the one-word alternative, Alliance.

Alliance Investment Funds Administrator would be the legal name, but the company would soon be recognized by Alliance. The name was catchy; everyone liked it. They had agreed with the previous owners to make the name change gradually. They would like to avoid making the investors nervous. They would have six months to eliminate the last name and any written or non-written communication to the market.

In the first week of February, Alexander and his team spent many hours talking to clients.
Rumors run fast in the Dominican Republic. We need to be ahead of it, he thought.

Many clients were very supportive, but a few important ones were concerned about not being backed by the strong headquarters in Jamaica. It was a concern Alexander himself had, but he assured all of them that many measures had already been implemented. Their investments were secure. That convinced many, but not all.

During the following weeks, some important investments gradually started to get canceled. Everyone worried about this situation. They would need new investors and work hard to bring more funds from existing clients. They did both, but they had to do it faster.

With the local shareholder who remained, Alexander was able to get new clients. He was a well-known community member in the market and helped Alexander open some doors with influential businessmen, but investments didn't come as fast as needed. He decided to call his US Investors and ask them for some contacts. Now, as shareholders, they might want the business to succeed as soon as possible. The Senator gave Alexander the name of a lawyer in New York City, partner of Christopher and him, Adam Branning. He asked Alexander to tell him that both were already investing. Christopher also recommended three friends and made the calls himself.

By the end of the month, Alexander had new clients and new funds from his overseas shareholders. Everything was moving smoothly. Investments were stable; a few were going out, but many were coming in.

They were able to increase their funds and many expenses were cut. New savings were expected in the following days. Everything seemed to be moving in the right direction.

CHAPTER 12

Fred Shultz vanished after his call to Alexander. He hadn't forgotten losing an excellent business to him and was planning how to hit Alexander as hard as he could.

When the sales team analyzed investors leaving Alliance, they realized that many were requiring wire transfers to bank accounts at Fred's bank. That sounded strange, as it was a medium-size bank, different from a large one where everyone usually had personal or business accounts. Additionally, all were wealthy clients with considerable high-value investments.

This looked like a laser-guided missile against Alliance. Once they noticed the situation, Alexander asked for the clients' names to verify whether he knew any of them.

After learning their names, he made calls to some of them to figure out why they were leaving. Once he called four investors he knew well, Alexander realized that Fred's bank was offering substantially higher rates than the one Alliance was offering.

It was clear that Fred was paying much more to get them, in some cases, up to thirty percent more. Stupid and expensive, but not illegal. Alexander knew then that Fred's threats were now a reality. And he wouldn't stop quickly. He discussed options to retain clients with the sales team, but they couldn't do much to convince them.

With mutual funds, you can't give different rates to specific clients. It's the same rate for all investors on each fund. Fred was paying much more than he could, registering a loss for his bank. Alexander could highlight this anomaly to someone there and he immediately thought of Serge Arden, but it didn't feel right to call him directly. He had to find another way to show this to him, to his board, or to anyone who could stop Fred Shultz.

Alexander remembered the regular politics game played between risk and sales units, and traditionally general managers played on the sales side. Growth was critical to their annual goals.

Leveraging on his contacts at Fred's risk unit, Alexander could bring it to their attention, and they would do everything else. They might point it out at a risk committee. Reputational risk for paying much more could signal a lack of the bank's liquidity. Or a market risk by reducing, without need, the spread between the cost of funds and client rates. All would be reasons to play hardball with him. That might not stop Fred, but it was worth a try.

Alexander moved forward. Three years ago, he'd met National Development Bank (NDB) risk manager at a convention in San Diego. Alexander invited him and other men in the same area from other banks to have drinks the following Wednesday to nurture relationships with his former risk colleagues.

Once at the restaurant, Alexander waited for the right moment to pitch some comments to the incumbent. After one had left and another had gone to the restroom, he began.

"I've heard you're paying very high rates in one of your products at NDB, up to thirty percent above the market average. Can our mutual funds invest in it? Or me personally?"

"Thirty percent above market? No way, you must be wrong," the risk manager said.

"Sure? A close friend recommended me to invest. He sent some money to you last Monday."

"Something must be wrong, Alex. I'll check on it."

"Let me know if we can invest," Alexander said, then changed the subject while the man typed something on his phone.

The three spent one more hour at the restaurant and left. Once Alexander was driving home, he thought of waiting some days to see if something happened. He would call his friend early next week and assert pressure on his request.

Two days later, he asked his team for an updated report on wealthy clients sending investments to Fred's bank. Clients were still leaving. It was too soon to expect results from his conversations with the risk manager at NDB. If nothing happened, he would have to think of something else.

***

Since the first news Alexander heard about the Coronavirus in mid-January, it appeared that the disease had escalated. Around fifty cases had been diagnosed in China and two deaths occurred. He thought many more died every day for other causes, so there was no reason to be highly concerned.

By mid-February, the disease was practically unknown in the western hemisphere by the vast majority of the population. Those digging more on the web or news channels knew more about it. There were just a few cases in China, and the government had taken actions to prevent its spread.

Alexander constantly reviewed any possible data about it. He became more concerned when registered cases were escalating gradually out of Wuhan. Newly infected people appeared in Beijing, South Korea, and Japan. In just one week, and just in China, cases had increased to about three hundred.

The World Health Organization became more involved and issued more information and reports than they had in the previous month. More cases occurred in China each week. He thought it was getting out of control there. When he heard about the first confirmed case in North America, he expected the disease to be easily controlled.

He didn't recall the city, but it appeared to have been somewhere in the state of Washington.

With an increased concern due to the disease's accelerated spread, China's government classified it as a delicate situation. Alexander didn't know by then the implications of this statement, but he started to connect the dots. New cases in Australia. Also, in American cities in California, Arizona, and Illinois. Some countries, such as Macau and Hong Kong, already with cases, were showing a rapid increase.

When is this stopping? If you add all the cases in all countries, it should be a lot by now, he thought.

Near the end of February, he was more alarmed. Not only for the increasing cases around the world, but for the measures taken everywhere. Rental cars and some passenger routes in China were suspended. Suspension of visas and flight bans came from Mainland China and Hong Kong.

Different world fairs in China were rescheduled, and many stores closed. Conferences and tournaments were or canceled. He recalled that months back, he had planned a trip to China that would now have to be canceled. Hotel cancellations were increasing. The disease was starting to have a variety of economic effects worldwide. He expected that financial markets would soon be hurt, despite that the Dow Jones Industrial Index had been at similar levels of 2019 year-end. He was curious why this hadn't affected it yet.

Scary was the increasing rumors that no known drugs or effective treatments against the virus were available. He became concerned about this.

If you get infected with the Coronavirus, what medicine would you take? "I don't know," the doctor would say, he thought.

In the western hemisphere, increasing cases started worrying everyone, but so far, it seemed to be that countries in this side of the world were not strongly affected. Governments were not taking decisive actions against it.

Alexander texted the Senator to get his view of the disease. He was more focused on the Republican reelection campaign of President Trump than anything else, but after some texts, he sent him a relevant text on the topic.

"Get prepared, Alex. Have many liquid assets. It's going to hit everyone around the world hard."

***

According to the Banks Commission's new rules in the Dominican Republic, risk managers now had to report to a board committee instead of to the general manager. This generated friction between both stakeholders at many banks. Now, more empowered, and even their bonuses not approved by the bank's main executive, they were able to work more independently.

Fred and the risk manager at NDB didn't have the best relationship. Fred didn't have a great relationship with anyone, but Serge Arden, who'd been his boss for many years and had been his supporter to get his present job.

The next risk committee would be held a week after Alexander's met with his friend at the restaurant. He would need to wait until next Tuesday to see if his plan had produced any results.

Meanwhile, clients kept leaving. By the end of the week, almost fifteen percent of the funds at Alliance had been transferred out, and everyone at Alliance was extremely troubled.

On Tuesday afternoon, a client requested his sales executive to cancel his investment and wire the cash to NDB. She was just waiting for him to sign a form, and the funds would be processed the following day. The client called back and asked her to cancel the wire transfer. He had explained to her that morning that Fred's bank was offering him an eleven percent rate. He didn't want to leave, but the additional income was too high, compared to the Alliance fund, where he received about eight percent.

"Why are you retrieving your instruction, Sir? What happened with the other bank?" she asked.

"Those idiots changed their mind. They called me back and told me they wouldn't offer those rates anymore. They did the same to my daughter."

When Alexander heard that, he was sure that his plan was showing some results, but more days were needed to confirm it. No more investments were transferred to Fred's bank that week that could be linked to this situation, just the normal ones with smaller amounts. On Thursday, he called his risk friend and asked him again if he could invest at such rates.

"Alex, you didn't hear it from me. It was a mistake. It's already fixed. We don't offer such rates anymore."

The bleeding stopped. Despite this, the damage had been done. Fifteen percent in fewer investments roughly represented the same decrease in income. That would affect any company, especially one struggling to become profitable.

After a month, the company had to deal with different challenges, but a huge one was caused by Fred Shultz. It would not be the last one. Concerns about the Coronavirus increased continuously. Alexander recalled the Senator's text earlier that month. He was sure this disease, added to NDB's attack, could affect his business sharply. It seemed they would have to live with both problems for a long time.

CHAPTER 13

On Saturday morning, Gabrielle prepared breakfast with mimosas to celebrate their first month as Alliance's partners.

"Last month was time-consuming at the office, and it looks like it'll be the same next month," Alexander said.

"Yes, I've seen it. You practically didn't have lunch at home."

"Right. I'm freezing the training and consulting initiatives for now. I need to focus on Alliance full-time."

"It's the best, Alex. All our savings rely on it."

Anyway, Alexander would evaluate the real estate initiative he'd been thinking about for some time. He knew various investors would be willing to get in, including George and other friends from Mexico. Alexander had been working in that sector for more than twenty years. He knew the business dynamics too. He'd spent many hours reviewing and approving loans to these projects countrywide in his last job.

He checked on a two-acre piece of land, analyzed by a developer, to build a project. It was presented to Alexander at the bank he worked for. He'd passed in front of the land days earlier and the property remained without any change. On three of its boundaries were streets and another piece of land belonging to a different owner on the fourth side. Winston Churchill Avenue, a main avenue in Santo Domingo, was one of the boundaries, where a commercial unit could be nested and, in the rest, several residential buildings could fit perfectly.

He remembered the landowner didn't want to sell it. Mr. Ramos had tried to partner with someone to develop a project, but it had been not easy to get someone, and financing as well. He was a wealthy man but with not many liquid assets. He and her sister had inherited the land some years ago. They were in their early sixties, and neither had the money nor the will to build a big project on their own.

Both were investors at the brokerage. Alexander called him to discuss the idea he had for the property. Mr. Ramos was surprised by the cold call, but when he heard that Alexander wanted to talk about the land, he accepted immediately. They agreed to meet half an hour later in a coffee shop half a block away from the owner's home.

Once there, Alexander told him a good project, in the right hands, could result in a great business opportunity for him.

"We're leasing the property to various small businesses, but all contracts will mature in the next two months. We haven't decided to continue with them or to sell the property."

"Do you have a buyer?"

"Not yet, but we're sure someone would be interested. It's very well located. We wanted to develop a project once, but we weren't able to do it."

"Would you consider that option again? Getting involved in a project with a developer?"

"If conditions are fair, we would think about it. We haven't been lucky with such alternative in the past."

"If you get a buyer fast, what would be the price, Mr. Ramos?"

"We haven't thought about it lately, but it should be around ten million."

Alexander opened his eyes wide. The price was too high for him.

"Uh, with a formal cash offer, we could think of something around nine million," Mr. Ramos said.

The quick response of the owner reducing the price gave Alexander a chance to pitch his idea.

"Sir, I have a plan for your land. I've made some rough numbers on it. If you're willing to join a developer in a project, you'll be able to get in a three-year time frame around the ten million dollars, even more. But it'll be difficult to get a buyer to pay you nine in cash for it."

"And what kind of project could it be?" Mr. Ramos asked, apparently interested.

Alexander didn't want to give him many details. "I need to make a deeper analysis, but a combination of commercial and residential could make sense. I would need to have a layout of the land to work on it."

"Let me think about your idea. I would need to discuss it with my sister and my wife. I'll send you the layout later, and I'll give you a call early next week with our thoughts."

"Perfect. I'll wait for it."

Alexander left some cash on the table and they left.

He went home with an estimate of the land price and a clear idea for the project to develop. With the layout, he would confirm it. He would need to think of the legal structure and get the initial capital required to start the project. The owner could contribute with the land in a Trust, or the land could be sold to a fund, lease it back, and develop the project before selling it to third parties.

He dedicated all day to making forecasts. He called his former risk analysts to get an update on construction costs, margins, and everything he could get from recent projects. Only one was available.

"Alex, you used to call us on Saturdays to ask for information. We thought that would stop when you left the bank. So naïve." They laughed, and Alexander replied, "Uh, sorry. I appreciate your help. This is important."

He had lunch at the studio to continue nonstop with the analysis. The faster he could advance, the better. Gabrielle went to her mother's home for a couple of hours, so he could focus on the project.

That weekend, his nephew returned to Santo Domingo from Punta Cana. The project he was working on was completed, and he was free now. Twenty minutes later, he arrived at Alexander's apartment. He had all the necessary information. Alexander could populate a spreadsheet with all the information needed with his help.

Ninety minutes later, Alexander had nearly the complete analysis; he just had to wait for a few costs his nephew would provide to him during the week, but he had temporarily used a rough estimation. He was sure now. It could be a great business opportunity.

He called George, his friend from university, to present the project.

"Ey, I'm getting involved in a new real estate business, and I need your expertise."

"Sure. When do you need, Alex?"

"I have a presentation. Let me send it to you, and maybe we can connect later to discuss it. Does six work for you?"

"Sure. I'll review it."

"Perfect. It'll be in your email in a minute. I'll call you later."

He was free for an hour to have some rest. He had spent the whole day reviewing everything about the project. He lay down on his bed and relaxed. After some minutes, he recalled what had happened during the week with Fred's bank. Something disturbed him. When he finished reviewing the whole situation, step by step, he had an insight.

How did these guys target our most wealthy clients so precisely? How could they know about them? We don't report investments to the credit bureau, only to the Securities Commission.

After thinking about it for several minutes, he concluded that someone must be passing on specific information of his clients. It could be someone on the regulator's side, or the external auditors. He froze with the last alternative he imagined. Wow. Wow. Or someone inside Alliance.

He became deeply anxious. He determined it was not probable that the regulators or the auditors could be involved in such dishonest action. He'd dealt with them many years and they'd never had a problem like this. Additionally, nothing similar had been heard with any other company in the market. He was sure an insider at Alliance had to be involved.

But who? Maybe someone who had left the company? Who had access to all these clients' information?

Gabrielle arrived a minute later when Alexander was thinking about who could be involved. After she came into their bedroom, she saw him looking at a fixed point of the ceiling.

"What are you thinking about with such concentration? I said hello, and you didn't answer."

"Sorry. I was figuring out something. I need to discuss it with you."

She knew what had happened between Fred's bank and Alliance. He told her what was on his mind.

"I agree," Gabrielle said. "Someone at Alliance, or someone at NDB who knows all those clients should be involved, but what are the chances of that? It must be someone at Alliance."

Alexander nodded.

"When I spoke to the two clients, I didn't ask them the name of Fred's bank executive. I will call them back and find it out," he said and added, "Maybe someone who used to work for us. I wish I could call today; I'll do it first thing Monday."

"If they didn't work for Alliance in the past, check if someone has any relative," she suggested.

Alexander passed the weekend hoping it had no relation to someone working at Alliance. That would be even worse. No matter what, they had to understand all the details of this case. He thought that knowing who had access to the system and the clients' information could bring some insights. He knew that many had: Operations, Technology, Sales. Checking on who had reviewed all clients who had left for Fred's bank could help too. He immediately scheduled a meeting early on Monday morning with those responsible for technology.

***

Late that afternoon, he called George.
"Hi, Alex. Back from the beach already?" After so many years, some still didn't know the nearest beach Dominicans went to was forty minutes away.
"Like every day," Alexander said, thinking that he and Gabrielle should visit any of the beautiful beaches in the country more often.
"Did you have a chance to review the presentation, George?"
"Yes, I just want to discuss something with you first."
He wanted to talk about the Coronavirus and its effect in the Dominican Republic. As Alexander had, he'd watched much news about the virus, and measures were escalating fast, affecting various industries.
"George, my view is that this industry is not going to be strongly affected here. People will need to find a home to live in. Young couples, no matter what, will still be getting married."
"Right. I agree. I'm more concerned about the commercial units. In addition to the disease impact, this sector is more affected every day. Online stores are killing them."
"If we decide to move forward, the commercial sector we lease to, needs to be well analyzed. The square feet used for that part of the project will be reduced, and remember, it's a great commercial location.

After their initial discussion, they spent an hour on the financials, which showed excellent profits. They agreed on including a third building. It made sense, more sales to use the same piece of land. He still had to validate density regulations in that zone to see if it was possible.

"So, the next steps, Alex. What do you propose? It would be excellent to present to our friends here. Some might have an interest in it. I'm so far," George said.

"Excellent. You're welcome. I have an important meeting on Monday morning and might be busy all day, but I'll get everything updated and send it to you on Tuesday morning."

"Perfect. That would be nice."

"George, thinking on it. I was planning to see my mother in Mexico City. Maybe I can be there on Thursday and present it. That fits for you?"

"Yes. Just confirm it to me and I'll make all the arrangements. You can stay at home."

"OK, thank you. I'll plan on it. We'll be in touch."

After hanging up, Alexander reserved a flight. He called his mother and Rachel, and neither hesitated for a second to see him there. They planned to get to Mexico City Friday morning. Alexander had to come back to Santo Domingo on Sunday, but his mother could stay there for the week and go back to Acapulco with Matt on Friday. Rachel could get back to Aguascalientes anytime she wanted.

He spent around two hours Sunday morning reviewing the project's financials. Then he relaxed. He and Gabrielle stayed at home all day reading and watching a movie after lunch.

At night, Gabrielle was kind of tired and went to bed earlier than she usually did. Alexander was worried about it. The same had happened in previous days. By seven, she was in bed sleeping.

***

Alexander arrived earlier than usual at Alliance on Monday.

Jeff Blake knocked on his door at 7:28 a.m. He was responsible for technology at Alliance. Alexander asked him to come in and apologized for the sudden and early meeting request. He told him their conversation needed to be kept strictly confidential.

"Of course, Alex," he said while Alexander passed him a list of the clients who had gone to Fred's bank.

"I need to know who in the whole company has access to this clients' accounts in the last ninety days."

"Alex, many sales executives at the company have access to clients' accounts."

"Right, but they normally review the accounts of their clients, not of others. Check if anyone at Alliance inquired about all the accounts. Also, check if someone who had worked for us in the last six months checked on them."

"When do you need this information?"

"Before noon."

"What? Why so fast? I have a couple of meetings later."

"Please, Jeff. This has to be your top priority. It's mine now. Anything else not critical has to be postponed. If not possible, delegate it."

"Uh, OK. I'll do it."

"And Jeff, please be careful. Please do this by yourself, don't ask anyone to do it, and don't speak to anyone about it. I'll see you at noon or earlier if you're ready."

After Jeff left his office, Alexander worked on different administrative matters until nine, a prudent time to call the clients he had talked with the previous week. He needed to find out the names of executives at NDB, relatives of them at Alliance, or any other helpful information. He called three of them that he knew well. He didn't want to ask the sales executives to do it to avoid alerting anyone. It was the same executive for both clients. His name didn't mean anything to him that morning, but what he discovered later would surprise him.

CHAPTER 14

Jeff was back at noon to brief him on his investigation. It had been difficult to consolidate the information from the databases by himself to avoid alerting someone. Still, he used an audit trail report with enough information to analyze what Alexander was looking for.

"Tell me, Jeff, what do you have?"

"I don't know yet it, but it might be part of the findings you're looking for. I looked at all the sales executives and then at all that had left in the last six months. I didn't find anything with either, so I extended the search up to one year, and nothing again."

"Nothing?" Alexander asked, disappointed.

"Nobody, present or former sales executive, got into the accounts of these clients often. Just periodic visits, when the clients' investments matured, or close to such date, and just on their clients."

Alexander sat on his chair and balanced it back, crossing his hands behind his head.

"So, we have nothing strange with anyone?"

"Yes, we have. When I reviewed who has seen all these clients' accounts in the whole company, I noticed that the assistant, a gal hired last November, has entered all the clients' accounts you gave me."

Alexander pushed forward, and with his hands on the desk thought about Jeff's finding.

"That should be normal. As far as I remember, she registers all personal data of clients for the executives."

"Right! That's normal. What is not, is that back in January, she searched in a specific screen that contains financial information of clients' investments, including maturing date and investments' balance of all the clients in the list you gave me. And thirty-seven clients more."

Alexander rose out of his chair as if the nylon mesh was burning him.

"What? How did you get all this information?"

"Do you remember the twenty thousand dollars I requested two months ago to buy a program license needed to prepare reports? The one that we held a long discussion on, and you said it was too expensive."

"Right, I remember."

"That tool helped to get the audit trial downloaded, clean it up, and order it in the way you needed."

After thanking Jeff for the valuable information obtained, Alexander spent several seconds thinking about what to do next.

"Jeff, did she enter on these or any other accounts today?"

"I'm not able to see it. The last report generated from the system is from Friday. To see today's inquiries, we would need to wait until tomorrow morning. Alex, we need to take her out of here right now."

"No. We can't do that. If we do it, we will alert people we don't want. Someone else is out there, or maybe inside, who is the real danger for us. We need to play this smart to eliminate this threat effectively."

"Did you check everyone in the company?"

"Yes, but she was the only one with this behavior. Even you appeared. But you just checked your account."

Alexander smiled and then appreciated Jeff for all the information. He asked him to review her inquiries every morning and brief him with any suspicious activity.

After the meeting, Gabrielle called him. He told her about Jeff's research. She was surprised. He would think about how to manage this situation properly.

Alexander called Hans Perutz, director of security at his former employer, someone he fully trusted and who had become a good friend. Alexander asked him for the phone number of an investigator who had done some jobs for them in the past.

They agreed to meet out of his office, in a minimarket two hundred meters away. Half an hour later, they discussed his request after Alexander gave him an envelope with information.

"I need to get any connection of the woman inside the envelope working at Alliance with the other two guys inside it or anyone at that bank. I just have the photograph of one of the guys."

When the investigator opened it and saw the women's photograph and name, he nodded. But when he saw Fred Shultz's photograph, he reacted differently.

"Wow. This is quite delicate."

"I know, that's why I'm calling you and not someone else. She's passing information of Alliance clients to someone there, maybe him, or maybe the other guy that works there in the sales unit. We need all the information you can get, as fast as possible."

"You know fast is more expensive, Mr. Stern. I need to pay higher incentives for the information," he said.

"How much more?"

"Don't know yet, but maybe up to … five thousand dollars."

"Uh, well. OK, but I need it right away."

Alexander nodded and agreed with the fee. He didn't have time to negotiate.

He walked back to his office. His lunch had already arrived. He closed the door and started eating the chicken salad Amanda had ordered for him and thought about the problem he had on his hands, and possible next steps to mitigate it. After lunch, he called Ryan to see if more clients had left, but since last Thursday, no one had.

At least the bleeding's stopped for now, he thought.

Despite the situation at Alliance, Alexander was eager to get that week's flight to Mexico City, not only to discuss the business opportunity with his friends, but to see his mother and Rachel. He would be free from Friday at lunchtime until Sunday night. Unfortunately, Gabrielle would not be able to join them. She had plenty of work with her new business.

The funds' balances were increasing again. He was curious about what had happened in that risk committee at NDB, but he had no opportunity to get that information. The last time he spoke with his friend, he appeared reluctant to say anything else about the bank. At six, he left Alliance. He had struggled to sleep until late the previous night, thinking who could be trying to damage the company.

The day after, Alexander arrived back at the office on time to meet with clients. His next meeting, now with the auditors, started when he received a call from Mr. Ramos. He excused himself and left his office to take it while the attendees continued discussing some aspects of the annual report with his team.
The call was short but pleasant. Mr. Ramos advised him that he and his family were participating in the project. If the estimated benefit was reasonable, they would move on with a formal letter of intention. Alexander told him he had completed the analysis and had presented it to some investors. He would have more news the following week.

Late at night, he received a call from the investigator. He didn't give him any details, but it was a message that calmed his worries.
"Hello, Mr. Stern. We found the relationship between the young lady and one of the other bank guys. It's not with the senior one, but from messages we were able to retrieve, we're sure the top guy must have planned it all."
"Fine," Alexander said. "Let's meet tomorrow at 9:00 a.m. in my office."
Gabrielle was already sleeping. He was not able to update her on it. She'd been tired again and went to bed

earlier that night. They usually retired after eleven every night, but she had her eyes closed before eight.

When the investigator arrived the following day, Alexander closed the door and they sat on the two couches steps away from the window. The investigator briefed him on his findings.

"Mr. Stern, a sales executive from NDB has been dating the woman at Alliance for six months. She's been passing him information about your clients, including the investment amount, maturing date, ID number, complete name, and phone numbers. The same executive also has texts on his phone between him and Mr. Fred Shultz. Nothing that could compromise both, but he texted the executive with something about calling clients of a company. Surely yours. He also referred to a special program that was being approved for only one month to bring clients."

Alexander was surprised. The investigator still needed to get the details of the program. He was expecting to have that information no later than Friday. They agreed that he would send Alexander a message when everything was done and would meet him at his office early next Monday, once he was back from Mexico.

***

Alexander took the 9:01 a.m. flight on Thursday, a direct flight arriving at noon. Walking out of Terminal B, he saw a man with his name on a small panel. George's driver was waiting for him to take him to his home.

He had met George's wife for many years. An adorable tiny woman, but with a strong character. Nevertheless, she had always been extremely friendly and warm with Alexander and Gabrielle.

After lunch with George and his family, they went to his office. Three of their closest friends from the university were interested in the project. They arrived ten minutes after four. Alexander presented the project to them, and George finally confirmed he would invest in it. Axel agreed too. The other two passed.

The next morning, Alexander presented the project to a couple of George's friends, but neither decided to step in. More than the project, they were concerned about the Coronavirus' impact, and they wanted to keep all cash they could. However, they agreed to stay in touch for future investments.

Once the meeting finished, they stayed to discuss the next steps, agreeing to formalize discussions with Mr. Ramos. In two weeks, George and Axel would travel to Santo Domingo to visit the property and sign all the necessary documents.

The lawyers would need around a week to prepare everything but would have to confirm the exact date. Alexander would be named managing partner of the company developing the project. The company name would be Adagio Associates.

They left George's office happy to finally become partners.

"George, I'm sure this would be an excellent business opportunity, and I'm glad to make it with you," Alexander said.

"Right, Alex. We've talked about it for so many years. It just took us more than twenty."

George left Alexander at the hotel. They agreed to have a conference call next Tuesday for an update on the project. Alexander had enough time to check-in and rest until his mother and Rachel arrived.

Fifteen minutes later, Rachel knocked on the door, and ten minutes after, his mother. They were glad to see each other, but were starving, so the three walked out of the hotel to the restaurant.

They had previously agreed to have lunch at Fisher's, a place he'd loved since he was young. It was not her mother's favorite, but he and Rachel liked it. He always ordered the Langosta Tacos with the house's special sauce and yellow rice.

Once they were seated, a waiter came, and after introducing himself, asked for their choice of drink—a Coke for her mother and a beer for him. Rachel also asked for a beer, and Alexander looked at her, disapproving of her choice.

"Come on, Dad, I'm twenty-one. Relax."

Minutes later, after their meals were ordered, they started a conversation that lasted for more than three hours. They spent valuable time updating each other on many matters.

Alexander had arranged to visit the church where his father rested in peace, beside his grandmother. A usual twenty-five-minute drive, because of the rush hour's traffic, took them one hour to get there.

When they were back, Alexander called Gabrielle and detailed his day, including George's meeting with his friends, which hadn't shown any results.

"At least George and Axel decided to invest in the project," she said.

"Yes, I was hoping to have more of my friends with us. Maybe in the future."

On Saturday morning, they visited the Casa Estudio Diego Rivera y Frida Kahlo, now a museum. The house was built with one section painted in red and white for the famous painter, and the other section in blue for his wife. The artist had asked the architect to build two houses, separate from each other, with a small bridge at the top of both. Both houses served as each painter's studio.

After an hour of walking through the property, they crossed the street to have lunch at a restaurant they loved.

Antiguo San Angel Inn had been Alexander's family's first choice every time they want to join or celebrate a special event in Mexico City. Its construction, dated 1616, had been converted years ago in the Hacienda de Goicoechea.

In 1917, it operated for some years as a hotel. The old cask of the property had been declared a Colonial Monument in 1937. But it wasn't until 1963 that a group of investors founded the restaurant on the premises.

After the main entrance, on the right side, was a small chapel, and in the center of the restaurant an interior garden with a nice fountain. The main dining room was in the back of the internal garden, and the bar was on its left. Steps away from the main building, a large backyard was handled every day with great care.

Once inside, they went to the section where the host stood at his post. The man, around sixty years old, had been at the restaurant for many years, rising in positions since he was a young waiter. Mrs. Stern had met him in the eighties. The gentleman was glad to see her.

After ordering drinks, everyone ordered their favorite meal. First, they shared Crepas de Huitlacoche and Ostiones San Angel Inn. Then, as the main dish, Mrs. Stern ordered the habitual well-done ribeye, and Alexander shared the Steak Tártara and Arrachera Norteña Marinada with Rachel. They finished sharing two delicious desserts that had been listed on the menu for decades: Crema Bavaria con Fresas and Crepas de Cajeta.

The musical trios that played during lunch and dinner were always pleasant to listen to. They were delighted with three of their favorite songs, requested by Alexander and granted, maybe, due to his generous tip. The first song, Gema, was one of the best songs he had ever heard.

They were out of the place, and after a short visit to Santa Fe Mall, they returned to the hotel.

On Sunday, Matt would pick up their mother and drive to Acapulco. Rachel's flight was on time, scheduled at 7:30 p.m. to Aguascalientes, same as Alexander's overnight flight to Santo Domingo. Both left for the airport, leaving Alexander's mother with tears in her eyes. All were expecting it. She was very sentimental when saying goodbye to their closest family members.

Forty-five minutes later, they arrived at Terminal B, where both flights were departing. She said goodbye to Alexander and walked to her gate. He had plenty of time. When he checked his messages, he saw one received from the investigator. It included a photograph of a document of Fred's Shultz bank. Somehow, he had skipped it earlier that day. It was a one-page memorandum detailing the special program approved and signed jointly by the business head at NDB and Fred. Now Alexander had all the dots connected.

During the long hours at the lounge, he thought extensively on how to manage the situation generated by Fred's bank. He had to decide what to do with the young lady still working at Alliance. Knowing how everything had happened would help him plan on Alliance's counteract.

CHAPTER 15

Alexander's flight arrived sharp by six in Santo Domingo. He slept only three hours. The previous days in Mexico had been pleasant and rewarding, but it was time to get back to his daily duties.

Once out of the airplane, he made a quick stop at the restroom to change his blue polo for a shirt and took his jacket out of the carry-on. Outside of Customs, the driver stood waiting for him.

"Do I take you home, Mr. Stern?"

"No, please take me directly to Alliance. I have a meeting early today. And I've told you many times to call me Alexander, not Mr. Stern. Mr. Stern is resting in peace in Mexico. I just visited him last Friday."

They smiled, and the driver said, "I've tried, Sir, but I can't. It's due to respect for you."

"My friend, respect is not shown by how you call someone. Please just call me Alexander."

"I'll try, Sir."

Once they got to Alliance, the investigator was already out of his office, sitting on the black leather couch. During the weekend, Alexander had spoken to Jeff, who confirmed that Dominic, the sales executive's assistant, was not getting in the accounts' screen anymore.

Alexander remembered a previous experience he'd had at his former employer that ended effectively; the same scene that Hans and his security team once performed would be replicated.

A meeting would be scheduled. The investigator will handle it and Jeff would just come in the room to detail the findings from the system inquiries, in addition to one uniformed guard would stand by the door. They would show Dominic all the information they'd obtained and pressure her to confess. She might ask for an attorney or just become quiet. But the investigator would push further and advise her that enough proof had been collected to lock her up in jail for many years. She had violated the confidentiality agreement. They would tell her that an immediate confession was needed, with all details and contacts at Fred's bank. With that document, Alliance would put in writing that she would not be sued, but she would be fired.

With a formal confession, they would have something against her contact at NDB. Depending on the results, Fred or the business head might be liable as well. They were not too optimistic about it. The memorandum signed by both characters didn't say anything about direct efforts against Alliance clients, so it couldn't be used against them, but a confession of Dominic citing this memorandum and explicit requests to contact Alliance clients could make a difference.

A small conference room generally used by auditors or to host clients was prepared for the meeting. It was past the elevators, away from everyone. A phone would be placed behind some books on a shelf before she came in to record everything. The camera would have a full view of the circular four-seat table. Another phone would record the conversation, but only as a backup.

Once all was set, Alexander's assistant would request her to wait for him inside that office, but just the three men they had planned to attend would arrive.

When Dominic arrived, Amanda called her out of the sales unit.

"Good morning, Dominic. Alexander asked me if you can help him with something at the office past the elevators. Please bring a pad and a pen to write his requests."

"OK, now?"

"Yes, he'll be with you in a minute. Please wait for him there."

"OK," she said.

When Dominic arrived, no one was there. She stepped inside and sat. She noticed that someone she hadn't met was meters away from the office, on the phone talking to someone.

A few seconds later, the investigator came in. He was the man she had seen outside. After him, Jeff and a uniformed guard came in too. The last one stayed on his feet by the door with his back slightly pressing it.

"Where is Mr. Stern?" she asked.

"He's coming in a minute," the investigator said. "He asked us to discuss something with you."

The investigator introduced himself and in the next five minutes told her some of the information he was able to obtain. With great accuracy, but showing nothing to her, he detailed some of his messages with her boyfriend at NDB, especially those that compromised her the most.

He stopped talking to let Jeff detail what he had found on the inquires of clients' accounts in the system. Her face turned pale. She realized that they knew everything.

"I have to go," Dominic said and stood up. She wasn't able to walk out as one side of the table was blocked by Jeff, the other by the investigator, and the guard was protecting the door.

"Dominic. We know you're a victim in this situation. We want to help you. Please sit down and hear what we can do for you," the investigator said calmly.

Dominic sat slowly back, and the investigator continued for a couple of minutes with some additional facts.

"Now, tell us how this happened. We know it all, but we want to hear your version. I'm sure it's the same as one of your friends at the other bank."

"Uh, I don't have anything to say."

For some minutes, she remained reluctant to speak about anything. She kept holding her hands together and pressing them to the table, where her perspiration constantly left a mark. The investigator insisted again.

Twenty minutes later, he increased his tone of voice upon her silence.

"If you don't cooperate with us, we'll have to put you in jail. Officer, please put the cuffs on her."

"Wait!" Dominic shouted. "Don't do this to me. What do you want to know? I'll tell you everything, but please help me."

The next half hour, she described exactly how everything had happened with broad details. Two executives at NDB had been informed by the business head that Fred Shultz would pay them a special bonus if they could bring some important clients from Alliance using a special approved program.

The bonus amounts were specified and were linked with the number of investments they could bring in. More money, more bonus. She had been promised good cash. Two thousand dollars had been deposited in her account, and more was promised.

Dominic was reluctant to put everything in writing, but after they told her that everything was being taped and showed her the hidden phone, she decided to write a two-page confession. She now had to trust they would not use it against her as promised.

The investigator and Jeff requested her to stay at her desk and avoid any communication with her boyfriend during the day and with anyone about it.

During the day, she would have more information on how they would proceed. They couldn't retain her, but she was so scared that she might decide to follow their instructions.

After the meeting, the investigator walked to Alexander's office. He was waiting to be briefed on the outcome with all the details. Now he had to decide what to do next. They could not retain her. The investigator recommended letting her go, requesting her to keep quiet about this matter. Otherwise, legal action would be initiated against her."

"My job here is done, Mr. Stern," the investigator said.

"Right. Thank you for your valuable help."

Alexander opened his desk and grabbed a white envelope.

"Here is the payment for your services. I added twenty percent for the last meeting. It was not agreed upon initially."

"Uh, fine. I appreciate it, Mr. Stern. You know you can count on me anytime."

Alexander stayed some minutes watching at his window and thinking what to do next. The first part of his plan was completed. Cancer would be eradicated from Alliance, and he had enough proof to complicate Fred, with or without legal action against him.

He called the human resources head and briefed her on all the findings. She was astonished. He told her that he would keep the written confession in his vault, along with a video of the meeting.

"What do you want to do with her, Alex?" she asked.

"Just take her out of Alliance right away."

"What about the severance package?"

"We have some days by law to pay her. We have time to decide on that. Just take her out of here today."

Alexander went home for lunch. At two-thirty, he had a meeting with William. He would brief him about the situation later. Ten minutes later, he entered his apartment with his carry-on, gifts, and tequila he had brought from Mexico.

Gabrielle was angry. She had met Dominic before at a Christmas party. She'd spent an hour talking to her about her food business. She was following Gabrielle's page on Instagram, and she had often sent her lovely comments about the appetizers she posted.

"How false she was, Alex."

"False and stupid. Fred and his gangsters compromised her for pennies. She could be gaining much more in a couple of years. She had a lot of potential. Now she's damaged her career. At least in the financial sector."

"What are you doing with her now?

"She's out."

"And with Fred Shultz?"

"I'm still thinking about how to move forward with him. That's more delicate. We'll see."

After lunch and a nap, he hurried back to the office. He got to Alliance just in time for his meeting with William. He knew already that Alliance was losing clients and substantial investments but knew nothing about the investigation process and its results. He was surprised.

"This is like a famous author thriller," he said.

"It's like a nightmare, my friend," Alexander said. "I scheduled a meeting with our local partners. It's fair to explain to them the situation. We'll be meeting at three today."

They met at Alexander's office. He summarized the investigation results after giving them some background on how they had stopped, so far, the bleeding of the funds. He ended by telling everyone that the month's preliminary results reflected they had replaced part of the investments gone with new ones.

Everyone felt a mix of astonishment and anger. All raised some questions and assumptions.

"What are we going to do? That's a bigger institution than us. They can damage us big time," one said.

"Why is Shultz doing this? Did we do something to them in the past?"

"We should report this to the authorities."

"We should call the cops and our lawyers."

When the conversation turned more excited, Alexander interrupted them all.

"Guys, guys! Relax. I want to bring Fred down, Fred's bank, and all involved in this scam, but that kind of noise right now will not help us. It would damage us more, and additional investments will go out. We need to play this smart."

When everyone calmed down, he continued.

"I wanted to keep you updated, but please, maintain confidentiality. This is very important. We'll come up with a plan shortly."

Everyone agreed but remained nervous. That afternoon, Alexander would have a meeting with a lawyer, a close friend. One he could trust.

The lawyer arrived at four. After a casual conversation, they sat down on a couch. Alexander explained the situation and told him all the information he had and what they had done so far.

"What can we do against this guy or his bank?"

"Not much, Alex. It sounds difficult to establish an effective legal action against Fred with the information you have. It appears that he was cautious in not getting directly involved, so he'll just deny everything, blame the business head, the sales executive, or both."

"And what about the confession?" Alexander asked.

"Your guys didn't follow the right process. Not a lawyer present with the young lady, too. Anyway, you don't need to have a noisy and costly process. It will damage Alliance more."

"I know. What else can we do?"

"Maybe you can informally use this confession, the video, the text messages. His board at NDB are very decent people; one is Serge Arden. I'm sure you know him."

"Yes, we're not close friends, but we know each other. Decent guy."

"If he and his board members know about this, they won't be happy. Not sure if with this they'll kick him out. I doubt it. He could blame others, anyway. Maybe some sort of reprimand. But he'll behave for sure, at least for some time."

"OK, I'll think about what to do next. Thank you for coming up here. I'll call you when we're clear on how to proceed."

"Anytime, Alex."

Alexander felt that all they had done would be thrown into the garbage. But he was wrong. Being unable to sue the guy or the bank prevented him from making a bad decision that would affect Alliance more, as the lawyer clearly stated. After some minutes of evaluating everything, he was convinced he would need to think of something else.

Human resources informed everyone at the sales unit that Dominic would not be working at Alliance anymore. They were surprised by the sudden decision and asked for the cause. Personal reasons, they were told.

All were out of the office at lunch when the guard escorted Dominic to human resources with her personal belongings and then to the underground parking, where she took her car and drove from the building.

After he met with the lawyer, Alexander spent an hour thinking about what to do next. At 5:30 p.m., he was exhausted and went home. He was not able to think about it anymore. He just made a quick call to the lawyer who was preparing Adagio Associates' documents to get an update on them. He confirmed that everything would be ready for Thursday afternoon. He wrote an email to George and Axel.

"Guys, documents will be ready on Thursday. We can review them on Friday to make any necessary changes. It's safe to plan your flight for next week, arriving on Monday. Please confirm to arrange everything. Take care."

Before he entered the elevator, his phone rang. The investigator was calling.

"Hi, Mr. Stern, I need to tell you something. My contact at the bank just told me that two sales executives were fired today. One was Dominic's boyfriend."

"Wow, that was fast."

"Yes, Sir. Too fast. I don't know if the girl talked or something else. I'll get more information and let you know immediately."

"Perfect. Thank you."

It appears Fred doesn't want to leave any trail, he thought.

At home, he spent half an hour updating Gabrielle on everything. Then he went to take a shower and relax until dinner was ready. Once he lay down on his bed, he saw a message from Susan, the corporate lawyer.

"Alex, please call me. It's urgent."

Alexander dialed her immediately, wondering what could be so urgent.

"Hi, Alex. Sorry to bother you at home. I went to your office, but you'd already left."

"No problem. Tell me, what's going on?"

"Sorry to give you this kind of news. We're not getting the Alliance's acquisition approval from the authorities."

"What? You're joking at me. What happened?"

"We don't know. They sent us a letter saying that the new shareholders were not adequate. And according to the new regulations, they need to be… blah, blah, blah."

"We surely didn't see this one coming," Alexander said.

"It's not the final decision, but it will be their recommendation to the National Securities Council, the final approver on the ownership change. They'll be meeting next Tuesday."

"Let's meet tomorrow morning. I'll schedule it right away with William and you. We need to think of something to do quickly."

"I'll see you tomorrow, Alex."

Alexander was not usually a drinker, but he decided to have a shot of tequila Jose Cuervo Reserva de la Familia. Kind of strong but perfect for that moment to absorb such news. Once in the studio, he sat to think how to deal with this new bomb. Actually, this could be worse than Fred's attack.

CHAPTER 16

Alexander arrived early at the office on Tuesday. Last night's news from Susan shocked him. He scheduled an emergency meeting with her and William. Alliance's acquisition approval with the Securities Commission was now their highest priority. He had been thinking about how to deal with this issue. So far, they would be rejected if nothing changed.

The only solution he had seen was to ask someone who could influence regulators to get the recommendation changed, and it had to be done in less than four days. Next Thursday, the Securities Commission was sending its final recommendation to the National Securities Council. Once the recommendation had been sent, nobody could change it, and it would be difficult for the Council, even if they were able to approve it, to go against their subordinate.

The meeting started on time.

"What's going on? Why the urgency?"

"Susan will brief you," Alexander said, while nodding to her to start telling him her findings.

She repeated the same explanation of the previous night. Everyone kept silent for some seconds, then William smiled nervously.

"Are you kidding me? That doesn't make sense. We spoke personally to the authorities, and everything seemed fine. What happened?"

Susan remained silent. Alexander started walking around his office.

"We don't know yet," he said. "It sounds strange, but we need to find a way to reverse the damn negative recommendation, and fast."

After walking and meditating for a few seconds, he added, "We have until Wednesday night to solve this."

"We need to request a meeting with the Superintendent to discuss it," William said.

"Amanda is already coordinating it. She's requesting it for any time today, for the three of us," Alexander said, and added. "We cannot depend only on that. We need to find someone who can pull some relationships in our favor. Ideally, with the Superintendent first, and if that doesn't work, with the President of the National Securities Council. Another option would be the Central Bank Governor, but that would be too much."

His office phone rang, and he rushed to take the call.

"Alexander, the Superintendent is not available until Thursday. Does Thursday afternoon work for you?" Amanda asked.

"If there's no other option. Explain to his assistant that this is an urgent matter. I need to speak with him as soon as possible."

After hanging up, he turned back to William and Susan.

"It seems we'll need Plan B."

William kept quiet for a minute.

"What's on your mind, William?" Alexander asked.

"Alex, do you remember that wealthy investor, a former Central Bank official, who we always thought was a friend of the actual governor?"

"Uh, Roberto Sued?" Alex asked.

"Right, him. Is he still investing with us?"

"I don't think he invests at Alliance. If he has something, it might not be substantial. I believe he still does at the brokerage."

"It might be worth it to call him and see if we can meet with him."

"Right. I'll research if he's friend of the governor or is someone who can help us there. I'll call you later."

He asked Susan to request a meeting with the department's director approving Alliance's request at the Securities Commission. They needed to understand better what was going on. All agreed to meet again at noon.

Alexander confirmed at the brokerage that he had investments, but the executive handling his account didn't know of any personal relationship between Mr. Sued and anyone at the Central Bank or any financial authority.

Following various attempts to find out something about him, he called a former sales executive who had managed Mr. Sued's investments for many years. He got lucky there. She was not sure how close, but she was confident they were friends.

This is the guy we need, he thought.

By noon, he had already talked to him. Alexander invited Mr. Sued for lunch that Tuesday, but he wasn't able to make it. Both agreed to meet that afternoon for a glass of wine. Everything was confirmed at 6:00 p.m. at El Catador, a wine shop with a nice bar.

He called William and Susan to cancel the meeting at noon and asked them to meet that afternoon. She would update both as soon as she had any news from the Securities Commission.

Before lunchtime, he called Ryan, the business head. He was sure that if investments increased noticeably, the authorities would have more confidence in approving Alliance's new shareholders. He asked him to make an additional effort during the week to make an important leap on the funds' balances. Once he finished the meeting, he left Alliance. He had lunch with an investor and a close friend. He was glad he didn't have to cancel him.

He arrived at the restaurant, parked, and walked in. His friend was already waiting for him. They ordered drinks, appetizers to share, and a main dish for each of them.

After two hours discussing the economy, investments, and some personal matters, both paid, and once they received back their cards, they left the restaurant.

Alexander walked back to his vehicle and saw a white paper on his windshield. He opened the note and was amazed when he read the handwritten words on it. First, he thought it was a joke, but then, with an increasing worry, read it back again.

"Alexander, if you don't leave the country, you're dead."

He turned back to see the back seat, then to both sides. No one was there, just parked vehicles. He looked around for several seconds, then hurried to the valet parking booth where two guys were standing.

"Hello, someone left this note on my SUV. Do you know who it was? Or did you see someone near my vehicle, the gray one down there?"

"No, Sir," one answered while he turned to look at Alexander's vehicle.

Then the other looked at the white paper and said, "Not me either, Sir."

"Are you the only two guys moving vehicles here?" Alexander asked.

One nodded and said, "Yes, Sir. Only the two of us for all these vehicles."

Alexander looked all around the parking lot but didn't notice anything strange. He went to his SUV again, started it, and drove back to his office six blocks away. During the ride, he looked whether any vehicle was following him. Nothing. Once he parked, he took the elevator and went directly to his office, preoccupied by the note he had received.

What the hell is going on? Is this just a joke? Not likely. Who would joke about something like that? he thought.

At his desk, he called his friend Hans, sent him a photograph of the note, and asked his opinion. He was asking someone who took any threat seriously.

"No one with a true intention to hurt you would be so stupid as to send you a handwritten threat."

"True," Alexander said, in an intent to calm himself.

"Anyway, Alex, you need to take care. It would be smart to take some additional measures. Someone who serves as driver and bodyguard is what I would recommend."

"You think so?" Alexander asked, reluctant to the idea.

"I know you don't like it, but you need to play it safe. At least for a while."

"You're right. I don't like it, but I'll follow your advice and hire someone."

"Who could want to send you such a note?" Hans asked.

"I recently had some problems with a bank's top executive, but I don't think he would go this far."

"Me neither. It would not be common to do this, but you never know. Ask the restaurant for the security videos, if they have any."

"I'll do that. Thank you, my friend. We'll be in touch."

"Yes, take care. Let me know if you need anything else."

After hanging up, Alexander was slightly less concerned. It made sense to hire a driver with protection skills.

He called the restaurant owner and explained the situation to him. The owner agreed to share the security videos, but he just had inside cameras. The only one outside was on the main entrance. He had two cameras that covered the whole dining area. He would send them the following day; the guy managing the system had not been there that afternoon. Alexander specified the time he had been at the restaurant to speed up the process.

He called the owner of the security company that managed those services at Alliance. He asked him to send resumes to evaluate.

"What's the profile you're looking for, Alex?"

"Someone who can drive and protect my family and me."

"You can get someone like a US Navy Seal, or someone who knows how to drive and use a gun, but smart enough to detect when something's wrong. The cost of each option is quite different."

"The last one sounds perfect, but he needs to be able to drive well. I don't have a formal driver because of that. I hate someone to drive me, but even more, if he does it badly."

"OK, I'll get on it. We'll send you some candidates, one day each for you to evaluate."

"Perfect. Please do it as soon as possible. If we can start tomorrow, perfect. I'm traveling out of the country on Thursday but coming back Sunday afternoon."

"OK. I'll call you back."

Before leaving for the after-hours meeting with Mr. Sued, Alexander and William met briefly with Susan. She had been able to schedule a meeting ten minutes before three with the Director of Approvals at the Securities Commission, a quick fifteen-minute meeting as he had another appointment at three.

Susan wasn't lucky to change the decision. Still, she noticed that the Director of Approvals referred twice to a particular statement, "The Superintendent has the final recommendation to the National Securities Council, positive or negative."

It seemed the Superintendent had intervened to recommend denial on the request, but she was not sure. The three agreed to discuss it after the meeting with Mr. Sued.

William and Alexander left for El Catador fifteen minutes after five. It wasn't far, but it was better to go earlier during rush hour. They arrived at El Catador on time, but Alexander's invitee wasn't there yet. They sat and asked the waiter to bring carbonated water, leaving Mr. Sued to order his choice of wine when he arrived.

Mr. Sued didn't know the purpose of the meeting, just that Alexander and William needed his advice in some matters in his area of expertise.

Fifteen minutes after six entered the restaurant. He apologized for the delay and blamed the rush hour.

"What do you want to drink, Mr. Sued?" Alexander asked.

"Wine, please. This is the best place for that."

"Right. Do you any preference?" William asked.

The sommelier came to their table and asked them to allow him to recommend some options. Alexander nodded, and the sommelier pitched a list of both wines and appetizers to share. At one option, Mr. Sued opened his eyes. Alexander noticed it.

"Do you like that one, Mr. Sued?"

"Yes, that's a good one."

"Please bring us a bottle and a tray of cheese and prosciutto," Alexander said.

Mr. Roberto Sued was in his seventies, a medium-size man with gray hair trending to white. His mustache was already white—an elegant gentleman. Always suited, or at least wearing a jacket, perhaps a custom from his previous years working at the Central Bank. He'd been a well-connected person in the past with all financial authorities.

He'd started his career there at a very young age after graduating in Economics. He worked in different positions until he'd been named Director of Economic Studies several years later. He had to be involved in several discussions due to studies and research he'd done jointly with different government Commissions, Ministry of Finance, Customs, and Tax authorities, mainly. He'd retired five years ago but was still well connected as he was a member of the country's ruling party.

Half an hour later, after discussing different topics, but mainly future elections and the economy, Alexander explained his case.

"We have an issue at the Securities Commission that perhaps you can help us with."

Alexander explained what had happened since they had acquired the company until the actual status with the regulators' approval.

"We need someone who can help us get this approved, Sir."

"Gentlemen, I think I can help you with such a matter," Mr. Sued said and sipped his wine.

William and Alexander turned to each other slightly, a discreet smile on their faces.

"Excellent, Mr. Sued. And how can you help us with this inconvenience?"

"The governor is a good friend of mine. He can make some calls and pull some strings to help Alliance receive approval. But I would need to ask him to do it as a personal favor."

"And could you do that before next Thursday?"

"Yes, I can do that. You helped me in all these years to increase my wealth. And your service has always been splendid since you were at the brokerage, Alexander."

"Excellent, Mr. Sued. Thank you."

I may need some help from you in the future. Would you be willing to do something for me?"

"It would depend on what, but we'll do our best for you, Sir."

"OK, I'll call him tomorrow morning and let you know during the day."

"Perfect. I'll wait for your call. Should we order one more bottle of wine?"

"Sure, why not?"

They left after the second bottle. Mr. Sued drove off in his car while Alexander remained outside with William.

"It looks like he can help us," William said.

"We have less than two days to get the recommendation changed. Not much time," Alexander said.

They agreed they would have to wait until Mr. Sued called back. They knew that if Mr. Sued was able to help them, it would cost something significant to Alliance in the future.

"No other option. We'll have to deal with that later," Alexander said while shaking hands with William.

He walked to his vehicle and called Susan to brief her. Then he sent a message to Amanda and asked her to insist on Wednesday for the meeting with the Superintendent.

When he arrived at his apartment building, he carefully checked the entrance and both sides of the building. He was sure no one was there. Then he drove in and parked. Inside his apartment, he asked Gabrielle to come to the studio to tell her about the shareholders' approval and the note he had received.

Gabrielle stood up, tapping her mouth with one hand. She didn't say a word until she'd assimilated everything.

"Who would be so stupid to leave you a handwritten note?"

"Right, it doesn't make sense. It might be Fred, or someone else trying to intimidate me. Anyway, I called the security company to get someone with personal protection skills to drive us."

She nodded.

"Tell me about the approval of Alliance."

Alexander made the long story short. They relied mainly on Mr. Sued, who appeared to be their best chance to move forward positively. Gabrielle was concerned about the approval and Mr. Sued's future request, but overall, about the threat note.

CHAPTER 17

Alexander did neither gym nor archery practice the next morning; he just wanted to rest. The past two days had been stressful. Too many balls to juggle with at the same time, and with the threat he'd received, he didn't want to be out much anyway.

Driving out of his building, he asked the security guard to stand at the entrance. He would pay careful attention to anyone or any vehicle nearby, until he had arrived at where he felt safe.

At his office, he recalled a gun he had bought many years ago in one of the leading gun shops in Santo Domingo, owned by a colleague's husband. A 9mm black Smith & Wesson. The three-grip option gave him the chance to fit his right hand best.

He loved to disassemble all its pieces, clean them one by one, and reassemble them again, especially after going to the shooting range. He remembered well the plenty of shots he was able to fire before reloading. Each magazine had a sixteen-bullet capacity.

He had to sell it in 2006 for a nice gain but deep regret. The cash helped to fund his first business with Gabrielle, the silver jewelry.

It would be good to have my gun back. It would make me feel safer, he thought.

That morning he had to review many items. Alexander's trip last week to Mexico and the messy previous two days had not allowed him to work on them.

He would need to be alert for any news from the authorities. Mr. Sued had promised to give him an update that afternoon. He was hoping to close that issue as he and Gabrielle traveled to New York the following day. He would eat dinner with his three primary investors in that country, two of them now shareholders at Alliance.

The Senator had scheduled a meeting with his lawyer, Adam Branning, and Christopher Mattis would be attending a conference during the weekend. They asked Alexander if he could join them for dinner and agreed to have it on Thursday. He'd accepted weeks ago, but now with all the rush at Alliance, he would prefer to stay in Santo Domingo. However, he wouldn't cancel; meeting the three gentlemen at the same time in the future would be challenging to arrange.

Since the trip had been planned, Gabrielle added herself immediately. She loved New York, and when possible, would be going there. Alexander usually flew around March for an annual risk conference he frequently attended.

Gabrielle had planned to dine with her cousin on Thursday while Alexander attended his dinner with the Alliance investors. On Friday, she had subscribed to a culinary course, and the non-reimbursed six-hundred-dollar fee was already paid.

Two weeks ago, they had discussed canceling the trip because of the increasing concerns with Coronavirus, but they decided to make it, taking proper preventative measures. So far, those measures included separating people three feet from each other and using antibacterial gel, while avoiding touching your mouth or eyes. Nothing else.

He stayed at his office for lunch. He would not move from Alliance in case any important call from the authorities or Mr. Sued came in.

Meanwhile, he reviewed an email he had received from the security company. It included three candidates' resumes. He was reluctant to get involved in this hiring, but he had to. The three were very good, with the necessary skills. One of them was too young, about twenty-five, and the other two were in their forties. He opted to interview the older one first, then schedule a meeting with the others the following week. His friend confirmed that all had been investigated thoroughly and were cleared.

Since he arrived at the office, he'd been constantly briefed by Amanda and Susan on any advance on each one's tasks related to the Alliance approval. Apparently, the Superintendent was neither granting him the conference call before Thursday nor effecting a change in the recommendation to the National Securities Council. His last option would be his plan B, Mr. Sued, a.k.a. plan A so far.

Concerns with Coronavirus were escalating, and they wanted to prevent any infection. Their usual attendance at a Broadway musical was canceled. Their regular visit to Eataly or Chelsea Market, too. He planned a long walkthrough Central Park while Gabrielle attended her course. Both agreed to rent a car on Saturday to drive to Long Island. Neither had been there before.

At four, Alexander was turning anxious. No news from anyone. He didn't want to call Mr. Sued. It hadn't been even twenty-four hours since their request.

He was signing different documents when he received an email from the lawyer who was preparing the Adagio contracts. He appreciated that the documents arrived one day early. He was planning to review them during his trip. He spent the next ninety minutes on them and sent them back to the lawyer, requesting some changes and questioning various clauses. The lawyer confirmed that all documents would be revised right away and sent to him later that night.

Immediately after he'd received the second email from the lawyer, Mr. Sued texted him, asking if he could call him. Alexander called him right away.

"Hello, Mr. Sued."

"Hi, Alexander. I have news for you," he said, sounding rather joyful. "As we discussed, I called my friend. He asked the President of the National Securities Council, who works for him, to review your case. This gentleman called me asking to explain everything in more detail and he called the respective unit at the Securities Commission to discuss it with them."

He was wordy in his explanation. Alexander wanted to get to the gist of it.

"After understanding the reason for the negative recommendation, he validated that the director and the Superintendent were too conservative with the minimum capital requirements. He agreed with both that a change in the recommendation could be granted, and so they did."

Alexander was walking excitedly around his office, "Excellent, so we'll be approved."

"Yes. They'll send tomorrow the recommendation to the National Securities Council to be included in next week's agenda. They'll also review a pending issuance you requested for one of your funds. I don't know the details, but I just wanted to tell you."

"Mr. Sued, we deeply appreciate your help. I don't know how to pay you."

The old man laughed and said, "Don't worry. We'll find a way to do so. It was my pleasure to help you."

"OK, we'll be in touch. Thank you again for all your help."

"Bye, Alexander."

Alexander called William and Susan. They met in his office and told both of them the details of his conversation with Mr. Sued. William almost opened a bottle of champagne, but they decided to hold on until final approval had been received. Instead, they crossed the street to the restaurant they frequented. Alexander sent a message to all local shareholders with the news and asked them to join if possible. Many did.

Once a table was set up at the terrace, he explained the good news in greater detail, and everyone proposed a toast. They had to wait for the final approval, but everything was moving in the right direction.

All were enjoying their get-together when Alexander saw Fred Shultz walking into the restaurant, accompanied by Jack Dowell. Minutes later, he saw Jack walking to the men's restroom on the terrace's left side. After thinking a few seconds about what to do, he decided to go inside and have some words with him.
Without telling anyone, he got up and walked inside. Alexander saw Shultz at the last table of the dining room and walked over to him, and six feet away, Shultz realized he was nearing his table. He didn't have time to do anything else but freeze, watching Alexander every second.
"Hello, Shultz, surprised?"
"Surprised at what?" His voice sounded exalted. He must have thought Alexander was about to punch him.
"Don't worry. I'm not making a scene here. I just want to tell you that I have compromising information on you."
With a nervous smile, Shultz said, "You have nothing."
"Oh yes. I have a video, a written confession, and a copy of a memorandum which, in the right hands, will break your bones."
"You have nothing," Shultz repeated, now without a smile.
"You'll see, coward. You'll pay for what you did to Alliance."
"I didn't do anything."
"Watch your back at the bank from now on. It might be your last day there soon."
Alexander didn't give him a chance to say anything else. He returned to his table outside. When Alexander sat, William turned to him.
"Everything OK, Alex? You seem troubled."
"No, everything's fine. It's time to celebrate."

Half an hour later, he left the crew still drinking and eating appetizers. Alexander apologized for leaving early, but he and Gabrielle had an early flight the next day. He crossed the street to his building.

At his office, he picked up his MAC, his car keys, and three books on the Dominican Republic, a limited edition he was giving to each of his US investors the next day at dinner.

Before leaving, he checked his phone to see whether the paralegal or the lawyer had sent him the modified Adagio documents, but they hadn't. He was expecting them anytime soon. He wanted to send them to George and Axel for their review before they arrived on Monday.

He drove home, satisfied, not only for the approval, but also for the pleasure to confront Shultz. Now he was taking a break during his trip, hoping to relax for some days.

At home, he prepared his carry-on, the ideal luggage for four-day trips, and his Swiss Gear backpack. Both were enough to travel with all he needed and to add some purchases. Gabrielle added a large bag. Kitchen gadgets typically occupied a lot of space, and she would attack these stores during their trip. Alexander, after many years fighting this, had thrown in the towel.

He received the Adagio documents late at night and did a quick review. Everything seemed fine, so he forwarded them immediately to his friends. He expected some minor corrections, especially from George who was meticulous with all business and legal matters, but he expected the main conditions to remain.

An hour later, he hadn't received George or Axel's reply. He texted both as he needed to confirm their flights to ensure all their hotel arrangements had been made accordingly. They were hoping to go out for dinner Monday, but Alexander wanted to have them at home.

Gabrielle would prepare some of their best appetizers, and the tequila options he had were not available at any restaurant in Santo Domingo.

Alexander sent the documents to Mr. Ramos. It wasn't a decent hour to call him. He would wait for his answer, most probable the next morning. Two hours later, he received a text from Mr. Ramos.

"Alexander, let's move on. We'll see you on Monday at noon to sign the documents, and we gladly accept your invitation to your home at night. Take care."

Even though he'd been traveling several days ago, he was willing to make this trip. On the last one, he had to pitch the project twice, deal with the traffic, and move from place to place in the city.

He hoped to spend these days casually with his wife, having dinner with his new investors and shareholders, and enjoying walking through the city. The previous three days of that week had been nerve-wracking enough to make him need a short decompressing trip soon. It was time for days of relaxation.

***

Shultz remained at the restaurant with Jack for two more hours after his encounter with Alexander. When Jack came back, he found Shultz quite disturbed. The waiter brought him another glass of whiskey, the third one. Jack was still finishing the first shot.

"You're drinking fast, Fred."

"I needed another drink after the scene you missed."

"What scene?"

"An idiot made a scene while you were in the bathroom. Alexander Stern. Did you know him?"

"I know who he is, but we haven't met. What happened?"

"We had a disagreement. Some clients from his company went to my bank," Fred said, not disclosing the whole truth.

"He looks like a nice guy. I heard good things about him and his company at the Construction Association. Did he make a scene just for that? Are you sure you didn't do anything else?"

"He's an idiot, Jack. Well, maybe we were a bit proactive taking those clients from his company."

"Fred, we've known each other many years. No one in his position will do something like that in a public place just for a proactive business initiative. What did you do?"

"OK. Maybe we pushed harder than usual."

"If you had problems with him recently, why did you choose to come to this restaurant? Just across from his company."

"This is the only restaurant that serves great zucchini carpaccio. I won't miss it because of him or his company. Look, let's change the topic."

Jack watched the ceiling for a second. He knew something else had happened, but he didn't care that much. He simply wanted to order another glass of whiskey and enjoy the night.

Shultz changed the subject. They finished their drinks, and several more.

It's time to scale this up. This is personal, against Alliance, and against Alexander Stern, he thought.

CHAPTER 18

The usual driver from Alliance picked them up on Thursday morning. Alexander valued the early flight, despite the hard time to wake up. Their flight was at 6:10 a.m. and it would land some minutes after nine.

Three hours and fifty-five minutes later they landed at JFK International Airport. Once at the hotel, they left their luggage at the concierge to start their short walk-through nearby to their hotel. After they visited some stores, they agreed to have lunch at Bareburger on Fifty-Seventh Street. They loved the bison meat hamburgers in this place.

After lunch, they left the restaurant, turned left at the next corner, then turned left again on Eighth avenue, and two blocks later were at Columbus Circle entering in The Shops. Gabrielle loved to go there and buy some kitchen tools and gadgets at Williams Sonoma. Alexander usually waited for her at Bouchon, drinking an espresso and a large macaron.

The early flight and the long walks demanded some rest. After check-in, they relaxed for two hours. Alexander checked on any urgent email or message, and only one was genuinely relevant.

Susan forwarded him an email from the Securities Commission. The recommendation for approval of the new shareholders of Alliance had been sent to the National Securities Council. He informed Gabrielle about it, and they were happy to hear the good news. He would inform his new partners later at dinner too.

Alexander's dinner was at seven. Christopher had made reservations. The four of them would meet at Daniel, an excellent restaurant of recognized chef Daniel

Boulder on Sixty-Fifth Street. Alexander stayed at the hotel until it was time to leave for his appointment.

At five, Gabrielle put on a jacket, gloves, a scarf, and grabbed her purse. She was going for an afternoon walk to visit more stores before meeting with her cousin at 6:30 p.m., a doctor who lived in New Jersey but worked in New York City.

"I'll see you tonight, Alex. Have a nice dinner with our new partners."

"Thanks. Enjoy your dinner too. Say hello to your cousin for me."

After a hug and kiss, she left their room.

Later, Alexander dressed in business casual attire. In the lobby, he ordered a cab, and five minutes before seven it stopped in front of the restaurant. He passed the main entrance and saw one of his partners at the bar, playing with a glass of whiskey. Christopher Mattis had arrived early and was waiting for all the attendees.

"Hi, Alex. Glad you made it," Christopher said when both saw Adam Branning, the lawyer and now investor at Alliance.

"Gentlemen, would you like me to guide you to your table?" A host asked.

"Yes, please. Take us there. We are waiting for someone else. He should be here soon. Please guide him when he arrives," Christopher requested.

The three partners were seated in a skybox with a unique view of the kitchen. More than willing to watch the spectacle of one of the world's most recognized chefs, they wanted some privacy. The small room, perfect for a party of four, was covered with frames in the upper part of the walls. One wall had nice mahogany shelves filled with books and knick-knacks. Another wall, in the lower half, featured a window that allowed them to see the kitchen, and a curtain that could be closed if privacy was needed. That would be the case later. The Senator was quite finicky about that matter. He often wanted privacy, unless he was campaigning or if he wanted to be seen with someone or somewhere.

Christopher already had his whiskey from the bar. Alexander asked for the same, and Adam ordered a glass of water. He would drink wine later when the first bottle was opened. After a short casual conversation about Tennessee, football, and the weather in New York City, the Senator arrived.

"Good evening, Senator. I'm glad to see you. How are you?" Alexander said while shaking hands with him.

"Everything is OK, Alex. Too many things to handle these days, but I'm done for the day, and hopefully for the week."

The sommelier arrived and recommended a variety of wine options. The Senator chose a Domaine Pierre Usseglio & Fills 2011.

"I guess you have more than one bottle," the Senator said.

"Of course, Sir."

Once he finished pouring the wine, he left and closed the door. He came back again to offer some bread, and minutes later, a server came to request their choices from the four-course prime-fix menu offered that night.

Alexander handed the books from the Dominican Republic to all. Everyone appreciated the opportunity to go through the book for some seconds. Then the Senator proposed a toast. They raised their respective glasses to cheer up when the Senator eyed Alexander.

"Alex, we're glad to have you here. We've agreed that everything we speak about is always kept strictly confidential. I mean, STRICTLY CONFIDENTIAL."

Alexander maintained full attention on the Senator and nodded to.

"We're trusting you because of the many years we've known each other, and now Christopher and I are shareholders at Alliance. We hope Brad can be soon too."

"Gentlemen," Alexander said. "I appreciate your confidence and your support. Count on my full discretion on all matters related to us."

"Perfect," the Senator said. "Having agreed on that, cheers, gentlemen."

After a sumptuous meal, the Senator, on his third glass of wine, started talking about politics and everything related to the November elections. He was concerned that President Trump's popularity seemed to be showing a downward trend, and with it, the Republican Party would be damaged too. This brought the conversation to the Coronavirus, widely discussed everywhere but not at an alarming level in the United States yet. At least in public opinion. The government had downgraded it with exceptional efficiency. When the Senator was asked to talk more about it, he opted to change the topic.

They discussed the financial markets, which had shown a strong downturn since February. The Dow Jones Industrial Index had come down about eight percent from last year's closing. Christopher was worried about it. He'd already lost several millions. Everyone was expecting some kind of correction after the strong growth in 2019, but nobody was sure how strong COVID-19 would affect the economy in the future and how neat the impact would be. So far, in the early days of March, they'd seen a slight positive reversal, but it was a minor one, and markets were still extremely volatile. Uncertainty was everywhere.

Two bottles of wine later, when they'd all finished their dinner, the Senator and Adam shifted to whiskey, joining Alex and Christopher.

"Tell us, Alex," the Senator said. "How's the business doing? Are you taking good care of us?"

"Everything's fine. We had a tough situation with some investors the last weeks, but we were able to handle it."

"What situation, if I may ask?"

"A targeted attack to our client's base. To some of our most important investors," Alexander answered to Christopher.

"And where did it come from?" Adam asked.

"From another bank, a medium-size one managed by someone who appears to lack any principles."

"But you solved it already, right?" The Senator asked, and before Alexander was able to answer, he added, "if you need any help, we will find a way to do it. Be sure of that, Alex."

"Thank you, Senator. I will. For now, it's been solved."

The conversation shifted again. The Senator spoke about many things going on in Washington. Campaign activities were increasing, but Coronavirus was a concern everywhere. And if the financial damage continued, he was sure President Trump's popularity would firmly decline.

"Gentlemen, if jobs are lost, the President will be affected. So far, he's fine, but there are many concerns about this disease. I expect it to get worse before it improves."

"But he said recently that it's just like a strong flu," Alexander said. The other three gentlemen smiled tensely.

"I agree with Brian, Alex. It seems to be getting worse, but the government is downgrading it. Remember, they're campaigning for reelection. I've heard that many strong measures are being discussed that would impact the economy. Am I right, Brian?" Christopher turned towards the Senator, waiting for his response.

The Senator crunched his face, in agreement, but didn't say a word.

***

Gabrielle agreed to meet with her cousin at 7:30 p.m. After a pleasant walk visiting stores, she arrived at the restaurant, nearby Columbus Circle. She carried her purse and two shopping bags. Alexander had reserved a table in her name. She was seated and immediately ordered a glass of pinot grigio. Then, a quick view at her phone to see if she had received any messages from the family, but nothing. The girls don't miss us very much, she thought and smiled.

Her cousin arrived ten minutes later. After a long hug, they both sat. They sputtered, pure Dominican style, and a minute later, the waiter approached to ask for her cousin's choice of drink.
"Glass of white wine, please. Same as she's having."
They spent the next two hours updating each other on everything. Gabrielle talked about her new business and how it started to gain traction. Alexander had requested she didn't give her cousin any details about his dinner with Alliance investors. They'd agreed to say that he was with some friends.
Their choice for dinner was fish and steamed vegetables for her cousin, and salmon and wild rice for Gabrielle. It was a great seafood restaurant where Alexander had eaten before and recommended it highly.

After two hours of speaking frenetically, they shared the check and left. Three minutes later, both stood on the street talking again, as if it hadn't been enough. Finally, they said goodbye to each other and started walking in different directions.
Gabrielle went back to the hotel. Twenty minutes later, she was in their room. After a quick call to both their girls, tired enough to even watch TV, she lay off on the bed and went to sleep.

***

Adam left the restaurant at nine. Christopher accompanied him to the entrance, and after discussing something, went to the restroom. Whiskeys had had an effect on him.

The Senator came back to the attack on Alliance, and Alexander added more details on what had happened, including the investigation and the confession episode.

"You managed it well, Alex. Especially the investigation. I agree with your friend that these situations are better managed off the record. A legal process is expensive and painful."

"Right, Senator. But I don't think this guy will stop there. I'm sure he'll try to affect us again, and maybe me directly."

"Hmmm. What do you mean, directly to you?"

Alexander told him about the threat left on his car at the restaurant days ago.

"Sounds kind of stupid, the handwritten note, but stupid people normally don't think well how to manage things, especially when they're full of hate."

"Right, Sir."

"Alex, give me some days to think about how to help you. Maybe I can get more information on him."

"Thanks, Senator. I appreciate it, but I don't want to bother you with this. I can handle it."

"Alex, this idiot is affecting our company. Remember, we're partners now. If I can help you, let me. It will be for good."

"Thank you," Alexander said, hoping to close the discussion, but the Senator continued.

"I have a close friend at the CIA. He's well connected in all the Latin-American countries. Many specialists work for him there. I'm sure he knows someone in Santo Domingo. Maybe he can retrieve some useful information."

While the Senator was speaking, Alexander felt rather anxious. CIA? Specialists? He thought this was going too far.

"Senator, I don't think this is something an agency like that one should get involved. Don't worry. I'm sure we can handle it, but thank you for your offer, Sir."

"Alex, don't worry, I just want to help. Let me see what I can find. Having more information might be useful for us, for Alliance, and for you. If you want to use anything we get, that would be your call to do so or not."

Christopher joined them, and the Senator made some hot jokes to him, and they laughed, breaking the tension Alexander had felt a moment earlier. A couple of minutes later, Christopher stood and said, "Gentlemen, I think I've had enough whiskey. I'm leaving for my hotel."

"It's time to go for me, too," the Senator said. "We're at the same hotel, Chris. We can go there together."

"Gentlemen, let me get the check," Alexander said.

"It's paid, Alex," Christopher said. "The next time is on you. Maybe in a nice place in Santo Domingo,"

"Thank you, Christopher. I was hoping to invite you all."

They left the room and went down to the main entrance. They put on their coats and went out of the restaurant. The Senator's driver was waiting for him in a black SUV.

"Alex, it was a pleasure to have dinner with you. We'll find a way to do it more often. Good night," Christopher said.

He walked around the vehicle and stepped into the back seat. He was followed by the driver, who closed the door and came around again, waiting for the Senator to finish speaking with Alexander.

"My boy, thank you for coming," the Senator said, kindly holding Alexander's arms and speaking with a parental tone. "We had a wonderful dinner. I'm glad you could make it. Feel free to text me anytime you want. We'll be in touch soon."

"Thank you, Sir. Glad to be here, and I appreciate your offer and support."

"Bye, Alex," he said while stepping into the vehicle.

The driver closed the door, stepped into the driver's seat, and drove off. Alexander stepped back, turned around, and started walking. He wanted to burn some of the several whiskeys he had consumed that night.

It took him twenty-five minutes to get back to the hotel. He thought about the Senator's offer, but he didn't think it had any significance. He assumed it was the mix of wine and whiskeys over several hours that perhaps had made the Senator say more he had to.

At the hotel, Gabrielle lay sleeping. He sat on the bed, and with her eyes closed, Gabrielle asked, "How was your night?"

"Everything OK. Get back to sleep. We'll talk about it tomorrow. Good night."

He kissed her, turned off the lights, and slept immediately.

Friday morning, he woke up ten minutes before eight with the sound of the coffee machine and smelling the aroma. He sat on the bed and stretched his arms in front of him. Gabrielle gave him a cup of coffee.

"Sorry, Alex, no milk. Just cream available."

He thanked her and asked, "At what time is your course?"

"At 9:00 a.m. I need to shower now. But tell me first about your dinner. How was it?"

"Excellent. I had a great time. We talked about the business, the economy, financial markets, politics, the Coronavirus. The food was great. I had roasted bison."

"Great. You'll have to take me there someday."

"Sure. The next trip."

"Sorry, Alex. I need to hurry up. You can give me all the details this afternoon. My cousin sent you a kiss and a hug. We had a great time."

Gabrielle walked to the bathroom and closed the door. Alexander spent the next half hour listening to Bloomberg's news and checking emails on his phone. By then, Gabrielle was ready to leave for her one-day culinary class. They agreed to meet there at 4:30 p.m. when it finished.

Once she left, he made a quick check of the funds daily report, and everything seemed to be fine. Growing was always a good sign, and no significant redemptions had been registered in the last two days, in all funds.

He hadn't decided what to do the rest of the day. Twenty minutes after nine, he was feeling slightly hungry. He took a quick shower, dressed, and left the hotel.

First stop would be a small cafeteria two blocks away. He liked the ham and cheese croissants there, with a glass of orange juice and a Hazelnut coffee. Twenty minutes later, he was ready to begin a long walk in Central Park. He had never gone through it completely. Checking an online map, he decided to start at Columbus Circle and through the interior trails to walk until the end at 110th St. After that, he would turn right until reaching Fifth Avenue, then another right on the park sidewalk to come back.

He thought it was a good idea to visit the Museum of the City of New York. Ninety minutes later, after enjoying Central Park's beauty, he arrived there.

Once he left the museum, the long morning made him feel hungry again. He decided to stop at a food truck on Fifty-Eight Street. After a large hot dog and a diet Coke, he was back on track.

Once at the hotel, he texted his two daughters briefly, but both were busy. He stayed there until ten minutes after four. He met Gabrielle outside the school. She was tired and didn't want anything to eat. Her group had been sampling different dishes all day, in addition to their lunch. They decided to return to the hotel and rest for the day.

The next day, they walked fifteen minutes to a rental car agency at Fifty-Fifth Street. Once they were inside their vehicle, they drove to the Hamptons. Both regretted spending so many hours, four in total, driving there to see the beach, eating something, and, after driving through the neighborhood, coming back to the city. It would have been much better to spend that day visiting a museum.

The following morning their flight was scheduled at 12:55 p.m. That didn't leave much time to plan something before it, so they went down at nine to the restaurant, had some breakfast, and ten minutes later, Alexander hailed for a cab for the airport.

They arrived at their apartment at seven that night. Alexander's friends, George and Axel, and soon-to-be partners in Adagio Associates, were coming the next day at six in the morning.

CHAPTER 19

Axel had visited Santo Domingo years ago for a regional meeting when he was assigned to Jamaica to lead a telecom company. It was the first time for George. They slept around three hours during their flight, but they would be able to rest before their meeting at eleven with Alexander, first to discuss the project highlights, before noon, when the signing of the final contracts would be done with Mr. Ramos.

After passing immigration, they walked through Las America's airport. Without documented bags, Customs was a quick stop. Alliance's driver was waiting for them at the end of the aisle where everyone is received.

"Hello, Mr. Fauch. Hello Mr. Cabrales. Mr. Stern asked me to pick you up."

"Thank you. How did you know it was us?" George asked.

"Mr. Stern sent me photographs of both of you."

"Uh, OK. Let's go," George said.

Axel turned to George while the driver was already walking three steps ahead and said, "I hope Alex didn't give him the full moon photograph at the pool in Cancun."

"I certainly hope not," George said. "Do you know? It's incredible how being so tired, you still manage to speak bullshit."

"Continuous practice and dedication," Axel said.

Later that day, they all would remember that joke.

The highway nested small businesses, warehouses, and some old houses on the right side. On the left side, the Caribbean Sea turned different shades of blue, including a lovely emerald closer to La Caleta, where some fishermen went out every day to catch fish, and where scuba divers were taken to dive to different undersea landscapes, including the wreck of the Hickory, a 108-foot tugboat about one hundred and twenty feet away from the beach, that served as habitat for coral and small tropical fish.

Other shipwrecks were found at La Caleta Underwater National Park, such as El Limón, Capitán Alsina, and Don Quico.

Fifty-five minutes later, they arrived at the hotel. Both were on the top executive floor of the building and would have to walk only a few steps for their meetings. They would be able to nap and refresh before their first meeting.

That morning Alexander was at the office at eight. He reviewed as many matters as possible before leaving to his meetings outside Alliance. As usual, he would first check the funds' balances, then a brief session to sign some documents with Amanda, and half an hour later a meeting with Ryan for an update on everything related to clients.

He left his office and went down with Colonel Robles, the new driver, to the underground parking. He had met him at home that morning to start a full-day test. He would be with him from 7:30 a.m. until late that night, a long shift but necessary to have more testing hours.

Colonel Robles followed typical security procedures. He stepped out of the elevator first in the underground parking lot, and after checking both sides, he walked beside Alexander to his vehicle. He opened the passenger front door and closed it when Alexander got in. He asked him to sit in the back seat, but Alexander declined.

"That's not for me, Colonel."

He never sat in the back. He used to drive whenever possible, but he would sit in the front if not. Otherwise, he got dizzy.

When he got to the meeting room, he waited until his friends arrived, five minutes later.

"Alex. How are you? Nice to see you," George said.

"Guys, nice to see you both. Glad to have you here. How was your flight?"

"A short overnight flight is killing," Axel answered. "We weren't able to sleep many hours, but we slept around two hours here at the hotel."

"After both meetings and lunch, you'll have time to rest until eight. A driver will pick you up to take you to my home for dinner."

"I don't know, Alex. I was planning to visit the city before dinner tonight. What do you recommend? This is my first time here, and I can't go back without doing some tourism," George said.

"That can be arranged. You can go to the old part of the city, make a quick walk where the Cathedral is, then visit the two museums at Plaza España. Dinner at home will be casual. You can go directly from there."

"Fine, I'll do that. Will you join me, Axel?"

"Of course. I'm not letting you have fun alone. I'm your escort today, remember that."

They spent the next fifty minutes discussing the deal. Everything was arranged for them to sign the contracts. They focused on the next steps and a potential timeline for the project. Alexander explained what was all needed to be done with the Trust to fund initial operations, authority's permits, and transferring the property.

Mr. Ramos arrived on time with his lawyer. So did Alexander's Notary Public. The fiduciary representatives came minutes later. Everybody understood the project and all legal matters; only minor details were reviewed. Once they were all in agreement, they signed the contracts. In a week, Alexander would send a chronogram for the whole project.

They all agreed to have lunch at the commercial center in the lobby. Alexander chose an Asian restaurant run by a well-recognized chef in Santo Domingo.

"Mr. Ramos, have you ever planned to develop a project like this in your property?" George asked.

"Yes. Many years ago, that was my wish. But lately, I've just been trying to sell it."

"It's better to develop a project on it," Axel said.

"I've had often been asked to sell it, and some weeks ago, a guy had insisted on buying it. When Alexander told me about the project, I got more interested in building something there."

"So, you had more offers?" George asked.

"Yes, one, but we didn't agree on the price."

"Sir, I truly believe we're the best option for you. You'll be able to have a much better return, plus the satisfaction to see something built on it," Alexander added.

"I know. Thank you for that. The next time Mr. Dowell calls, I'll tell him it's off the market.

"Who, Sir?" Alexander asked back.

"Jack Dowell. He's the one trying to buy it."

When Mr. Ramos said the name, Alexander didn't say anything. He didn't know that Jack Dowell, Fred Shultz's friend, was trying to buy the property.

I think I gained another enemy, he thought.

Mr. Ramos excused himself at 2:30 p.m. He had another meeting to go to, and he was already late. The remaining partners stayed at the restaurant. George, quite sensitive in these matters, noticed Alexander's reaction when Mr. Ramos mentioned the potential buyer.

"Alex, is it my perception, or were you surprised when Mr. Ramos told us the name of the guy interested in the property?"

"You´re right. I don't know that guy, but from weeks ago, I´ve been having problems at Alliance with someone he knows well."

"I hope nothing serious," Axel said.

"I don't think it could get more serious. Everything has been improving lately, but he's someone I have to take watch closely."

Alexander paid and reminded them that the driver would pick them up at four, and they would visit the Colonial Zone. Alexander asked both to evaluate the driver's driving skills and tell him their opinion later.

"Why, Alex?" George asked.

"We're evaluating to hire him at Alliance, and he'll be with you guys during the afternoon."

"We'll charge you a fee for that service," Axel said and smiled.

"Right," Alexander said and hit his arm. "See you guys later. Enjoy your afternoon as tourists."

***

Gabrielle was in charge of the event with Mr. and Mrs. Ramos, their Mexican friends, and themselves. Alexander invited William, but he wasn't able to make it. He offered to participate in the project, but he passed on it due to other commitments. His investments overseas, combined with the recent capital injection at Alliance, had limited his cash.

As planned, the driver picked up his friends and took them to the recommended sights. Some hours later, they arrived at Alexander's home. He was in the studio checking on wine options to offer. He thought Mr. Ramos and his wife might prefer wine, and he was sure his friends and Gabrielle would choose tequila.

"Pero ven acá. Como tu ta?" Axel said when they came into the studio. All laughed instantly.

"Oh, now you are talking Dominican," Alexander said.

"After two museums, a beer at a restaurant, and some interactions while walking there, you have to learn these phrases," Axel said.

"Hi, Alex. You need to give Axel tequila. Maybe we can shut him down for a while. He's gunfire talking bullshit," George said.

Everybody laughed, and the waiter came into the studio and offered different kinds of drinks and cocktails.

Five minutes conversation about Santo Domingo passed. George and Axel told Alexander how much they liked the Colonial Zone.

The doorbell rang twice.

"It must be Mr. Ramos and his wife," Alexander guessed.

"Axel, please behave. We don't want our business with this guy to die before it starts," George said.

"Just watch me," he said and laughed.

That didn't sound as good as George and Alexander wanted.

"Good evening, Mr. Ramos. We're glad to have you at our home. Nice to meet you, Mrs. Ramos. Let me introduce you to my wife, Gabrielle."

"Nice to meet you. Thank you for the invitation, my wife and I appreciate it. We have much to celebrate."

"That´s right, Sir. Please come into the studio. Our partners are waiting there."

After introductions had been made, they all sat.

"Excuse me," Gabrielle said. "I have to finish something in the kitchen. I´ll be right back."

For the next forty minutes or so, they extensively discussed Mexico and the Dominican Republic. Mr. Ramos had been in Monterrey many years ago. George offered them a nice view of the best cities to visit and a list of the must-see museums and sites to enjoy in Mexico City. He loved to make those summaries to everyone he knew from overseas. He was an avid promoter of his home country.

Dinner was served at nine. Gabrielle had arranged a classily setting, with a large variety of her most tasty appetizers, dished elegantly. Mrs. Ramos congratulated her; she was impressed. All men ate as if it were their last meal. When asked what they liked more, all agreed on the dates filled with goat cheese and covered with caramelized bacon.

An hour later, a set of three different desserts prepared in Gabrielle's kitchen arrived. Drinks didn't stop coming all evening. The waiter knew Alexander's guidelines.

After some drinks, Mr. Ramos told Alexander he had spoken with Jack Dowell that afternoon. He called him insisting on buying his property, but this time he told him it was not for sale any longer. A project would be developed in partnership with three investors, two Mexicans and Alexander Stern. Jack chided him why he hadn't been told before, something he wasn't entitled to. Mr. Ramos told him he could do with his property whatever he wanted, and so he did.

Twenty minutes before midnight, Mr. and Mrs. Ramos left. The party of four stayed in the studio consuming tequilas until one in the morning. The story of the photograph at Cancun came up. It wouldn't have been a weird one if it hadn't been taken with all their buttocks, and the ones of a bunch of women. They took off their swimming suits momentarily at the pool bar for such a photograph. Of course, that generated a strong warning from the manager on duty that afternoon.

George was practically sleeping on the couch, and Axel seemed tired too.

"Axel, it's time to go. We need to catch an early flight tomorrow," George said.

"Yes," Axel said quietly as both stood up.

"Guys, it was a pleasure to have you at our home," Alexander said. I'm pleased that we got in this project together, something we've been hoping to do twenty-something years ago."

After some hugs and several minutes of saying goodbye, they were taken back to the hotel. Alexander and Gabrielle went to their bedroom. They checked on the house alarm. They were still concerned with the recent threat and checked the alarm regularly to make sure it was correctly set up.

***

Fred Shultz and Jack Dowell set up a meeting on Tuesday morning, as Jack requested. He was bothered about losing such an opportunity, and he recalled Fred's discussion with Alexander. Now he was interested in receiving more details and seeing what he could do to buy the property. He regretted not paying more before. Now he had lost much more. He needed to find a way to take out Alexander of the deal with Mr. Ramos, and Fred could be the best advisor on such a matter.

Jack arrived at Fred's office at eleven.
"Thanks for receiving me on such short notice. I know you're busy as hell."
"No problem. When you called me, you said it was something urgent. And if it's related to Alexander Stern, I want to hear about it as soon as possible. What's on your mind?"
"The son of a bitch just excluded me of a good business I've been looking for. It's a piece of land well located. I offered a lower market price, and I wasn't willing to increase it. Alexander and his partners closed a deal with the landowner, and now I'm out."
"What kind of deal?
"I don't know the details of the transaction, but he told me it was closed."
"You're sort of fucked by this idiot, Jack. You need to find a way to take him out of the deal, leaving the landowner no other option than to reevaluate your offer at a price he would be willing to sell."
"Right. But I need Alexander to be cut out of the deal first."

"We'll find a way to do that," Fred said.

They stayed for an hour trying to find a way to make Alexander and his partners get out of the deal, but so far, they hadn't found a way to do it, at least not a legal one. Fred had to run to another meeting. They agreed to think about it and discuss it later.

Fred had already thought of something he'd been planning days ago that could indirectly help his friend.

***

Alexander was being driven to his office on Tuesday morning by the second candidate he was evaluating. George and Axel's flight was scheduled at nine. He called them before departing to check on them and agreed to be in touch during the week.

Alexander was close to Alliance when his phone rang.

"Hello, William. How're you doing?"

"Hi, Alex. We're being hit again. Ryan just told me that two important clients are leaving, in addition to three from yesterday."

"Who are the clients?"

"Haven't you seen the report? We lost four percent of our portfolios yesterday with those three clients. We have six percent less in funds managed in addition to these two. In just two days," William answered excitedly.

"I just arrived at Alliance. I'm going up."

Alexander hung up and got out of the vehicle at the building's main entrance. He pressed the elevator button to get up to the Alliance floor. While waiting, he looked at the email with the client's portfolio. When he saw it, he opened his eyes wide and took a deep breath.

These are not regular runoffs, but significant investments. What's going on? At this pace, we'll be out of business in less than two weeks, he thought.

CHAPTER 20

Once at his office, Alexander called Ryan and the executives in charge of the departing clients' accounts. William joined them. Alexander was briefed on all the information they'd been able to retrieve. Four of the clients were requesting wire transfers to Fred's bank. There was only one difference from the previous attack. This time, Fred's executives were not offering exorbitant interest rates, just slightly higher ones, but nothing that could be considered strange or inappropriate.

They agreed that these clients usually move to better rates' options, even if the difference was relatively small. It was clear to all that the targeting of Alliance's wealthy clients had started again. All clients who had left were in the list generated by Jeff.

They had to think of something fast. There was no time to lose. Some clients had been contacted already. A significant amount of investments could be gone, leaving the company in a difficult situation.

"Alex, maybe you can call Fred directly," one of the executives said.

Alexander said it wouldn't be helpful. He let them know that two executives involved in the previous attack had been fired, but it was obvious someone still had the list of Alliance's wealthy investors. Maybe Fred himself had passed it to other executives.

All the executives were requested to contact all their clients immediately. They would invite those on the list for lunch or drinks after work. During the week, they had to deepen their relationships with them. Ryan would be joining them in this task. Same with Alexander and William. Clients wishing to go would be asked to wait for some days, or to make just partial retirements until all their investments were gone. That might not stop the bleeding but could reduce the pace until a definite solution was found.

Alexander called three banks to request a credit line. He offered his shares as collateral, but the banks were not willing to grant it. William and Alexander spent all day calling former clients and financial institutions. New investments to substitute those flying out were vital to mitigate the accelerated reduction of the funds' balances.

They decided to absorb some of the losses when they sold securities to honor redemptions, but it wasn't possible to cover all if everything continued. Soon an impact would affect the funds' profitability, and more clients would leave even if they had not been on the deadly list.

Alexander arranged lunch with Ryan and two brothers who were investors at Alliance. Both were on the list. Combined, including their mother's investment, represented four percent of the total. Lunch was going well. There was no news related to leaving the company, so far. It was just until the last of his dessert that one of them brought up the topic for discussion.

"Gentlemen, maybe we'll have to cancel part of our investments with Alliance."

"Why is that?" Alexander asked.

"We need to increase our investments' profitability and we received a good offer from another bank."

"But that rate will be momentarily, only for one or two months. Rates in the market are coming down fast, and we've locked some medium-term investments in our funds that will assure your actual returns," Alexander said boldly.

"I haven't thought of that. But I already agreed to take part of it to another bank. Maybe they would maintain those rates longer than two months."

"I wouldn't take that risk. No doubt rates are dropping fast. You would earn less in the future with that option than with us."

"I'll check on it later," the investor said and changed the subject, clearly not willing to speak more about it.

Minutes later, everyone left.

"It's clear they'd been approached," Alexander said to Ryan. "I hope we can keep them, or at least part of their investments. Keep me informed about any request from them. As soon as we arrive, please check if any new clients are leaving."

Ryan nodded, not willing to speak much.

The restaurant was near the office, and Alexander arrived soon at the main entrance of their building. Alexander sent his nephew a message rescheduling their meeting until the weekend. He had to concentrate on Alliance. He asked his assistant to reschedule some appointments until next week, too. His main priority would be to handle this situation, and everything else could wait.

Ryan called him twenty minutes after they arrived.

"Alex, two more clients are leaving. We lost three percent of the total portfolio."

"Damn, three percent," Alexander said quietly.

After this news, he remained in his office, watching the city through his window and thinking deeply about how to manage the situation. Minutes later, he recalled the Senator's offer.

Maybe it's time to call him and accept his help, he thought.

He was hesitant to do so. He spent another half an hour thinking of a way to stop it, but no options came into his mind.

"Good afternoon, Senator. How are you?"

"Hello, my boy. I'm fine. How was your flight back to the island?"

"This week has been complicated. We are under attack again, Sir."

"Same as the last one? Same guy?"

"Yes, Sir. Missiles are hitting us every day."

"Do you want me to call my friend and ask him to call someone there?"

"I don't see any other option. We need to stop this fast."

"Don't worry. We'll handle it. Keep resisting; it might take a few days."

"Thank you, Sir."

"I have to go. We'll be in touch soon. Bye."

Alexander wished that soon meant truly soon. After a minute, his instinct told him it was not the best thing to do, but he didn't have any other alternative.

William came to his office ten minutes after he'd texted the Senator. He briefed him on everything but left out the Senator's part. He and William discussed different ways to handle the situation. Alexander waited to receive calls from his assistant. She was dialing to potential new investors. Then Ryan came to his office and informed him that the clients from lunch had asked him to cancel twenty percent of their investments, but they would wait until next Tuesday.

"At least we have one week to replace them," William said.

"Right, but every day the funds are going down. We need to work on something bold fast," Alexander said while answering his phone.

"Alex, I haven't been able to reach the investors. I'll keep trying," Amanda said.

"OK," Alexander said, disappointed.

That afternoon, the sales executives were able to get new investments to cover half of the money they had lost that day. Despite a negative net, this was good news. The impact for that day was not all that they were expecting.

The driver he had to evaluate that day was a mess. As stated in his resume, he had good protection skills, but he was the worst driver Alexander had ever had.

"This guy drives like he's driving a motor cross," he said to William. "He stops suddenly and takes off as if someone is chasing him. Terrible. He makes me dizzy, even in the short drive from the restaurant."

"Let's continue with the next candidate."

Alexander sent the driver back to the security company immediately after coming back from lunch.

Amanda called him. "Alex, an assistant at the security company is calling you. Do you want to take the call?"

"Yes, please."

"Mr. Stern, the driver is here. Is something wrong?"

"I decided to hire yesterday's driver, Colonel Robles. Please send him to my home tomorrow morning. You need to help today's driver with some lessons."

"OK, Sir. Regarding Colonel Robles, is 7:30 a.m. fine?"

"Yes. Thank you."

Alexander was able to end the task of finding a driver. He had a good feeling about Colonel Robles. Something he would be grateful for, since the following days.

Alexander stayed in his office. Amanda was able to get a couple of potential investors, but just one would invest. He finally went home at seven.

No driver had been assigned until the following day. Taking the short ramp down to the street, he saw a parked black SUV, but he didn't pay much attention to it until the next corner when he saw it was tailing him. At the next corner, he made a right, then a left because there was traffic ahead on the main avenue, so he decided to take an alternate route.

He was surprised to see the same black SUV behind a sedan behind him. He felt a shock through his system. This could not be a coincidence. It must be following me, he thought.

He made an abrupt stop, running the risk of having hit by the sedan, then accelerated fast and turned left at the next intersection. He sped up again until the next corner. He was about to turn right again when he saw the black SUV coming fast. He was already about two hundred feet away from it. He accelerated, and after seven blocks, he arrived at his street. Once in front of his building, he opened the gate, hoping to have time to enter before the black SUV got closer.

When the gate finally opened enough, he drove fast through the ramp and stopped the car in front of the elevators. He grabbed his phone and home keys and ran up the four floors through the stairs to his apartment. He opened the door and closed it fast. Once he locked it, he rushed to the studio balcony to see if the vehicle was there. He saw it about a hundred feet away from his building, driving fast.

The security personnel at the lobby called immediately. Alexander was already back from the balcony and answered the intercom.

"Mr. Stern, you left your car on the ramp, out of your designated space. Are you OK?"

"Yes, I'm fine. Someone was following me. Please check if some unauthorized person is at the lot or at the lobby, or if someone you don't recognize is on the street."

"Yes, Sir. I'll call you back."

Three minutes later, the guard called.

"Mr. Stern, no one's there. Do you want us to call the police?"

"No, thank you."

"Do you want us to park your car and send up your keys?"

"Yes, please."

"We'll pay close attention to anything strange, Sir. We'll keep you informed."

"OK. Thank you."

Minutes later, someone knocked. He walked cautiously by the door and saw the concierge through the peephole. He opened and got the SUV keys. After thanking him, he closed the door and locked it again.

That experience confirmed he had to do something. It was becoming more dangerous by the hour. He was concerned for himself and his family. Many questions came up to his mind. Was Fred Schultz behind this and the other threat? Or Jack Dowell? Or both? It doesn't make sense.

He went to the bedrooms and relaxed after watching Andrea and Gabrielle there.

Gabrielle saw his face and asked, "What's wrong?" What happened?"

He explained everything to her, and she became deeply concerned.

"Wow, Alex. Now I'm scared. A stupid note is one thing, but this? This is something else."

"Yes, I know. I'm worried too."

"Who could be behind these?"

"I don't know. Maybe it's someone just trying to intimidate me."

"Yes, but who?"

"Fred is the only one I can think of, but I'm not sure. I never thought he would go this far."

"What should we do now?"

"First, I'll have a whiskey. I need one."

He walked to the studio and she followed behind him. Once there, he served two glasses, a whiskey for him and a shot of tequila for her.

"Gabrielle, tomorrow, the driver will be here early in the morning. I'll brief him on everything, and I'll talk to my friend in the security company now. He'll take me to Alliance. I have to be there all day, and he'll come back here if you or Andrea want to do anything out of the house."

"What? Forget that. Andrea and I aren't going anywhere. The driver can stay with you all day," she said emphatically.

"OK. We can decide whether to hire another driver or take a different action. We'll see."

They remained there for half an hour and one more round of drinks. That night they went to bed very late. Finally, around two in the morning, they were able to sleep.

***

Colonel Robles arrived earlier than the time he'd been requested, but he wanted to review everything. He checked the vehicle, including the chassis, the engine, and seats. He wanted to make sure everything was in order.

He studied both vehicles' entrances to the building, the main door to the lobby, and the personnel access. He spent several minutes in the lobby checking the security cameras and made sure the electrical wires were working.

He left the building, walked to the adjacent properties to study them, and went back to the building's main entrance, where he did a complete review, making sure to visualize everything one hundred feet away.

At 7:45 a.m., Alexander called him. He summarized everything; he'd already been briefed the previous night.

They drove out to Alliance; no vehicle followed them. Nothing strange. They agreed to take a new route to the office. They would park and would go up to Alliance together. Same when they left. They would be together whenever they were out of the apartment or Alexander's office.

Once Alexander was at his office, Colonel Robles took the SUV to the security company. He spent the day adding some light armor to the doors and a special plastic to all the windows. Meanwhile, the bulletproof glass would be installed.

Alexander spent the whole day on the same duties as the day before, except lunch out of the office. He had something planned at a restaurant, but it was canceled. Instead, Amanda arranged a nice lunch in the conference room with a client and Ryan. This time William would join them, as he knew the client very well. Another one on the famous list.

After a nice meal, the client told everyone he was not leaving. He was loyal to Alliance. So far, he had made good money during many years with the brokerage, and he was comfortable there. He had been contacted by another bank lately and they had been very persistent, but he would stay.

Colonel Robles arrived ten minutes after seven. The vehicle was heavier but safer. The security agency could get special windows for the front and rear passengers but were pending the remaining ones. Now the side windows were immobilized. The four doors now had a half-inch steel plate inside.

The agreed security protocol was strictly followed. Fortunately, they experienced nothing strange or risky that day. At Alexander's apartment, Colonel Robles gave him the vehicle key and left.

On Thursday morning, Alexander was still at home when the phone buzzed. The Senator was texting.

"Hello, Sir. I'm his assistant. Can you text now?"

"Good morning. Yes, of course."

"He wants to see you as soon as possible. He asked me to tell you that he has a solution for your problem. Would you be able to have dinner with him this Friday?"

"You mean, tomorrow?"

"Yes, Sir."

"Where?"

"Nashville. He's assisting at a wedding on Saturday, but he'll be there tomorrow morning."

"OK. Yes, I think I can find a flight."

"Perfect. As always, he wants full discretion. Please make a reservation for dinner in your name at The Palm. 7:00 p.m. Choose a booth at the bar, not in the main dining room."

"OK, I'll do that."

"Perfect. Safe flight. He'll see you there. Bye."

Alexander confirmed that the only available and fastest way to get to Atlanta, and then to Nashville, was to take a flight later at 3:31 p.m. He could sleep in Atlanta and drive early the next day to Nashville. He could reserve a flight back to Santo Domingo from Atlanta at 10:00 a.m. on Saturday. Still, he would have to drive back from Nashville to Atlanta at 3:30 a.m. on Saturday, or drive on Saturday to Atlanta and take an early flight on Sunday morning to Santo Domingo. He decided on the last option.

When he told Gabrielle, she didn't like it. She always hated those quick trips, but she understood, and if Alexander could find a solution, he had to make it.

He filled a carry-on, no backpack this time. He took his passport, and after lunch Colonel Robles drove him to the airport. Once at the office, he made a hotel reservation at the same one he'd stayed at with Gabrielle on a previous trip to Nashville.

He spent that morning thinking about what the Senator's solution could be. He thought it could be more investments from them or friends, but a quick mysterious trip would not be requested only for that. Something else had to be hidden on such arrangement.

CHAPTER 21

Alexander finished his roast beef sandwich and left Alliance for the airport. Having previously done check-in online and without a documented bag, he went fast to the airplane, which departed on time.

Once in Atlanta, he walked the long aisles to Immigration and was able to pass quickly. He picked up the vehicle he had rented and went directly to the hotel. Once in his room, he checked for any news from Alliance. Only Gabrielle and William knew about his trip. Everyone was notified that he was out of the city to meet with an investor. After speaking with Gabrielle, he watched the news on TV for a couple of hours and then went to bed. The previous long night was taking its toll.

On Friday morning, he ate breakfast, and half an hour later, he was on the road to Nashville. About an hour before his destination, he saw a signal with Lynchburg's directions. He suddenly recalled that Jack Daniel's distillery was there. On his last trip with Gabrielle, they'd seen a similar signal on the other side of the highway when they drove back to Atlanta. Maybe on Saturday I can visit it on my way back, he thought.

Once at the country music capital, he drove directly to the Union Station Hotel, a restored 100-year-old structure with a stunning stained-glass ceiling. Many years ago, it had been the main building of an old train station. The lobby featured a perfect blend of modern and classic objects that formed an elegant decoration. He liked the contemporary art deco metal-horse sculpture at the lobby, and the fireplace with two medieval-style hall chairs on each side.

He asked the hostess if he could stay in the same room as his previous trip.

"Oh. So, you've been here before?"

"Yes, I spent three days here last year with my wife. We loved your hotel."

The hostess asked for the room number, and after confirming it in the system, she smiled and nodded to him.

"Oh, lucky you. It's available. You have a better room now, but I'll make the change if you want."

"Yes, please. I liked that room, its decoration, the view of the train railway, and the landscape you can see from the window; it will be nice."

"Perfect, let me arrange everything."

Five minutes later, he entered into his room, a nice regular-size fully restored space with warm modern furniture, not typical of the Southern-style, but featuring a nice touch of country music objects and lithographs.

Once he hung up his clothes in the closet and looked at his phone for any urgent messages, he took the elevator down to the lobby. He stepped out of the hotel, passing by the big rock guitar at the main entrance, made of various screws, nuts, and many other metal pieces.

He walked down Broadway Street, and five blocks later, he was at the heart of the Honky-Tonk district, with many bars and plenty of live music performances all day. It was almost time for lunch. He decided to pay a visit to Rippy's, the bar he and Gabrielle liked.

Live music had started at eleven in the morning and would not end until very late at night. He spent the next three hours listening to music and relaxing. He had plenty of time before his dinner with the Senator, which would take place just steps around the corner.

He went back to the hotel and checked on Alliance. He had received an email from Ryan; two more clients had told their sales executives that they were leaving, both with significant investments. Ryan had tried to retain them, but he couldn't do so. The bleeding continued. William had been advised, too, and was texting him. They chatted for some minutes and agreed that

Alexander would call him after his dinner with the Senator. He was anxious to hear about his solution for Alliance's predicament.

Alexander called Gabrielle later. He didn't want to worry her, so they just talked about her business, Andrea, and Rachel.

He spent the remaining hours before dinner reviewing other Alliance matters, including a sales plan, some incentives estimations, and the company's financials.

He left his room with enough time to walk to the restaurant. At the hostess booth, he confirmed his reservation at the bar. The Senator hadn't arrived, but Alexander was guided to his booth. He ordered a whiskey and a Nashville brewed beer while waiting for him.

The Senator arrived ten minutes later. He entered the restaurant and told the hostess someone was waiting for him at the bar. He signaled the way himself.

"OK, go ahead, Sir," she said.

He wore a black jacket, a scarf, glasses, and a brown beret. His face could barely be seen. He did not want to be recognized if possible, even in the city where he was born.

Once he saw Alexander, he nodded to him and approached where he was sitting. Alexander had left him the side with the least view from the bar.

"Hi, Alex. Don't stand up," the Senator said.

"How are you, Sir?"

"Fine. Thank you."

"Perfect. Did you arrive today?"

"Yes, my boy. This morning. I passed all day relaxed. Just personal matters, thankfully. Nothing from Washington. Well, there's always something from Washington."

"I hope everything is fine, Sir."

"Yes. I see that you already ordered. I'll have a whiskey too."

Alexander called a blond waitress standing in a corner, watching nearby tables.

"Yes, Sir. How can I help you?"

"Miss, I'll have a whiskey, same as him," the Senator said, pointing to Alexander's drink.

"Thank you for calling me Miss, Sir. I'll bring it right away. Do you want something else? A beer, water?" she said while both smiled at her comment.

"That'll be all for now, young lady. Thank you."

"You know, Alex. I love Nashville. Wonderful city. Since I was young, I've enjoyed it a great deal. Country music is the best. You need to have a taste for it. I love it. This part of the city reminds me of many good stories with friends. Too much fun. It´s nice to visit Centennial Park and see the Parthenon. You can't miss the Country Music Hall of Fame. Too much history there, and the old cars exhibited, belonging to some famous musicians, are just great."

"Yes, Sir. A nice city. I was here last year with my wife. We enjoyed it, and I agree with you, country music is great. We both love it. I liked the live performances very much presented at many bars."

"Oh, great. So, you know the city. I'm glad to hear that, my boy. Tell that to Chris, too. He'll love to hear it."

"Sir, why did you choose this place? It's crowded. I thought you would like something more private."

"You know, Alex, The Palm is perfect. My friends and many people I know don't come to this restaurant on Fridays, and whenever they come, they don't come here to the bar. They book regularly at the main dining room. I´m practically an unknown here. And with this nice beret and glasses, and without a suit, I pass unnoticed."

"You have a point there," Alexander said.

"Also, people who come here from Nashville normally don't care too much about politicians. Not all, but many are more bohemians, instead of being interested in politics or business affairs."

"But it's louder here."

"Yes, and it's better that way. In these booths, if you get closer, you can speak quite normally, and no one can hear you."

"You're right, Senator. I see you're all set up."

The waitress came back with the Senator's whiskey. After serving it to him, she asked if they were ready to order. Alexander had looked at the menu while waiting for the Senator, so he was ready. The Senator knew precisely what to eat. The waitress took both orders and left. After a sip of whiskey, the Senator started to speak, this time on the night's central theme.

"My boy, you're having a difficult time back home."

"Yes, Sir. We are under attack again. It stopped momentarily, but now we're being hit again. Same bank, same guy, the one I told you about."

"I know. Since last week we've made some inquiries. My friend at the agency has someone there helping to retrieve some information about that guy. It´s already done. We just want to see if he can add something else to his investigation, something more relevant and of greater impact."

"OK. What do you have so far, Sir?"

"I can tell you this, Alex. You won't have to worry anymore about this guy or his bank."

"Sir, everything will be done … uh, how can I …"

"Legally?" The Senator asked.

"Well, yes, Sir."

"Of course, my boy. As everything I do. Don't worry about it. Let me eat some of this fresh bread while it's warm."

After several minutes of discussing the tasty bread and beer served in Nashville, they were interrupted by the waitress. She was accompanied by a man handling a black round tray with various dishes.

"Gentlemen, your food is ready," the waitress said. "May I serve it?"

"Of course, my dear. I´m starving," the Senator answered.

"For you, Sir, the prime boneless rib-eye steak, medium, and a side of brussels sprouts. And for your sir, the prime New York strip, well done, and a side of three-cheese au gratin potatoes. I hope you enjoy your meal."

Both thanked the waitress, and after a blessing by the Senator, they started to eat their meal. Half an hour later, while talking of many casual topics, including the great meat served in Nashville, they finished. The waitress removed the dishes while offering desserts. Both passed but chose another round of whiskeys. Once she brought both glasses, the Senator continued with the conversation Alexander was expecting.

"Alex, let´s talk about your problem," the Senator said after a sip of his whiskey. "So far, the inquiries that my friend's friend has made, a specialist down there in Santo Domingo, were very productive. We have compromising information about this guy, and some of his board members, not all. Pretty decent people in general, but everyone, everywhere, has a little secret. These guys are not the exception."

"That´s good news, Sir."

"It's excellent news. The plan is to take him down from his bank position using that information. His board will not have an option other than to kick his ass out."

"And what is that information?"

"Hear this, Alex. We detected fraud in his bank. Nobody inside the bank knows about it yet. He's been taking money from some abandoned accounts, closing them, and sending the money to an account in The Bahamas in his name, with a quick scale in another local bank. He's sent close to a couple of million dollars in the last seventy-four months, small amounts each time to stay under the radar. We know his annual salary the same years back, and his lifestyle, credit card payments, everything. There's no way he could save that much money."

"Yes, that's fraud. He could go to jail."

"Yes, he could. But I'm not sure his board would want to do that. It would indicate the lack of controls they have. If all this becomes public, they'd have to explain a lot to the financial authorities, external auditors, and clients. Their image would be severely damaged, and hundreds of clients would run out fast."

Alexander was impressed. He had to assimilate all this information provided by the Senator.

"I never thought this guy could be robbing his bank, and for so many years," Alexander said.

"My boy, our guy there is still retrieving some information, just to complete the investigation and be better prepared for everything. But we can move forward right away with all what we have."

"How can we use that information?"

"The specialist is formulating a plan. He'll contact you back in Santo Domingo with all the details."

"OK, Sir."

"Alex. I haven't finished."

The Senator ordered two more whiskeys, and Alexander also asked for tonic water. Minutes later, the waitress was back with everything. The Senator leaned forward again to continue his conversation.

"Alex, you have all our support. Chris, Brad, and I are committed to help you with everything you need on the island or here in America. We can do many things together, you'll see."

"Thank you, Sir. I'm glad to hear that."

"To move everything forward, we need your help with something. We need to increase our Alliance's ownership and maybe participate in that new adventure in real estate you're working on with your Mexican friends."

Alexander was surprised at the Senator's last words. He hadn't said anything to him about Adagio Associates.

"Wow. You are well informed. I feel as if I've been bugged," Alexander said lightly, but he was worried.

"Come on, Alex. We wouldn't do that. It was done with the banker who's making your life miserable. The specialist retrieved a conversation between him and someone called Jack Dowell. Some details about your project came up. As we speak, they're both planning how to hurt you at Alliance and with that project, to the point that you'll lose both. And with that, my boy, we could lose our money too. We're not allowing that to happen. This guy is going down."

"Sir, I'll need to speak with the other shareholders. That's not my call. How much are you willing to put in?"

"Don't worry about it. We don't want that much. A thirty-five percent total would be a decent number."

"That's a very high number. I don't know if I'd be able to arrange that."

"It's a fair number, Alex. You can think about it, but you don't have much time. Our business is suffering. This would be a good tradeoff for the other shareholders, as well as for us. We're able to send the equivalent amount for the additional twenty percent on Monday, plus two times that amount on long-term investments. That would help the business to stay afloat while we stop this idiot banker."

"Let me think about it, Senator."

"My boy, think about it while I go to the bathroom. I'll be back in a minute."

The Senator stepped out of the booth. Alexander thought about his offer.

He has a point; we don't have time. Without their help, we won't have a business in two weeks, maybe four if we get more new customers. Keeping sixty-five percent without problems is better than eighty-five percent of nothing, he thought.

The Senator came back, and they continued their conversation.

"Sir, our situation doesn't leave us another option. You know that, and I know that. I'll address the other shareholders to see if they're aligned. I'll be in touch with you early next week. I'm fine with moving forward with your proposal, but I need them to be too."

"Good. Wise decision. Not only to save this business. We'll do many things together that will make us very happy and wealthier. We'll always take good care of you, son."

"Thank you, Sir. About the real estate project, we need to leave it out for now. It's in a very early stage, anyway," Alexander said.

"OK, we'll leave that for a future discussion."

They had another round of whiskeys, and half an hour later, Alexander paid the check; this time, it was on him. Both walked out of the restaurant where a driver sat parked, waiting for the Senator.

"Alex, do you want a ride to your hotel?"

"I appreciate it, Sir. But I'll walk."

"My boy, thank you for everything."

"No problem. Thank you, Sir."

"You'll be contacted in Santo Domingo. Take care, bye."

The Senator entered the car and it drove off. Alexander walked back to the hotel. During the five-block walk, he kept thinking about how to address this with the local shareholders. Finally, he decided to discuss it with William first. So far, he was the second-largest shareholder. Alexander knew him very well, and he would not be comfortable with the situation.

He didn't expect much discussion from the other local shareholders as long as he or William stayed in the company. They trusted them and would agree to whatever decision they made regarding accepting or not the offer.

Alexander discussed things briefly with Gabrielle. She was sleeping when he dialed the, so they agreed to have a fresh conversation once he was back in Santo Domingo.

The next morning, Alexander woke up early. He went downstairs to the lobby and walked through the nearby streets to the hotel. He was back at eight and sat in the cafeteria to have a light for breakfast. He showered, closed his carry-on, and went down to check out. At nine, he was on the road back to Atlanta. He forgot to visit the Jack Daniels distillery; too many thoughts were dancing inside his head.

Suddenly, he remembered the handwritten note. He was certain Fred was behind it.

What would this idiot do if he was fired and knew Alliance was behind it? He could definitely do something stupid, he thought.

CHAPTER 22

Four and a half hours later, Alexander arrived in Atlanta. He stopped for lunch and sat near the bar. A TV has tuned CNN. He couldn't hear it, but he could read the captions at the bottom of the screen. Apparently, a discussion was taking place about the Coronavirus among top government officials, including President Trump. Alexander knew it was continuously getting more complicated around the world. He would search online for more news that night.

He arrived at the hotel at five and hurried to his room, constantly thinking about the Senator's proposal. He didn't want to get diluted by letting him and his friends come in, but at least he and William could not get much more cash to inject as capital and avoid a collapse.

His conversation with William on Monday had to bring a final solution to this inconvenience, but maybe an unexpected one.

Once in his room, he took a quick shower and lay off on his bed, turned on the TV, and searched for the same channel he'd been looking at in the restaurant. He was surprised that the channel was still on the same theme, just with different hosts.

***

Only a strong flu, as President Trump called the Coronavirus, was later named COVID-19. It was in all the headlines, on many TV channels, in newspapers, and other media networks.

In the United States, registered cases were nearly three thousand, and just that day, six hundred new cases were added. These data immediately drew his attention. He recalled that early that week, maybe on Tuesday, someone had said the United States had around one thousand cases. Now they had almost tripled in just a few days. It was rising fast. And the same was happening all around the world.

The TV host presented a summary of people infected in some countries. Spain reported 5,753 cases that day. Italy, 21,157, and just that day, only in Italy, more than three thousand people were infected.

On Friday, President Trump announced he had declared a National Emergency, and funds had been secured and approved by Congress to battle the disease.

If Congress works in coordination with the White House, this issue must be grave. It seems to be out of control, he thought.

The Dominican Republic's first case appeared on the first days of March. So far, just eleven cases had been registered, and no deaths. Alexander felt calmed and thought his country might not be strongly affected, but the way it was growing everywhere else worried him. There was no vaccine for it yet. Nor a definite treatment to help people infected fight the virus effectively.

That day, China announced that everyone arriving from overseas would be quarantined for fourteen days. This surprised Alexander, and he concluded that if these measures were replicated in the whole world, soon they would be taken here. He needed to get back home fast.

Alexander arrived in Santo Domingo on Sunday at one. He was glad to be back home. Colonel Robles and Gabrielle were waiting for him at the airport entrance. He didn't know she was coming to pick him up. It was a pleasant surprise.

They crossed the street to the parking lot. Alexander opened the SUV's left rear door for Gabrielle while Colonel Robles placed the carry-on in the trunk. When Gabrielle stepped in, he closed the door and walked around to get in the front passenger seat. Colonel Robles was standing behind the SUV vigilant.

Suddenly, a man approached them as Alexander was walking behind the vehicle. When Colonel Robles saw the man coming directly at them, still some twenty feet away, he grabbed his gun with his right hand and half took it out of the holster, with a bold intention to take it out completely if the man came any closer.

When Alexander saw that, he froze. Colonel Robles held him between the SUV and the other vehicle, using his left arm to stop him. Then, he turned to the man nearby.

"Hold on there."

The man stopped, a smile on his face.

"Relax, Colonel. Calm down. I just want to give a card to Mr. Stern."

The guy turned to Alexander and held it up.

"Mr. Stern, I have a message from the Senator."

Alexander thought about what to do.

"It's OK, Colonel, let him come closer."

The man approached, gave him a white business card showing the name Antonio, and a phone number below.

"We'll be in touch, Mr. Stern."

The man walked off while Alexander turned the card around to see the other side. He started reading the message on it.

"Mr. Stern, text me when all documents are ready to be signed by the US shareholders' representative. Then I'll give you details to solve your problems with the banker. We'll meet soon."

Gabrielle didn't realize what was happening. She was on her phone speaking to Andrea. Earlier, when they were walking to the vehicle, they had agreed to eat lunch at a restaurant both liked, and she was calling her to see if she would be joining them. Andrea declined. She had some other plans at home already. Alexander stepped into the front passenger seat. Colonel Robles got in the driver's seat and drove out of the airport.

Forty minutes later, they arrived at La Scarpetta, a little Italian restaurant in an open plaza near Alliance. The place frequently took more time to serve meals, but everything was made fresh. At least, that was what the host often said when they took too long.

Just eleven tables. Colonel Robles sat at one table and Alexander and Gabrielle sat in the corner. After ordering their main dish and an appetizer for both, Alexander gave Gabrielle a summary of his dinner with the Senator.

"What are we going to do, Alex? Gabrielle said. "Is there any other solution? Maybe we can find something to stop the attacks from Fred's bank."

"I've been thinking about it all week. This guy is not stopping until he's brought us on our knees, and we're forced to sell, or maybe worse, to become broke or intervened by the authorities."

"I don't like this movie-wise espionage," Gabrielle said. "Sounds dangerous."

"I know, Gabrielle. But if we don't find another way soon, we won't have any other option, or we'll lose everything."

Gabrielle nodded. After some seconds, she said, "You're right. It seems we have no other option. Do you think the other shareholders would sell some of their shares?"

"I don't know. I thought of different scenarios: all selling part, only some selling them, or just let them in, issuing new shares and all getting devalued. The truth is, the US investors and we have a majority. Or William and we have a majority. Or the local investors and the team members and we have a majority."

"Right. In the end, the decision will be on us," Gabrielle said.

"Yes. The question is, who will be joining us and who won't?"

They talked extensively during their meal. Alexander decided to speak with William early the following day. Alliance required a final decision as soon as possible. If the attack continued, the following week could do a lot of damage, and there was no sign that it would stop.

Alexander texted William, "Hi. I need to talk to you in person. Can we meet tomorrow morning? Is nine, OK?"

"Hi, Alex. Yes, see you at Alliance tomorrow," William answered.

After lunch, Colonel Robles took them back home and was dismissed. He would be back early the next day. Alexander would hire another driver to alternate with him until the dangerous situation had dissipated and all family members were able to drive by themselves again.

Alexander spent that afternoon drafting and calculating different scenarios. He thought long about how to address it with William, the local shareholder, and the team members. William would be the first one to contact, but all the other discussions had to be planned as well.

The next morning, Alexander arrived early at Alliance to review any pending items before his meeting with William. He told Colonel Robles that someone else would be alternating with him in the following days to let him rest properly and have a regular schedule.

At eight, Alexander arrived at Alliance. Amanda was already there. She handed him some documents requiring his signature and both reviewed his schedule for the week. Same as last week, just meetings with clients. Any other meeting, unless it was urgent, would be postponed. He told her about his meeting with William and he didn't want any interruption.

William arrived at nine sharps. After coming into Alexander's office, he shook hands with him, and Alexander offered an espresso from the silver-plated coffee machine in one corner of his office. William accepted and sat in one of the couches. A minute later, Alexander passed him the cup and sat as well.

After discussing Friday's remarks at Alliance, they talked about the difficult decision they faced. Alexander explained all what the Senator was requesting and his suggested solution. William didn't like it, as Alexander expected. William highlighted the offer's risks, and Alexander weighed having them as friends and partners, or not having them at all. Additionally, if no other solution was found soon, there was no other option than to accept the Senator's offer.

"Alex, these guys could be close friends until they lose interest in us, or until we can't contribute to their best interests. And that might be the best, losing interest from them, because they're quite powerful, and we don't want them against us."

"I agree with you. It's something we'll have to deal with in the future, I'm sure, " Alexander said. "The fact is that right now, I don't see any other solution. I've spent days trying to find one and nothing has come to my mind. If you or anyone else has an idea, I indeed want to hear it."

They spent the next forty minutes deliberating. Finally, they agreed they would have to let the US shareholders in; Alliance didn't have any other option.

"Alex, how could the deal be settled? They want thirty-five percent, so we need to discuss this with all the shareholders, including us, to give them twenty percent of our shares. If all the others agree, how much will you and I have combined?

"Fifty-two percent," Alexander said.

"So, combined with all other shareholders, we lose at least the sixty-seven percent minimum needed for some decisions, based on our shareholder's agreement," William said.

"Yes, we lose it."

William nodded.

After discussing different scenarios, Alexander and William agreed to schedule a meeting that afternoon with all local shareholders and explain everything. All needed to be at the meeting. It would be scheduled at six in the evening. They agreed to see each other at Alexander's office at four to discuss some details before the meeting started.

Alexander would spend all day at the office. He prepared a short presentation with the company situation, the US shareholders' offer, just the financial data and banning the espionage part, and an example on how the shares could be redistributed. By noon, he was done and ready for the meeting.

William left and went to his office on the other side of the floor. He called home and told his wife that he was staying at Alliance for lunch, without any details of what he had discussed with Alexander. He thought deeply about their situation, trying to find another solution, but again, nothing came up.

I don't like this. Sounds risky. Too much power that can pass us a bill, later on, he thought.

He called a close friend in Argentina, someone he trusted, and told him about their problem. After half an hour of discussion, his friend didn't offer him a different solution. Both agreed that at that moment they would help Alliance, but it was playing with fire.

"William, fighting with a local banker is one thing. Having to fight with a US Senator, an extremely wealthy businessman, and a New York-recognized lawyer is another story," he said.

After his call, William kept thinking for another hour. He had to make a decision. He would discuss it with Alexander, and then he had to move forward and learn to live with his decision.

After lunch, Alexander sat on his couch drinking a coffee. He kept searching for another solution, but still nothing. After he met with William, he received an email from a sales executive, copying Ryan. Another client was leaving, another one from the same list. Funds were going to Fred's bank. A stop to him and his bank was needed, and the only solution was the Senator's deal. Alexander decided to go for it. He tried to convince himself it could be a good option. Maybe instead of it being a risk, it was a huge opportunity. Future would tell.

Several minutes later, Alexander answered a call from an investor and went for a walk-through inside Alliance. He passed in front of Dominic's desk and recalled he hadn't decided what to do with her regarding the severance package. He'd focused only on stopping the bleeding.

He passed by Susan's office. The approval of Alliance's new shareholders was still pending. He smiled at the thought that they would have to send them another request for a new shareholder. Walking back to his office, he received a text message. It was from the Senator.

"Hello, my boy. How are you doing?"

"Hi, Sir. Everything's OK. I received your message at the airport."

"I know. Why do you have a security guy? You hate that."

"Sir, someone was chasing me early last week. I finally decided to hire someone to take care of my family and myself."

"Do you know who could be? Maybe that idiot banker?"

"Maybe him, but I'm not sure."

"Don't worry about it. He might only be trying to intimidate you. It must be him. We'll deal with that later. How's our request moving?"

"Working on that. I have a meeting later with the other partner, and then another one with all the other shareholders."

"How is that partner handling it?"

"He doesn't want to get devalued, as do any of us."

"My boy, I don't see another option. But in the long term, it would be better for all. Trust me."

"Yes, Sir. I hope."

"Do you want us to handle anything with him?"

"No, Sir. I'll handle it."

"Good. Let me know as soon as you have the final decision. Bye."

"Yes, I'll do that."

Alexander was hoping to finish everything related to the solution required that afternoon. To have the meetings, to decide on final percentages of all shareholders, and to move forward. He was closing that negotiation later, but not in the way he expected.

CHAPTER 23

Susan, the legal counselor, called him as soon as she got back from lunch.

"Hi, Alex. I have good news," she said with excitement. "We received the approval we were expecting. The letter from the Securities Commission just arrived. Alliance's new shareholders are finally approved."

"That's excellent news," Alexander said, smiling. Everyone was waiting for it.

"I'll arrange everything. We still need to complete the last part of the process. See you later, Alex."

Somehow, Alexander felt he was finally an actual owner of Alliance. It felt good. He called Gabrielle and Andrea to tell them the good news; they were part of it too. He would put a formal communication about it on hold. He wanted to see how it all ended with the shares to be sold to the US investors.

William came to his office at four. He knew him very well. A serious but calm face was not typical of his friend. Alexander decided not to anticipate his thoughts. They agreed on making espressos. Once they finished, Alexander moved to the office door, closed it, and walked to the couch. After a sip of his coffee, William started the conversation.

"Alex, we've been friends for many years. I loved when you brought the idea of buying out the previous shareholders and becoming owners and partners of Alliance ourselves."

"Right. By the way, we just received the final approval. Now we are formal shareholders."

"Yes, I just heard that from Susan. She let me know earlier."

"Alex, I made a decision. A difficult one. Trust me, it took me a to get to it. I don't want to sell part of my shares."

"Come on, William. We don't have another option," Alexander hurried to say.

"Let me finish, Alex. I want to sell all my shares."

The expression on Alexander's face said everything.

"What? Are you serious? You can't go out of Alliance. You're one of the cornerstones of this company. The partner I trust the most."

"Thank you, Alex, but I'm not comfortable with this new proposal. Letting them have fifteen percent was one thing. Up to thirty-five, I found too much."

"But William, what else could we do? We've been looking for alternatives and nothing else came up. We're under attack. We're struggling. This is the only option we've seen that will keep the company running."

"I know, Alex. But I've decided already. It would be better for all of us, including you. Of my twenty-seven and a half percent, I'll sell twenty to them and the other seven and a half to all the other shareholders."

"But William, we can't let you go. We need you here. Again, you're important to Alliance."

"Thank you, Alex, but I truly think it's best for all this way."

"William, I don't think things should end this way. There must be another option. Why don't we just get devalued proportionality?"

"Alex, please don't insist. It's time for me to let this go. The company will make it. I'm sure of that. These guys will help to pass this phase, and other difficult moments, for sure."

They stood silent a moment, then William excused himself and went to the bathroom. Alexander thought about how the other shareholders would view this. Indeed, some would acquire more shares. The question was whether some would shift to a similar position as William's. Alexander didn't want more friends leaving the company.

When William was back, Alexander said, "William, if that's your final decision, I respect it. It's something I wasn't expecting and surely something I don't like. This is a sad moment for me. I thought we would retire together, many years from now."

"I know, Alex, but right now, this is the best for my family and me. I'm involved in other business initiatives, and this cash will help."

"Well, if that is your final decision, let's have the meeting with all shareholders at six. I'll prepare a summary of how the distribution of shares would end."

"OK. Alex."

"We'll have to have a drink this afternoon, William, after the meeting. I need to take this in with something strong. May I invite you?"

"Sure, Alex."

They shook hands, and William walked out of Alexander's office. He sat back on the couch and thought about all the implications of this decision. The market knew William well. Some would ask why he was leaving. An excellent speech would need to be prepared before announcing it.

He went to his desk and calculated a new proposal. It might change depending on all the other shareholders' decisions. That would come to light during the meeting.

Alexander called Gabrielle to tell her everything, and that he was getting home late that night. She was shocked William would not be part of Alliance anymore. She was sad too, and requested him to be careful and make sure Colonel Robles would be with him all night.

Alexander had a few savings to buy part of William's shares, but he would need a loan to complete the payment of all the remaining shares assigned to him and Andrea.

At six, the local shareholders met in the conference room. Alexander had prepared a spreadsheet to change any share distribution that could result during the meeting. He explained the situation to everyone. William was stepping down for personal reasons, and the new shareholders could help end their problems with the other bank.

Questions were raised as a set of alternatives, many utopias. An hour later, they all agreed to move forward. Just four shareholders and Alexander decided to buy the seven and a half percent remaining. Alexander prepared a summary of the final distribution. His family group would own forty-four percent of the company. He disliked how he had increased his holdings, but it was necessary to maintain as much of the company as possible. These additional shares could make a difference in the future.

After everyone agreed, thirty minutes more were dedicated to wishing farewell to William. They had all known him for a long time. Alexander would be the most affected, but they had to move forward and protect Alliance and everyone working there.

Alexander went to his office with Susan to plan how to inform the regulators of the new changes.

"Wow, Alex. We just received the approval from the Securities Commission," she said.

"What can I tell you. That's life. I'm sure they'll understand. I will visit them to discuss it."

"Two shareholders were already approved. The new one might be easier; he's a wealthy lawyer in New York City," Susan said. "I'll have the documents prepared tomorrow morning for everyone to sign."

"Perfect. The overseas shareholders' representative will be here when we'd confirmed with them."

"No problem, Alex. Count on it."

Per the request of the financial controller, one of the shareholders, Alexander sent the final share distribution to her. She would validate all incoming funds from the shareholders investing more. He called the bank to complete the process for the loan he would need. Now he had the final amount. He would have to put up part of his shares as collateral, the unique way to have a forty-eight-hour approval for such an amount.

Everything set up, he texted the Senator. He wanted to tell him about the final agreement and ask him about sending the funds. First, it would be done as investments in any fund. Once everyone signed, the cash needed to pay William's shares would be converted to capital. These funds were important, but it was more important to stop Fred Shultz.

"Hello, Sir."
"My boy, I'm glad to hear you."
"Sir, we have an agreement with all local shareholders. Documents are being prepared. We can sign them anytime on Friday."
"Perfect. I'll call our friend, the lawyer. He'll contact you to make all necessary arrangements."
"When do you estimate you'll send the funds as investments while we sign and make the capital injection?"
"My boy, the money's ready. We'll send it tomorrow morning to one of the funds you have."
"Perfect, Sir. About the other subject?"
"About the banker?"
"Yes. He's still hitting us."
"Everything is set up. Our friend there is waiting for your go-ahead once we sign."
"OK, Sir. I'll call him."
"He has all the details. Soon he'll be out of your way. Sorry, I have to go. We'll be in touch. Bye."

William waited for Alexander at his office. He didn't have an executive position at Alliance, but as the second main shareholder and his friend, Alexander agreed that he had an office there. He was a board member and was a pillar of the company. He always offered great advice, and his market relationships were extremely valuable.

With his new shareholder percentage, Alexander had the opportunity to have three board seats in the board. He would propose William stay on as a member.

***

La Cassina terrace was a nice place to have drinks after work, enjoy great food, and smoke a cigar. Nine blocks away from Alliance, Alexander and William could get there in seven minutes without traffic. It was one of the best restaurants in the city, frequented by businessmen during the day, and family and friends at night and weekends. It was a preferred choice for the wealthy society and executives living in Santo Domingo.

Alexander selected the venue, he was inviting. But he knew his choice was one that William also liked very much, mainly because he could smoke his variety of excellent cigars produced countrywide.

Colonel Robles left them at the entrance. He would stay until they were ready to go. The hostess seated both at a four-party table. William took out two Arturo Fuentes, one of the best cigars of the Dominican Republic and worldwide.

"Are we allowed?" he asked the waitress.

"Of course, Sir."

Seconds later, a waiter asked them for their choice of drinks. They agreed to have a single malt scotch whiskey Alexander liked very much: The Balvenie. Once the first round came, they ordered two appetizers. William handed Alexander a cigar. They lit them, one behind the other. After all was set, they would speak and gossip long.

They spoke about the lovely terrace, not crowded that day; just two tables occupied, one with four suited men, another with three young ladies in their thirties.

"This is a great place, Alex. I'll miss it if I have to leave the country one day."

Alex nodded. "William, I hope you and your family stay here for many years."

"Thank you, Alex."

"We've known each other for twenty-five years."

"Right, and we had worked together four times, in four different companies, including Alliance. What a history."

"I hate seeing you out of it. I hope we can have you back soon," Alexander said.

"Thank you, but it's better this way. Moreover, it helps me to fund other businesses. A piece of quick advice, Alex. Be extremely careful with these new partners. Never show all your cards. Be cautious."

"Yes. I know. I've been thinking about that for days. Trust me, I'm prepared for any outcome."

"Perfect," William said, and grabbed his glass.

The waiter brought the three appetizers they had ordered. He placed them on the table and described both, "Burrata Amalfitana, Korean barbecue ribs, and pork belly buns. Enjoy."

They recalled many stories from all the companies they had worked for together. Their mutual friends' list was extensive.

Coincidentally, some crises had occurred when they had worked together: Mexico's Tequila crisis in 1995, the Dominican Republic financial crisis in 2003, the World economic crisis in 2008. They spent an hour discussing all of them and the challenges they had experienced. They ended wondering if COVID-19 disease would derive in another crisis. No doubt it would.

After another glass of whiskey and ten minutes past eleven, they agreed it was time to leave. Alexander left William at his home. The next morning, his wife would take him to the office. At Alexander's home, Colonel Robles took his vehicle and went home too. Gabrielle was already sleeping. Alexander got a glass of water from the kitchen, re-set the alarm, and went to bed. The rest of the week would be a marathon of unique situations to handle.

CHAPTER 24

Susan sent the documents on Tuesday. Alexander reviewed them and requested a few changes in the Shareholders Agreement, slight modifications which might protect them in the future. He hoped the US shareholders would not have a problem with them. Wrong. It was something that started a discussion.

After sending them to Adam Branning, he answered Alexander back in less than half an hour. He thought they were expecting them by the minute when he saw his email requesting a call to talk about the document. Once he called him, after greetings, they proceeded to discuss the terms.

"Let me get to the point," Adam said. "Our friends in Washington and Nashville would like to take out the new clause you included in the Shareholders Agreement."

"That minor change?" Alexander asked.

"At some point, that could not be a minor one."

"It applies the same for any shareholder. We need to leave it that way."

"Alex, I recommend we go back and rewrite it or take it out," Adam said vigorously.

"Adam, that clause protects the minority shareholders, including all of you. We have to leave it. It's common in many contracts like this, at least in this country. I'm sure you know that."

"Let me call you back, Alex."

Adam hung up instantly, leaving him no chance to say anymore. The money had finally arrived and invested. Alliance was now in a more comfortable position. Besides other investments from new clients, the funds received had offset the substantial redemptions requested by clients going to Fred's bank.

That morning, Alexander watched CNN and a local news channel. In addition to some measures the US government had taken since February, they announced several flights had been banned. Everything was being tightened up. Alexander needed to move fast and complete all the documents.

After hanging up, Adam texted the Senator and Christopher. After a short discussion of the clause, they agreed to move forward. The clause protected them as well. The Senator added that if they wanted some advantage over the other shareholders, they would pressure them differently. Christopher emphasized that any necessary negotiation could be arranged with Alexander. He liked him, and he was confident that their relationship would matter more than that specific clause.

The Senator asked Adam to sign the contracts soon. He couldn't give many details, but he expected flight bans to intensify anytime in many countries. Both the United States and the Dominican Republic would be affected. Christopher offered his company jet to make a quick trip, if necessary, to Santo Domingo or any other airport in the country that would allow a landing. He would keep the airplane and the crew on hold in Nashville.

At three, Adam texted Alexander telling him they were OK with the clause, but he needed to review the rest of the documents. He advised him that the three companies' representative was with him in New York City, and they would be flying there when everything was ready. One hour later, both were discussing it by phone.

"Alex, I reviewed everything, just minor changes but only on legal wording, nothing related to the essence of the document."

"Perfect. What do you want to do?"

"Let's review them, and if we agree, we'll make arrangements to be there and sign on Friday."

They spent the next twenty minutes on it. Alexander agreed to everything. He sent a final draft to Adam and printed eighteen copies, one for each shareholder and four additional ones if they needed them for any purpose.

That afternoon, Susan arranged with Alexander's assistant to print all documents and coordinated with all the local shareholders to sign. She was sending the documents to Alexander's home for him and Andrea to sign when everybody else had done so. Adam would call Alexander that night after their travel arrangements had been made.

A messenger delivered the documents to Alexander's home and left. Alexander hadn't spoken yet with Adam. They agreed to talk after the Dominican President addressed the country that night. They expected additional measures to fight COVID-19 in the following days.

Around four minutes after his conference started, the President announced that an Emergency State decree enforcing many lockdown measures would be sent to Congress for approval. All frontiers were to be closed, effective Thursday morning.

Adam had already made arrangements to fly on Friday when Alexander called him.

"Hi, Adam."

"Tell me, Alex. What did the President say?"

"Many measures will be taken, but for us, the most important is that all flights will be banned after Thursday morning."

"What? I already reserved a flight for Friday."

"I'm not sure if you'll be allowed to come in and be able to leave the country after that."

"Right. We need to make different arrangements. I'll call you back."

Adam checked whether any flights were available for Wednesday, but all were fully booked. He called Christopher to explain the situation. A minute later, his assistant instructed the pilot to fly Wednesday morning to New York. Adam and the representative would be waiting at Teterboro airport, and then they would fly to Santo Domingo. After an estimation, he called Alexander back and asked him to be available around noon. Antonio would call him early the next day to coordinate everything. They would sign the documents, the representative would fly to Panama, and Alexander would discuss with Antonio the following steps to neutralize Fred Shultz's bank attack, and Fred Shultz himself.

After hanging up, Alexander instantly remembered his conversation with the Senator about CIA specialists, and how to neutralize someone. He didn't like it. He hoped that everything would be done legally, as the Senator had affirmed, but he doubted it. He wasn't able to discuss all that with Gabrielle that night. She was at her mother's home with her sisters, making arrangements for her to cope with the government measures.

Colonel Robles was taking her back home. Alexander recalled that he hadn't made arrangements for the additional driver to alternate with Colonel Robles. He sent an email to the security company asking them to send the third candidate on cue. Despite the late hour, his friend agreed to do it Thursday morning. The candidate would be at his home at 10:00 a.m., the same time Colonel Robles would be arriving. He would instruct the new driver with all logistics related to the Sterns.

Alexander was not going to Alliance that morning. He updated Gabrielle on all matters going on and they decided to move forward, hoping things would be for everyone's benefit.

Antonio called him that morning to inform him the jet was already on its way and was expected to arrive at 12:25 p.m. at Presidente Dr. Joaquin Balaguer International Airport, located in northern Santo Domingo.

They agreed Alexander would pick him up at noon at the underground parking of a mall, then they would drive to the airport.

Alexander left home in time to pick Antonio up. Once at the mall, he waited five minutes until he arrived. He came from the back and knocked on the rear seat window, behind the driver's seat. Colonel Robles unlocked the vehicle and he stepped in. He began to drive, took the ramp in the back part of the mall out to the street, and drove to the airport.
"Hello, Antonio. Is everything set up with the plan?"
"Sir. It's better to talk about it when we arrive," he said, not wanting to say a word within Colonel Robles hearing.
"Perfect," Alexander said.

It was a quiet journey, except for Alexander's comment on the weather. After they arrived, Antonio asked them to park in front of a gate that allowed vehicles to get to the end of the runway where some hangars were located.
"Wait here, please," Antonio said while getting out of the vehicle.
He walked to the gate and talked to a guard standing there. After a couple of minutes, he came back.
"Everything's set up. When the airplane arrives and stops near that white hangar over there, we'll be allowed to drive in."
"And then what?" Alexander asked.
"Then we'll stop fifty feet away from the jet. The door will lift down, and we'll get in. Colonel Robles will have to wait for us here in the vehicle. I expect it'll take us about half an hour. Then we'll come back and leave."
"OK," Alexander said.
Colonel Robles eyed Alexander, waiting for his instructions.
"Don't worry, Colonel. It's fine. We'll be back soon."

They saw the jet approaching the runway. Landing would take a few seconds. When the aircraft arrived at the expected point, the guard waved his right arm, signaling them to come, while opening the gate. Colonel Robles drove to the section pointed by Antonio.

When they stopped, Alexander admired the nice G450 with double turbine. He loved jets, and one of his dreams was to acquire one someday. He knew a lot about them. This one had a capacity for up to sixteen passengers, depending on each owner's customization, and had a range of eight thousand kilometers. It had no company logo, only two blue navy enlarged letters, CM, on the left side between the cockpit and the door.

Antonio stepped out of the vehicle, followed by Alexander, who carried two white legal-size envelopes. They walked to the jet. The cabin door was opened from the interior and a young and attractive flight attendant appeared.

"Good afternoon, gentlemen. Please come in. Be careful on the stairs."

"Thank you," Alexander said and stepped up.

Adam and the representative sat in two of the four seats with a table in the middle. After quick greetings, Alexander chose the left aisle seat in front of Adam, and Antonio walked to the cabin's end.

"Do you want something to drink, Sir?" the flight attendant asked.

"Water, thank you."

Once she left, Adam began to explain arrangements for their speedy arrival in Santo Domingo. After a couple of minutes, they started the signing process.

"Alex, do you have the documents?"

"Yes." He took them out of the envelopes.

The flight attendant was back with Alexander's water. She served it in a glass while Adam checked all the documents with the representative.

"Everything is fine. We can proceed to sign them, Alex."

"Let's do it."

Ten minutes later, all documents were signed. Adam would be a shareholder with the new agreement. Adam asked Antonio to come closer.

"Please excuse us. We need to discuss other non-legal matters," he said to the representative.

"Yes, Sir. I have to get to another meeting here in Santo Domingo, then take a flight to Panama."

Alexander let him walk out and sat back again. Adam moved to the window seat to leave the aisle one free for Antonio.

"Bye, gentlemen," the representative said, picked up his carry-on, and got out of the jet.

"Alex, Antonio will explain all the details of the investigation and the plan to stop the attacks Alliance is suffering," Adam said.

"Antonio, you have our go-ahead. Please coordinate everything with Mr. Stern once you leave the airport."

"Yes, Sir. I'll do that."

"When do you figure this problem will be neutralized?" Adam asked.

"In less than two weeks, but pretty sure by next Tuesday. I just need to confirm something to complete the puzzle."

"Please keep us informed."

"Yes, Sir."

"Gentlemen, I think our meeting is done. I need to fly back to Nashville to meet with Christopher. Remember, Antonio, we need to finish with the problem as soon as possible."

"Yes, Mr. Branning."

They stepped down from the jet and the door was closed. As they walked to the SUV, Antonio told Alexander that he needed to sit with him in the back to discuss the plan. Alexander nodded.

As the jet began to speed up to the runway, he opened the door of the passenger's front seat and placed the envelopes on it.

"Colonel, I'll sit in the back. Please take us to the same place where we picked up Antonio."

He opened the rear door and stepped up. Antonio already sat behind the driver. He turned left to Alexander, and with a smile on his face and a quiet voice, said, "Mr. Stern, you'll be pleased with the plan we've set up."

I hope what he says is legal, Alexander thought.

CHAPTER 25

Colonel Robles accelerated slowly to the speed limit permitted inside the airport. Seconds later, the guard opened the door. He went out and took the avenue to the mall. Meanwhile, Antonio detailed his plan to Alexander.

"Mr. Stern, as the Senator told you, we have compromising information on Fred Shultz, two board members, and two employees at the bank. We just got information about the employees this week. All committed a monumental fraud inside the bank, planned and executed for many years. First, they made withdrawals from abandoned accounts, mainly those with attractive balances. The cash ends up in another account in another local bank and then is transferred to an account in Nassau, The Bahamas."

"Yes, the Senator told me something about it."

"Initially, we thought they were writing off those balances, but we found that it wasn't that. They're just robbing these accounts. Plain as that. The second scam is with a group of loans granted periodically by a credit officer. Not significant amounts, all less than ten thousand dollars. The bank approved them, and after five monthly payments, to skip some early warning controls, the loans are not paid anymore. Six months later, they're written off.

"How many loans were approved?" Alexander asked.

"On average, four loans every month since at least five years ago. All were granted to real clients who don't have a clue they had those loans, until another bank told them when it appeared in their credit bureaus. It's a typical case of theft identity."

"And nobody asked about them at the bank?"

"Due to the small amount, nobody cares about them. When clients claim, they just clean the credit bureaus after a vague investigation process. There are only a few claims. Many were to senior people, who no longer go to banks to request loans, and some are dead by now."

"Are you kidding me?" Is Fred Shultz approving them?"

"No. The two employees involved in this scam are a credit officer and a sales executive, which resulted in Fred Shultz's nephew. We have in our possession compromising chats and taped calls between both of them."

"We can put them in jail with that," Alexander said.

"Maybe we can, but we would have legal proof only against the nephew, and maybe on the credit officer. It would be difficult to prosecute Shultz and forget about the board members. And the bank would not be willing to do that."

"How are the board members involved?" Alexander asked.

"We also have conversations and some compromising texts between Fred Shultz and them. That's how we knew about the account in The Bahamas, opened in Shultz's name. It was initially opened for other legal purposes, but at some point, that changed."

"And how will we use this information?"

"The plan is as follows. Before the bank's next board meeting, we'll deliver a set of documents to each board member. The ones involved will receive all, and the other ones will receive documents about Fred Shultz and the other employees, but nothing about the board members involved in the scam. A request to fire Fred Shultz and the employees will be included in all packages. If immediate actions, meaning the same day, are not taken, a similar package will be sent to the financial authorities and various contacts we have in the press.

"Wow, that's playing hardball."

"We're certain they would want to avoid the scandal, the regulatory fines, the legal actions they would be liable to, and for sure, the loss of many clients, who would be concerned about their controls and illegal practices."

"Are you sure that would stop the attacks to Alliance?"

"Yes, Mr. Stern. It should. But to be completely sure, we're sending another note to Mr. Arden telling him that a complot is in place from his bank against many financial institutions, but mainly yours. If it doesn't stop, the actions I listed would be taken anyway and would be sent to the Bank's Association as well. A similar note would be sent to both board members and recommending them not to even think of resigning. Both are part of the Executive and Risk committees. They would help your business going forward. Trust me."

"And Serge Arden? Could he be involved?"

"We haven't found anything on him. He's a decent man. The only one who doesn't have a secret, or at least we haven't found it."

"And do you have something on Jack Dowell, a very good friend of Fred Shultz?"

"We're investigating him, Mr. Stern. Nothing yet. But it's just a matter of time. Everyone has something. Nevertheless, I'm sure with all what will happen next week with Shultz, he won't be wanting to mess with you."

"Do you know who sent me the threat note and followed me the other day? Did something about that came up?"

"No, Sir. We're pretty sure Mr. Shultz planned everything. But we're not a hundred percent sure."

Alexander was impressed, but still assimilating the whole plan while Antonio paused to check his phone. He thought it could work, but he was analyzing whether it could generate more problems for him and Alliance in the future.

He expected to hear with more certainty that Fred Shultz or Jack Dowell was behind the threats.

"Mr. Stern, it's confirmed. The next board meeting at NDB will be next Tuesday. If you agree, we'll set up everything."

Alexander thought about it for several seconds, then nodded in agreement. He didn't like to be involved in

these situations, but he had to protect Alliance, his partners, and his family.
"Perfect. I'll keep you informed in the following days."

A minute later, they arrived at the mall. After a quick goodbye, they stepped out of the car. Antonio walked far from the vehicle and Alexander stepped into the front passenger seat. Colonel Robles accelerated and made a U-turn in the next aisle to take the ramp out of the mall.
"To your home, Sir?"
"No, to the office, please."

Ten minutes later, they arrived at Alliance. When Alexander got to his office, Amanda gave him some documents to sign, and he handed her the two envelopes.
"Please give these to Susan."
"Yes, Alex. Ryan is looking for you."
"Thank you. I'll call him."
Ryan would tell him later about two more clients who had requested their funds. I hope next week this problem will be history, he thought.

Checking his emails, he saw one from George. He and Axel asked him to schedule a conference call to discuss Adagio. He replied to both, proposing next Monday. He needed to finish the chronogram, and now with the Emergency State declared in the country some assumptions had to be updated.

Everything was arranged to receive the new driver the next morning. He asked Colonel Robles to be with Gabrielle and Andrea, and he would evaluate him. He had lunch with a client and a meeting at one association, both outside the office.
Alexander met with all top team members to discuss the Emergency State and lockdown measures enacted in the country. Human resources would prepare a plan on

how to move forward, and arrangements to send part of the team members to work from home. Another meeting would be held on Friday morning to decide the final plan.

Before ending the meeting, Alexander checked to see whether the funds from the loan were deposited in his account. He had signed everything on Tuesday, and the payment of William's shares was pending. The money had not been deposited yet. He immediately called his executive at the bank.

"Hi Mr. Stern, how are you?"

"Fine. Thank you. I'm checking on the funds from the loan. I signed everything yesterday."

"Yes, it's being processed. Should be in your account in any minute."

"OK, perfect. For a minute I thought it was not approved."

"Everything is fine, Sir."

"OK, we'll talk later. Thank you."

Alexander called the financial controller. The other shareholders had already transferred the money. He was the only one pending. He would confirm to her when it was finally deposited, but William's payment would have to be done early the next day. He would update him, so he walked to his office.

"Hi, William. Can we talk?"

"Yes, please come in. How was your meeting? Everything signed?"

"Yes, finally."

"That's it."

"Not so fast, my friend. Now that you're not a shareholder, you can be an independent member of our board."

"Right," William said, knowing already what Alexander would be asking.

"William. Please stay on the board with us. It's imperative to have you at Alliance."

"Alex. I need to think about that. I was planning to work full-time on other initiatives."

"It would be great to have you here, William. When do you think we can have an answer?"

"Give me until next Monday. We can have a coffee as soon as we get to the office and discuss it."

"Perfect. I'm hoping to hear a positive answer on this, my friend."

"Let's see. I'll think about it during the weekend."

"Perfect. See you on Monday."

Alexander went back to his office with a strong feeling that William didn't want to stay as a board member. He had that strange sensation in his stomach that was right almost every time.

He left Alliance almost immediately. At home, he joined Gabrielle in the studio. She was watching a culinary class. Alexander grabbed a beer and sat by her side. He continued thinking about William's response, but he needed to wait until next Monday to have a final verdict.

Once the program finished, Gabrielle turned off the TV and prepared to hear the important update Alexander would be giving to her. Ten minutes later, she was shocked.

"I can't believe a guy like Fred Shultz could do something like that," Gabrielle said, astonished. "He could go to jail."

"Maybe, if all the evidence is presented and accepted by a judge. But the bank has to sue him, and that won't happen. Do you imagine the mess that would create? Too much noise for them in the market."

"You're right. I don't think they would take any legal action against him," Gabrielle said. "I don't like the way this is being handled, but we don't have any other option. We're at risk of losing almost everything. And the threats, Alex, any idea who's behind them?"

"Nothing. Fred should be behind them, but Antonio's not sure of that."

"That worries me. I was hoping to know who was responsible. And now Fred is going to be affected, and who knows what he can do."

"That's the same concern I have. But we'll need to deal with that after next Tuesday morning, Gabrielle."

"Right. What about the other driver?"

"He's coming tomorrow. He'll be with me for the evaluation."

"Alex, what if the threats are not coming from Shultz or Dowell? Who could be behind them?"

"I've been thinking about that and no one comes to mind. It sounds obvious, and so naïve, if they're from Shultz or Dowell. And neither are naïve, nor stupid."

Brenda came to the studio and asked if they wanted dinner served in the kitchen or the studio. Both were so comfortable they decided to take it in the studio.

"What about William, Alex? Did he accept keeping his board position?"

"Not yet. He's thinking about it. We'll know next Monday."

"Why? I thought he would accept it right away."

"Same thought, Gabrielle. But he hasn't decided. We agreed to meet on Monday, but my impression, so far, is that he'll reject it."

"I think the same. If he hasn't accepted yet, I think he's just finding a diplomatic way to tell you without affecting our friendship."

"At least on my side, that wouldn't be a problem," Alexander said.

"I know. It's strange. Let's see what happens next week," Gabrielle said, skeptical.

Alexander shifted the conversation to Gabrielle's business. He wanted to avoid talking about Alliance anymore. Her entrepreneurship was growing. She had excellent ideas and looked to see which products could be increased for mass production. Her menu of appetizers, pastries, and sauces has been offered. At least one product in each category was being ordered frequently by different clients.

Gabrielle started to watch another cooking program while waiting for dinner, and Alexander went to their bedroom to review the Adagio chronogram. He was convinced that the Emergency State would take more than the fifteen days described by the President. He had checked to see what was happening in other Asian and Middle East countries, and lockdowns were already longer. It would be crucial to understand what the government office of public registration of properties would do. If they closed, as expected, the project would have to be paused, as the property would not be transferred to the Trust. He expected to have more information regarding it next week.

After thinking about it before dinner, he was sure that his professional life would change next week. At Alliance, everything was expected to improve. Adagio could be delayed, but eventually would move forward. However, he never thought that next week could turn extremely dangerous for him and his family.

CHAPTER 26

Antonio had spent a week investigating Jack Dowell. He and one of his associates had been following him the previous days. His car was bugged, but not his office or home yet. He still needed to find out if he was plotting anything against Alexander, Alliance, or his real estate project.

Alliance's US shareholders didn't have any particular interest in that business, but it appeared promising. And more than promising, it was a business that could grow and thus serve their interests.

Nothing compromising had been identified yet, but it was still early in the investigation. So far, no illegal actions had yet been found. Maybe some bribes were given to some authorities in the past, but not recently, and would be difficult to verify. He just had found that Dowell had a lover. The relationship had lasted for three years and was acknowledge by his wife and two sons. Mrs. Dowell had an agreement with him.

"Do all you want to do, but not in public," she said, and was recorded by the bug planted inside his vehicle while he was driving, and the phone was connected to Bluetooth, so Antonio's associates were able to hear that conversation. However, that was not the kind of compromising information they were hoping to find.

Home and office phones, as well as his lover's phones, would be required to intercept. There was no rush on it as in Shultz's case, but something would surely come up that could be useful in the future.

On the other hand, everything had been set to take Fred Shultz down.

On Friday, Alexander agreed with his team on the plan to manage the country's lockdown. Their company was not required to close its doors but would need to respect the restrictions on schedules as to when people would be allowed to travel. Otherwise, they would be detained. From 5:00 p.m. to 6:00 a.m. the next day, no one would be allowed to be on the streets unless they were authorized by the government. This measure was implemented to maintain social distancing and to limit spread of the disease. This brought some challenges for the team, but they had to plan around it. Part of the team would be sent to work from home, and part would stay at the office, shifting every week.

Once everything was arranged, they focused on maintaining close interaction with clients using online tools, especially those included in the famous list. When they agreed on this, Alexander recalled he hadn't decided what to do with Dominic. She was already out of Alliance. He decided that nothing else would be done against her, and the severance package would be paid.

Everyone was worried about the lockdown. Nobody knew how much it would affect not only their business but also all companies countrywide. Closing frontiers, industries, and limiting free travel would have a strong economic impact.

The world was suffering the same. Now, without tourists coming to the beautiful Dominican beaches and remittances impacted by the same situation, the country would be affected even more. If it was only for fifteen days, it would not represent a significant problem, but if it was extended, the impact would be more significant every day. Unfortunately, that was the most probable scenario.

That Friday, Alexander knew that the Adagio Associates project would be delayed. There would be no chance to initiate with such conditions. Anyway, he would be working online with his nephew again on a new chronogram. Only some activities could be scheduled for the fifteen days of the lockdown. He would add two more weeks as a cushion.

George and Axel were already informed of the Emergency State in the Dominican Republic. The three talked that afternoon and agreed to complete the chronogram and have the conference call next week. With all that information, they could agree on the next steps. Alexander told them he would need to manage Mr. Ramos' expectations. Once he hung up with them, he called him.

"Hello, Mr. Ramos. How are you?"

"Not so good with this situation."

"Yes, Sir. This is going to change everyone's plans. A delay of our project is now a fact."

"What do you think about it, Alex?"

"During the weekend, I'll work on the chronogram to have greater clarity on how the project can move forward. My concern is that we don't know many variables yet. We don't know if we'll be able to transfer the land to the Trust. And without that, we can't move forward with the bank."

"Yes, that's one of the first steps," Mr. Ramos said.

"We'll be prepared, and immediately after we can continue with our project, and if the market conditions are fairly manageable, we'll move forward. Maybe instead of building all at once we'll need to start with the first building only, then the others. We'll see."

"Right, Alex. That's what we need to do. Please keep me informed on everything."

"Sure, Mr. Ramos. We'll be in touch."

Gabrielle decided to take additional measures on COVID-19. They would send Brenda home temporarily; she needed to be close to her family. Gabrielle and Andrea's businesses were both put on hold. They would follow the lockdown measures completely.

Everyone was concerned about the spread. It could get inside their homes from anywhere.

Gabrielle had made a full shop at the supermarket, enough to supply them the next fifteen days. When

Alexander saw the charge on their credit card, he thought it was for at least forty days or more.

Home dynamics changed. Now Gabrielle did the cleaning and cooking. Andrea and Alexander cleaned the bedrooms and washed the dishes. Alexander had enough shirts to wear, but he might need to iron them suddenly after they'd been dried, a practice he'd learned well when he was young and would soon be reinforced. No gym. No restaurants: all were closed. No family or mall visits. Not even gassing up their vehicles; anyway, it would not be needed. Alexander would use his vehicle during the week to go to Alliance, but only half a day. Colonel Robles would work just half those days too. All these measures would be implemented at least for the next fifteen days. Hiring the new driver was put on hold, but Alexander had liked him.

Alexander recalculated the Adagio estimations during the weekend. Commercial units would be built after the residential part. It didn't make sense to start with them with the present situation. Agreements with unaffected companies such as banks or pharmacies had to be closed before launching.

The apartments' plan had to change as well. Instead of building three towers simultaneously, they would have to begin with one. Depending on sales and available banking loans to buyers, the other two would be developed gradually.

On Monday, Alexander went to the office early. He would work on some pending items until William arrived. He spent the next hour signing documents and approving different requests. The office looked empty: fifty percent of the staff was already working from home, and after some technological complications were solved, at least an additional fifteen percent more would be gone the next fifteen days too.

Five minutes after nine, William came into his office. Alexander served a couple of lattes, closed the door, and sat down. They talked for some minutes about the weekend, until the conversation naturally changed to the subject both wanted to discuss.

"Alex, I thought deeply about your proposal, and trust me, I did. I've decided to pass on it."

"Why, William? We want you here."

"Trust me, I thought long about it. I decided to move forward with my other businesses and leave my long professional life in finance. At least for some months, maybe years, or who knows, maybe forever."

"Is this because of the new shareholders?"

"Not really. I didn't like that, but that was needed. I just want a change. I want to do something different. It's time for a change. I'm particularly excited about a vision of me not being involved in financial matters."

"William, I expected you to accept. I genuinely wanted that."

"I know, Alex, but please understand. What I'm doing is important for me. It was a difficult decision, but I prefer it this way."

"If that's your final decision, I respect it, my friend. We'll arrange everything around that, William."

"We'll still be friends. And anytime you want to talk, about anything, just give me a call."

"Sure, I will. And I'll still go to those Saturday barbecue nights at your house," Alexander said back.

"Of course. I'll schedule one as soon as I'm back from Punta Cana."

William left.

There's nothing else I can do. I need to decide who to appoint as a board member, he thought.

There was no news about investors leaving, which was always good news. COVID-19 lockdown was just experiencing its first whole week.

Alexander was concerned about the days to come. Nobody knew how people would react, especially regarding their investments. Some had already said they wanted to have more liquid assets instead of medium and long-term investments. He watched the money market funds increase sharply.

He went home at one, and would not come back until the next morning, as he'd arranged with other team members. Anyway, the lockdown started at five in the afternoon. He would stay at the office only those days when he would have lunch there, and he would be out no later than four. New times and new customs, as for many others in the country.

When he entered his apartment, more new rules had been implemented. Now shoes were left at the entrance, behind the door. At the front wall, over the Parsons table, Gabrielle had installed a tray holding antibacterial spray and alcohol, leaving space for keys, wallets, money, and used masks. No watches or rings were allowed the following weeks.
Then a mandatory shower, and all clothes used were to be deposited in a basket. After that, everyone was allowed to move freely inside the apartment. This routine will drive everyone crazy in two weeks, he thought.
Groceries would have to go through another process. All packages would be washed or cleaned with alcohol, and then placed in the refrigerator or stored.

That afternoon, he had an online meeting and several calls with different team members. Documents requiring his signature would be left for the next morning or sent to him if urgent.
The following days he would realize how productive one can be when avoiding commuting. He lived nearby the office, but at least one hour was lost every day, and when he added the time lost driving to meetings or lunches or

any other activity outside the office, more unproductive hours were added.

He made a rough estimate. He calculated that at least one full day was lost in travel, twenty percent each week. Incredible.

Around seven, he and Ryan were still discussing about a client investment. Suddenly, a message from Antonio appeared on his phone.

"Hello, Mr. Stern."

He knew what he was texting about. He ended his call with Ryan immediately. Once he hanged up, he texted Antonio back.

"Hi, Antonio, any news?"

"Yes, Sir. How can I tell you? The bomb has exploited."

"How's that?"

"All individual envelopes for each board member have been sent. We know all but one has seen the documents. The two compromised board members have already seen them and agreed not to talk with Fred Shultz about it."

"OK."

"I'll keep you informed later tonight on any advancement. They must be speaking with each other right now. I'll call you back."

Alexander called Ryan back. They agreed to talk again the next morning at Alliance. He waited until Antonio called later that day. Meanwhile, he distracted himself by watching CNN. News regarding the pandemic was being discussed everywhere. Alexander wanted to be updated on any news and information about it. It was essential for Alliance and Adagio.

He took a break to have dinner with Gabrielle. He told her what Antonio had mentioned to him. Now it wasn't just him, but she was also anxious to hear a new update.

They had to know NDB's position on this matter, but most likely, they would know the conclusion the next morning.

***

Rachel was in Aguascalientes, shifting between her small business and her studies. She was half in the ninth semester of ten at the university. Her small business was growing slowly but steadily. She was now focusing more on being a distributor instead of just selling products to retail clients directly.

Alexander felt quite tense about her. In Mexico, COVID-19 had not yet spread as it had in many other countries, but it was expected to be soon. He was concerned that the government was downgrading it, and many citizens were not implementing strong preventative measures. Just a few companies of the hundreds of thousands had been taking some proactive actions.

Rachel had an everyday life. Alexander had to be emphatic with her regarding this matter. An intense discussion between them rose when he saw her making cheers with a spoon to another boy. He saw the photo she had published on Instagram and became angry. After his many warnings to be careful, she hadn't understood.

He told her finally that the credit cards would be canceled if she didn't learn the importance of this matter. She joked about it, and Alexander canceled one of her credit cards immediately. She didn't believe it until she tried to use it minutes later. She became angry, but he didn't care. He had decided to discipline her on this matter. Or at least he would try to. That was his responsibility.

***

Antonio called again five minutes after nine.

"Mr. Stern, we're working on obtaining more information. It could take some hours for another brief. I'll have to call you around eight tomorrow morning."

"Anything new so far?"

"Nothing relevant, Sir. I´ll call you tomorrow."

"OK," Alexander said, disappointed.

CHAPTER 27

Alexander decided to start his bow and arrow practice again in a park near his home. He couldn't go to the gym; it would be closed during the lockdown. That Tuesday, he was incredibly anxious. Alexander woke up, and after a cup of coffee, he found himself thinking about what Antonio's update would reveal.

Colonel Robles arrived, so he put on with sports clothes and went out with him. Fifteen minutes after seven, he was shooting the first arrow. Having arranged with Colonel Robles to come early in the mornings would allow him to have enough time to practice or exercise before getting to Alliance.

He hadn't practiced lately, but he hadn't lost his previous accuracy. A minimum of six rounds of twelve arrows each was his daily regimen. He had bought an optic bow sight that he had not used yet. This morning would be the first time. Once he calibrated it, he gained considerable improvement in the percentage of close hits right at the target's inner circle. He liked this discipline. Every round he stepped back one meter, and after adjusting with the first two arrows, he would then hit the next ten arrows more accurately each round.

Colonel Robles was driving him back home when Antonio texted, asking him if they could talk. Alexander was almost at the underground parking, so he waited until he got there and texted him back.

"Hello, Mr. Stern. I need to update you."
"Right, what do you have?"
"The board is asking Mr. Shultz to resign today."
"Wow. That fast?"
"Yes, Sir. They don't want him one more day at the bank. They want him out before the end of the day."
"And if he doesn't want to?"

"Then, he'll be laid off. They would encourage him to avoid such a shameful situation."

"Maybe he deserves it," Alexander said.

"That's not all. The two executives will be fired this morning too. One is his nephew. They're not letting them get back into the bank."

"And the two board members?"

"Nothing, Sir. Remember, we're not putting them in a compromising situation. We want them to help you in the future. That's the plan."

"Right, just confirming this. But when Shultz sees he's lost, what might he do regard them?"

"We don't know, but he's not likely to do anything. Mr. Shultz needs them there to avoid some of the hotheads sitting on the board to push on taking some legal actions against him."

"That makes sense."

"It's not yet confirmed, but the chief financial officer is going to take Shultz place temporarily."

"OK. I know him. He's a decent man."

"Mr. Stern, one important matter. When the executives were fired, Mr. Shultz may think you're behind all this. His nephew is the one focusing on getting Alliance clients."

"He might. Or he might not. He can't be sure," Alexander said.

"Remember that we told the board members not only about his fraud schemes, but that he was also targeting clients of other companies, including yours, Mr. Stern."

"Okay, we'll see what happens then. Thank you for the update, Antonio. Anything else?"

"No, Sir. I'll keep you informed."

Apparently, that Tuesday would be the last day of Fred's employment. After his conversation with Antonio, Alexander updated Gabrielle and went to the office.

***

That morning, Shultz got up, prepared some coffee, and read both newspapers delivered every day at his home. After breakfast, he showered and dressed smartly for his all-day board meeting. Twenty minutes after eight, he was out of the house walking to his car. His driver was already waiting for him.

Shultz lived alone, was recently divorced for a second time, and had no family. A maid had worked with him since the divorce and arrived every morning at seven. She left Shultz's home before five in the afternoon on weekdays and at noon on Saturdays. He used to play golf with his usual foursome at the country club. Eighteen holes later, he showered and had lunch with whoever was available.

It took thirty minutes to get to the bank from where he lived at rush hour, not in the center of Santo Domingo but relatively close.

Before walking to his office, he habitually passed by the Treasury Department. That day he wanted to see how the market was performing with the pandemic. He had some investments in local bonds, both with the Central Bank and the Ministry of Finance. He wanted to sell them but doing it that day would cause a considerable loss, so he decided to wait. Ten minutes later, he went to his office.

The scheduled board meeting was initially planned to be a strategic session, so it would take all day. They had many matters to discuss to face the pandemic and the expected impact on the bank. He was hoping to be out of the meeting and be home before the lockdown.

***

Once at Alliance, Alexander made himself an espresso. He watched his phone for any text from Antonio, but nothing. He felt anxious now, knowing what would happen to Fred Shultz, but he didn't leave him another option. He had to protect Alliance and everyone working for him.

At 9:43 a.m., he received a call from an unknown number.

"Alexander, this is Serge Arden."

"Oh, hello. Please hold a second."

Alexander was not expecting that call. Serge Arden calling him was not usual. He wanted some seconds to think about how to manage it.

"Hello, Sir, how are you?" Alexander said politely, as he respected him.

"I've had better days. Can we speak a minute?"

"Yes, please go ahead."

"I need to meet with you. During the last twelve hours, it has been brought to my attention that some activities, not according to our best practices, have been happening lately here at NDB."

"Yes, Sir," Alexander said, and waited to hear more.

"I need to meet with you to clarify everything. Can we meet later today? Are you going to the office with this COVID-19 situation?

"Yes, I'm at Alliance. Anytime, before the lockdown hour."

"Perfect, I have a meeting at ten, which will end before noon. Can I come to your office at twelve-thirty?

"I'll be here."

"Excellent. Thanks, Alexander."

***

Fred had arrived at his office minutes before his meeting started. He hadn't seen any of the board members. Usually, one or two passed in front of his office and said hello before meetings, but not this day.

Two minutes before ten, he asked his assistant if any board members had arrived. She confirmed that they were all in the conference room, had been there twenty minutes at least. He was surprised; he didn't remember a meeting when everyone had such anticipation.

He put his jacket on and unplugged his laptop. Once he had all his equipment, he walked to the conference room.

He opened the door and said hello to everyone. No one answered, three members just nodded at him. His usual seat was the right one beside Serge Arden's. He noticed that the board's secretary took it, and two other members had moved left without leaving any space.

Serge was seated at the head of the table, and three members sat on each side. The remaining four seats on each side were unoccupied. When Fred realized this, he said, "Mrs. Secretary, you took my seat."

"Fred, we're changing seats this time," Serge said, and he pointed to the unoccupied seats on the right side. "Please choose any available."

It was an awkward moment for Fred and everyone. Fred nodded to Serge, and blushed. He noticed everyone had a letter-sized white envelope in front of them, which seemed to be packed with documents about one inch thick. All the envelopes were closed, but Serge's was open, with the documents removed from the envelope.

The waiter was still serving a glass of water to one board member and coffee to other three. He asked Fred if he wanted to order something. Fred shook his head. Serge asked the waiter to serve the remaining cups and wait in the kitchen until he was called. A minute later, the waiter left and closed the door behind him.

"Are we ready to start the meeting?" Fred asked.

"Fred, I'll take the lead on this one," Serge said, picked up the papers in front of him, and in a serious tone said, "Fred, we need to have a conversation with you."

CHAPTER 28

After his meeting, Alexander spent half an hour reviewing the financial markets. Last Monday, 23rd of March, had been one of the worst days in the New York Stock Exchange. Some indexes have reached their lowest level since 2017. The main index he followed, the Dow Jones Industrials, had closed the day before at 18,592 points, with a thirty-five percent loss since the last business day of December.

His concerns increased significantly. He recalled the 2008 crisis. It was expected a slight recovery, and the US government finally announced financial support for the families and companies. Still, there was too much volatility and uncertainty now as to what would happen in the future.

He didn't have direct exposure in the US market. He was lucky to have sold all his investments in different companies to fund the acquisition of Alliance, but he was concerned about how everyone would be affected by all the measures taken worldwide.

Everyone was expecting Alliance to be affected, but nobody knew the magnitude. It would depend on how much time companies worldwide remained closed, as in the Dominican Republic. Many would suffer in all sectors.

He spent some thoughts on Christopher Mattis' companies; a food producer focused on middle-class segments. His business would be impacted in subsequent months. Gabrielle's business focused more on the upper-middle class and wealthy clients. After analysis, he thought that she could partner with Christopher to scale up her business in Santo Domingo and the United States in the future.

He recalled his trip to New Orleans, Nashville, and Atlanta. The last two were places they could gladly live.

They had been able to drive through various neighborhoods and had loved them.

He smiled, thinking that the Senator could help him get the visa that he hadn't been able to get years ago.

After the black SUV followed him, he'd discussed with Gabrielle that maybe it was time for them to live elsewhere. They loved New York and Connecticut, but Georgia or Tennessee were good options too. If a good business opportunity arose, they would evaluate it.

Alexander was signing some documents when Ryan stepped into his office.

"Alex, do you remember the clients we had lunch with? The two brothers?"

"Yes, what happened with them?"

"Both were retiring twenty percent or more of their investments this week, but they recalled the request they'd sent."

"That's excellent. It was a substantial amount."

"Yes, a huge amount. And that's not all. Another client to who we sent his money yesterday is coming back too. He wasn't even able to invest at NDB today."

"Why?"

"The sales executive he'd been working with is not there anymore. His account was assigned to another executive, and when he tried to open the investment today, the rate she gave him was considerably lower. He immediately decided to send the funds back to us."

"That's great."

"Right. I hope this change in rates at NDB is maintained. That would stop clients flying out, and some would come back to us soon."

Ryan left his office. Alexander felt relieved upon hearing what was occurring. He thought that the bleeding might be controlled, but they had to wait to confirm it.

Fifteen minutes later, Ryan called back.

"Alex, this is strange. I don't know what's going on. "One more client is coming back. He's not one of our previous wealthier investors, but anyway, he's back. What could be happening? This is not normal."

"If it's for the same reason as the previous two brothers and the other client, rates at NDB have been adjusted. Tell all sales executives to proactively call all clients we've lost. Make sure they highlight our actual rates."

"OK, we'll do that."

Alexander called Antonio. He hadn't received any information from him, and he wanted to get an update on Fred's bank, especially now that good news was coming in.

"Antonio, do you have an update? Investors are coming back."

"Our plan might be paying rewards, Sir. The meeting is still in progress. I know the executives were laid off, but we don't know anything about Mr. Shultz yet."

"OK, let me know as soon as you know something."

"Sir, we found out that both Fred Shultz and Jack Dowell have registered guns in their names."

"In this country, everyone has a gun, Antonio."

"Right, Sir. But not everyone has a motive. Mr. Shultz might have one soon. I recommend you keep Colonel Robles close, just in case."

"Thanks, Antonio, I'll do that. I don't see Shultz doing something stupid with a gun, especially if it's registered in his name."

"Me neither, Sir, but it's always better to anticipate something. Remember, Mr. Shultz is being fired today."

"Right, but I'm sure neither Fred nor Jack would do something stupid."

"OK. I have to go, Sir. I'll keep you informed."

After hanging up, Alexander thought about their conversation. He felt concerned about Fred being armed. He was being kicked out of his bank for fraud, but a general manager, even one like Fred, would not do anything with a gun. Also, he would not lose his nice loot in The Bahamas by doing something stupid.

George and Axel had the conference call with Alexander at eleven as scheduled. Alexander sent the final draft of the chronogram. The business looked good even if it had to be developed slower.
"Guys, how are you?"
"We're fine Alex, how's everything in paradise?" George asked.
"I hope you´re not in shorts at the office," Axel said.
"Why not? Otherwise, I'll need to go home before going to the beach today," Alexander said.
George, usually the more serious one, said, "Eh, back to business. I have a meeting later."
Alexander began to explain all the changes they'd made.
"As you can see, we completed some pending information. Everything's included now."
"I saw it, Alex," George said. "We just want to discuss the situation with COVID-19 in the Dominican Republic. We're quite concerned about how it would affect the project."
"Right, it's going to have an impact," Alexander said. "Many businesses and workers are going to be affected for some time. The advantage is that even with just one building we can maintain good prices, and good profitability. And we're putting in pause the construction of the commercial section."
They spent the next forty minutes discussing the market impact. Finally, they reached an agreement on how to move forward; just one building at a time and hold on with the commercial units until agreements had been reached with some tenants.
They spent the next minutes talking casually about other matters. Both told Alexander they were willing to go back with their families, but the next time, in addition to

Santo Domingo, they would visit some of the lovely beaches promoted everywhere.

After hanging up, Alexander continued thinking for some minutes about the project. He required an excellent real estate broker with expertise in apartments and in the zone where the project was located. Also, various banks were important to preapprove the project, not only for the development loan but also to preapprove mortgages. He was convinced that at least two or three financiers were recommended. Exclusivity usually was less cost-effective for developers and clients.

Alexander was quite enthusiastic and optimistic about the project even with this situation. People would need new apartments as centrally located as possible. They would marry. Grown children want to live alone. There would always be a market for modern and new apartments.

He always had the dream to be a developer. He had built two houses, one in Monterrey, and one in Santo Domingo. His father was a civil engineer, always focused on huge infrastructure projects, but he was not very ambitious, at least initially. But it had to be soon; he didn't have much time to do it later in his life.

***

His new meeting attendee arrived sharply at noon. He asked him to wait for a minute in his office. Alexander had to call Ryan for a quick update on clients.

"Sorry, Mr. Sued, I had to make that call."

"Not a problem, Alexander. I was enjoying the view. I could drink wine for hours here."

"Would you have wine this early, Mr. Sued?" Alexander joked.

"Not at all. If we were meeting later today, I would accept one. Or a scotch."

'The next time we meet here, we should have the meeting in the afternoon. I'll arrange some drinks for both of us."

"Perfect. I'll be here tomorrow afternoon."

"Sir, tomorrow, I–."

"I'm joking. I can't tomorrow."

"OK, we'll plan on that, Sir."

"Alexander, thank you for receiving me."

"Don't worry, Mr. Sued. It's my pleasure. What can I do for you?"

When Alexander said that, he knew it was payback day. He hadn't received news from Mr. Sued in several days since their wine session with William. But surely, this was the time to receive a request. He only wished that it was something he could grant.

"Alexander, I want to see if you can help me with something."

"Mr. Sued, if it's in my hands, consider it done."

The old man kept dancing at his request. Alexander was willing to tell him to cut the crap and just ask for it. He had an important meeting at 12:30. Finally, he pitched it.

"Alexander, my son is graduating from university. He studied Economics and has been an excellent student; he graduated with honors. I suggested he could take a job at the Central Bank, but he's not willing to. He doesn't want to follow his old man's career and desires.

"Mr. Sued, do you want me to help him get a job in the private sector?"

"Yes, please, exactly that. And if it can be with you, I would be thankful."

"No problem. We need to follow a process: an interview, some tests. But as you said, he must be excellent. I'll see what I can do for him."

"Excellent. I'll email his resume to you. I appreciate this. I'll go now and let you work."

"No problem, Sir. Anything you need, just let me know."

"Thank you, Alexander."

Mr. Sued walked out of the office almost when Alexander was to have his meeting with Serge Arden. He was glad he didn't have to make him wait. He was curious if Mr. Sued's son could fit in the company.

Alexander didn't have any news from Antonio. He imagined Fred Shultz's reaction, with his well-known explosive character, pushing back and forth with everyone during his board meeting. He hoped to have more information before he met with Serge Arden, but most probably, he wouldn't have it on time.

His US shareholders hadn't been very communicative lately. He knew the Senator had been deeply involved in many meetings between Congress and the White House. The Democrats had raised their voice often with the way President Trump had managed the pandemic, attacking him every single day.

The Senator was not closely affiliated with Trump, but anything he did could affect the public's perception of the Republicans. That could damage him, making the days of his Washington assignment numbered. Neither the Senator nor Christopher could allow that to happen.

The Senator was at Washington more for power and priceless relationships than money. Well, for money, tons of it, but not coming in his regular paycheck. Something someday would come up.

CHAPTER 29

Serge Arden had worked in the financial sector for four decades, first in Miami for eight years, then assigned by the same bank to its branch in Santo Domingo, a city he loved and decided to stay his whole life. An economist with a double major in finance and marketing and a Kellogg MBA, he got married twenty-nine years ago. He had worked in several banks his whole career and was recently named President at his present bank.

A recognized banker in the country and a decent man, he was known to be fair with everyone, despite being an avid negotiator, who did not deserve what was occurring under his watch.

This was not the first time he had dealt with fraud during his career. He had seen many cases, and because of this, he was a keen supporter of risk and control units, established to protect banks, their employees, and their clients, from internal or external aggressors. By far, this scam was the most difficult he would have to manage, the first one with someone who had been his protégé, his recommendation for general manager, and his friend.

The night before, he received the first envelope of seven delivered. He opened it and started reading the documents inside. Seconds later, he held his breath and grabbed the door of his library. He sat in one of the two black leather chairs in front of a table with small sculptures.

Once he read the summary and looked at some of the proofs stapled behind it, he placed them on the table and went to the bar and poured himself a whiskey. Glenlivet eighteen years was his choice. He usually drank it with one big ice cube, but this time he would have a double straight one.

He reviewed all the documents three times. He held his grayed hair with both hands, unable to digest what he was reading, thinking again and again about it.

Not Fred. I can't believe it. Why? he thought.

After an hour of reviewing the documents and thinking how all this mess had been allowed, he accepted it sadly and decided to move forward, to take bold action on the matter, and to accept all the consequences. He was convinced his primary responsibility was to protect his bank, clients, and shareholders.

He wrote some notes in the next half an hour and began calling other board members. He expected them to already know about the situation; a note clearly stated that everyone was receiving a similar package that night.

He made the first call to the board's vice-president, who had already received his envelope and was willing to take his car and go to Fred's home to punch him. Serge asked him to calm down and to consider all the consequences. Minutes later, the vice-president was able to listen to Serge's plan.

The next call Serge made was to the Secretary of the board. She was alarmed, worried about the risk to the bank's reputation, and also concerned about the regulatory implications. She was more than willing to hang Fred. This situation would highlight a lack of controls. Nobody had found anything in so many years, not the internal audit, nor operations, nor risk units. Not even the external auditors.

When Serge explained his plan, she agreed to it immediately.

"No other option, Serge," she said.

After that, all other board members agreed to Serge's next steps to handle the situation, including the two involved in the scam. He didn't know that then, and they were not telling anyone about it at that moment.

Everything was settled, and a decision was made. Everyone just had to maintain full discretion, wait until the next morning, and pray to God it worked out as visualized.

***

Fred froze at the bank's board meeting when Serge boldly said that statement. He thought about what they wanted to tell him as he looked at the serious faces around the table, including his two partners in crime. He soon realized he had lost all his friends in the conference room and remained silent, looked at his phone, and then paid attention to Serge when he continued speaking to him.

"Fred, we've been acknowledged about information regarding irregularities at the bank with different clients' accounts and loans," Serge said, lifting the documents and looking at him. After a short pause, he continued.

"These documents are strong proof that over many years someone has organized and executed a plan to rob clients' money in abandoned accounts, and to approve unrequested loans, paid for some months before written off, and keeping the remaining cash disbursed."

Fred was shocked, but he managed to maintain his composure. How did they know all this? Nothing implicates me directly, he thought. After thinking about it, he decided to deny everything.

"What? What are you talking about, Serge? What accounts? Loans written off?"

"Yes, Fred. Many accounts were robbed. And many loans fabricated. Let me finish. I have proof of both scams here. All board members have proof. We all received it last night."

Fred's heart began to pump fast. Immediately after Serge's last words, he watched at his two supposed friends, seated on the other side of the table. He didn't say a single word, just looked to the papers in front of them. He felt betrayed, asking himself why they hadn't called him when they received the documents. The reason was obvious. They wanted to save their asses.

He'd been careful to manage everything without approving a single case or transaction personally. His relative had been in charge of the scam's operation, coordinating all details with a credit officer who approved the loans, each one for a six-hundred-dollar commission. More in some cases, when the amount approved increased. A result-driven variable compensation program.

Fred himself would not be implicated directly unless his nephew talked. But he won't do that. Such action would immediately link him to the scam and be legally prosecuted. The credit officer could claim that the loans approved had all the necessary documentation. Clients taking the loans had good credit bureaus, but they didn't know they were asking for them. The loans fabricated were just a few of the thousands granted at NDB every month. They passed unnoticed.

The cash stolen from abandoned accounts was another story. Withdrawals were made using the regular slips with false authorization of the client. His signature had been practiced for some days by Fred's nephew. Using a false ID, someone received the money from a cashier at any branch, and then the money was handed to him, minus the commission. He deposited the cash in another bank account in Fred's name.

Virtually no one ever claimed on these accounts. Clients just forgot about those balances. Many were leftover cash after the last payment done to loans, and others belonged to clients who had died, and relatives didn't know about the account.

No controls on these accounts' withdrawals were in place. The system had an automatic block if accounts were not used in the last twelve months, but Fred made minimum deposits of less than twenty Dominican pesos to keep the account unblocked. When the account had reached two years without transactions, they cashed out the total balance.

After a significant amount, most of the cash was transferred out of the country to the account in The Bahamas. The remaining amount was used to pay the first monthly installments on the loans.

"Serge, I didn't know anything about it. Who did this to our bank?" Fred said.

"Let me finish, Fred," Serge said. "We have evidence of who is involved. Both were detained at the reception this morning and were laid off. One is your nephew, Fred, and the other one is a credit officer."

"What? What did he do?"

"Fred, please. Don't deny it. We know everything."

"You know nothing, Serge. Everything you're got there is wrong," he said.

"Relax, Fred. It's better for all that we stay calm. Otherwise, you'll be in jail later today. Everything is arranged."

When hearing jail, Fred got frozen. He thought it was better if he had a lawyer in the meeting, but he chose just to wait and avoid saying anything stupid that could incriminate him even more.

"There is another matter that needs explanation," Serge said. "How can you explain the almost two million dollars you have at a bank in The Bahamas?"

Fred was shocked once more. Until that moment, he didn't expect they knew about that account.

"What account, Serge?"

"We don't have time for this, Fred. The documents are right here. I double-checked this with a good friend in Nassau who has a good friend in your bank. The account is in your name, Fred."

"Serge, many of us have overseas accounts. That's not a sin."

"Of course not. We want an explanation of the two million dollars sitting there. We're known each other for many years. Unless you have a very profitable side business that you haven't reported to us, which is against our policies, with your lifestyle and your bank income, there's no way to add that amount."

"That's for investment purposes. I have some partners."

The two board members looked at each other. One nodded discreetly at the other, signaling to his phone. He picked it up and typed a quick text to Fred: "Pal, don't do something stupid. Let the meeting flow. It's better for us all."

When his phone vibrated, Fred opened it and read the text. He decided to restrain himself as the board member recommended.

After some seconds of silence, Serge continued.

"Fred, the account is in your name. No partners registered. You would need to prove where those funds came from in a trial. I hope you have a good explanation because being prosecuted for money laundering could make for a very long sentence."

Fred became alarmed, hearing that a lawsuit could follow. It could become a nightmare for everyone, including the bank. But the bank would be punished by authorities with a fine, and a request to release various employees would come. Then would move on.

He could go to jail. He knew he couldn't prove that the money had come from a legal source.

He walked to Fred's seat and handed him the documents.

"Check this, Fred. Your account balance as of yesterday. Too much money."

Serge walked back to his seat without saying a word, allowing Fred to review the documents. He checked all the information in the two sheets he'd been given and acted as if he validated something. He remained silent, waiting for someone to say something.

"I don't know if anyone else has additional comments on this matter," Serge said. "I'm clear about everything going on here, and I'm pretty sure that if we continue investigating this fraud, internally and with the authorities, it will confirm what we already know."

He looked at the other board members to see if anyone wanted to say anything. The vice-president, deeply troubled the previous evening but now calm, added some words to Serge's conclusions.

"Fred, how were you able to do this to us? To this institution that gave you so many opportunities. To our shareholders, but first of all, to our clients? Didn't you think you could go to jail?"

Fred remained quiet in his seat. He was careful not to say anything that could compromise him further.

"Fred, let me add something," Serge said. "We also know that you have conducted a full complot, not quite a best business practice and against our corporate values, to affect other financial institutions, mainly Alliance. Do you know the risk you've placed us in if others in the market realize that an attack is being made on our bank by another financial institution? How do you think regulators or the Bank's Association would see this?"

"Alliance? I haven't made such an attack. We've been aggressive in making promotions to clients, nothing more."

"Do you think I'm stupid, Fred?" Serge raised his voice and looked directly into Fred's eyes.

Fred wasn't able to maintain eye contact with Serge and looked down at the table. Who's behind these envelopes sent to these guys? Could it be someone at Alliance? Alexander? he thought.

These questions spun in his head. He had been focused on the documents, but now he realized he had to know who was behind them.

"We've been aggressive bringing in clients. No one can blame us for that."

Serge looked at the ceiling and tilted his chair back while passing his right hand through his hair. Troubled, he was too tired to argue longer with Mr. Fred Shultz.

"Let's cut this here, Fred. Give us ten minutes to discuss this with the board members."

Fred took his phone and left the conference room. He walked back to his office and waited there until he was called again.

Serge addressed all the board members. The plan was moving as discussed. Through Fred's reactions, they had confirmed that he was involved in both internal scams, the attacks on other financial institutions, and that he didn't have a reasonable explanation about the funds in The Bahamas account. Finally, Serge asked everyone to approve the proposal for Fred's dismissal and everyone agreed to it.

Fred stayed in his office. He told his assistant not to forward any call, only if it came from the conference room, and closed the door. He spent his time guessing who could be behind the unmasking and what to do next. He had gained some enemies in the past, but he had a harsh relationship with Alexander only recently. He wasn't sure whether he was behind all this, but he seemed to be. He would try to confirm it later.

He reached for his phone and texted the board member who had sent him the message minutes ago.

"What's going on? Why didn't you tell me yesterday about those envelopes?"

"Tough situation, Fred. Don't worry about what's going to happen. It's much better than the alternative, for all. We're watching your back."

"What do you mean? What's going to happen?"

"I can't write now. Just accept the proposal and move forward. We'll talk later."

He didn't like his answer, but he couldn't do anything. He had to stay calm and wait.

He checked his phone for other messages and saw one from his nephew.

"Uncle Fred, something happened at the bank. I got fired. They asked me many questions, but I kept quiet. They gave me a letter. I need to talk to you."

"OK. Don't worry. I'll call you later. Don't talk to anyone. I'm in a meeting. I'll call you back."

He had to focus on his imminent problem now. It was safer for both his cousin had kept quiet, but he wasn't sure about the credit officer. He would have to check on that after his meeting.

Ten minutes later, Serge called Fred's assistant and asked him to come back. She dialed his phone extension, but he didn't take the call, so she walked to the door and knocked.

"Come in," Fred shouted.

"Sir, Mr. Arden just called. He wants you to join them back in the conference room."

"OK. I'll be there in a minute."

She closed the door. Fred grabbed his phone and walked out of his office to the conference room, expecting the worst. After he entered, Serge asked him to take a seat by pointing to the same chair he'd sat in earlier. Two members who were standing returned to their seats, and the uncomfortable session began again.

"Fred, the board members and I have discussed all the information we have in our hands, in addition to what we've retrieved from other sources."

"What other sources?"

"That's not relevant. Let's move forward, and please let me finish without interruptions. What happened in our bank is something we can't tolerate. It's something that has put us at great risk. The board has unanimously voted to request your resignation, effective immediately."

Fred remained silent for a few seconds.

"Why, Serge?"

"Fred, you know why. We don't have to give you more explanations. Here are the conditions. You will resign today. You will be paid based on what is requested by law, only that. We'll determine the amount for you to pay back to repair all the problems you've generated. That amount is being estimated as we speak. If you accept this, you might avoid going to jail for the rest of your life."

Seconds later, Serge said, "Fred, you have ten minutes to decide."

CHAPTER 30

Fred left the conference room thinking about Serge's proposal. It was now a fact he was leaving the bank and had to do it in the best way possible, and as safely as he could. A better option had to appear in ten minutes, but nothing came to his mind. He wasn't even able to concentrate on the proposal, guessing if Alexander was behind everything or who else could be. Fred passed from worry to anger in seconds, especially when he thought of whom to blame. Finally, he considered what the board had offered him.

He had no other option than to accept his resignation. There was no way to explain the amount of cash he had overseas, and he also had some easy-to-trace personal investments in the country. Credit cards complicated the scenario even more. He had paid many expensive luxuries with it.

Additionally, if a legal process against him started, his nephew would be included. It wouldn't be merely a public shame; he would be banned from his own family. He thought of his mother, and this would kill her. There was no alternative but to receive a small severance package and reduce the amount to transfer back to the bank as much as possible. He still needed that number from Serge.

How the regulators would take this sudden resignation and leave the same day worried him. Still, the board could explain that it was a mutual agreement due to personal or health reasons, and that another seasoned staff member would be taking his place temporarily. He wasn't sure who that could be, but he had an idea.

Twenty minutes later, Serge knocked at his door.

"Fred, we need your answer right now. We can't wait anymore; time to come back to the conference room."

"Yes, I was getting ready to go there."

"Let's go," Serge said, and they walked to the conference room.

Serge entered, and Fred closed the door.

"I accept your offer. I'm resigning and leaving today. I just need your commitment that no legal action will be taken against my nephew or me."

Serge nodded, then asked, "What about the money?"

"I'll transfer it to the bank today. I'll keep only the amount owned by other investors.

Serge handed him a paper containing some calculations.

"This is our estimate. That's the amount you have to reimburse to the bank, and then we'll do it to clients, plus the amount needed to pay the written off loans."

When Fred saw the number, it was slightly less than what he'd expected, so he agreed.

"Fred, you'll need to transfer that amount no later than 2:00 p.m. Send the money to the local bank you used before sending it to The Bahamas, and from there to us. Let me give you the resignation letter."

Serge walked to the conference room's back door, opened it, and called someone who handed him some documents. Then he closed the door and walked back to Fred again.

"Sign where the marks are," Serge said.

Fred hesitated for several seconds, but finally he signed.

After he'd signed, all the board members expressed relief. They would have to wait for confirmation that the wire transfer was done. Serge would handle that personally.

"Board members," he said. "Please allow me to remain with Mr. Shultz." Everyone walked out of the conference room in seconds; nobody wanted to spend more time in there. After the last one had left, Serge closed the door.

"Let me get an espresso," he said. "It will take just a minute."

Fred didn't answer. He waited until the machine poured the coffee into a small cup, and Serge sat back down.

"What a scene you made here today, Serge," he said with deep resentment.

"Fred Shultz, I deeply regret I've treated you as family for so many years. The shame you put on me is something I've never experienced in my whole life. You failed me. You failed me big time."

Fred remained silent.

"You had a great future at a great bank, with my trust, and the trust of many board members. You would have earned a lot of money. In a few years, you would have saved the same amount or more of what you have in your damn account in The Bahamas. What the hell were you thinking?"

"Sorry, Serge. It was a mistake. And I regret what I did."

"You've thrown your life, your job, and our friendship into the garbage."

"I know, Serge, and I'm sorry for that."

"Fred, go to your office, make the wire transfers, and send me the confirmations. Let's meet here in an hour. You should be done by then."

Fred went back to his office. He wanted the storm to pass as soon as possible. Once he received the confirmation of the wire transfer from The Bahamas, he would need to wait around half an hour to receive the funds in his account, to be able to transfer them to NDB.

He had time until he had to do the second wire transfer, so he went to the lobby where the commercial mall was and called the board member he had texted with.

"Why didn't you tell me about this last night?"

"Look, Fred. I don't know who set up this trap. But whoever it is, is blackmailing both of us too. Our envelope had another note, in addition to all the information Serge told you. They know we're partners. The only way for us to help you was to keep our positions on the board and to influence the decision to your benefit. And that, Fred, means keeping you out of jail."

"Is that right?"

"Oh, yes. Various board members wanted you in jail, your nephew, and the credit officer, too, not giving a damn for the reputational and regulatory risk. We were able to save your ass. I recommend you do whatever they want. Right now, the board is quite divided about whether to take action against you. I strongly recommend you leave the bank quietly."

Maybe he's right, Fred thought.

He felt upset about losing too much and didn't hesitate to ask the board member about the source.

"Do you know who's behind all this?"

"No, but it appears to be someone at Alliance or someone who cares a lot for that company."

"Why do you think that?"

"Your aggressive strategy to gain clients was focused on them, and some examples were included from that company."

"And how are they blackmailing you?"

"They asked us to support any initiative with Alliance, or we would be exposed to other matters in addition to our partnership with you. Fred, I have to go. But I want to give you some advice. Just leave all this in the past. I suggest you leave the country for some time, as soon as possible. If something goes wrong with this situation, and believe me, many things could go wrong, you will suffer, and I'm sure you'll end up in jail."

"Okay, I'll do that."

He hung up, sure that Alliance was behind the plot against him.

Fuck you, Alexander; this is not going to end here. You'll regret it, he thought.

He received an email confirming that the wire transfer had been completed and the money had been deposited at the local bank. He returned to his office, went online into the bank's website, validated that the money was there, and approved the second wire transfer to his bank. His loot accumulated for many years was now lost.

He stayed there for some minutes feeling miserable, until he was interrupted by someone knocking on his door.

"Come in."

"Mr. Shultz, someone is here with five carton boxes. I told him it must be a mistake, but he insisted," his assistant said.

"Ask him to leave them here. Come in. I need to talk to you."

"OK, Mr. Shultz."

She closed the door and walked to his desk. Fred explained to her why the boxes were there.

"This is my last day at the bank."

"Why, Sir? I didn't know you were leaving."

"It was planned that way. It's better. Thank you for everything."

She expected to have a more extended conversation, but Fred wasn't going to talk too much that day.

"If someone looks for me, I'll be with Mr. Arden," Fred said.

"Ok, Mr. Shultz."

She left his office and closed the door. Fred waited five minutes inside his office and printed the wire transfers' confirmations. He took them and walked to the conference room, the last time he would do this in his whole life. Serge was still waiting for him there.

"Do you have the bank confirmations, Fred?"

"Yes, here they are," he said and pushed them over the table to him.

"Now that everything is completed, I just want to tell you two things. First, I hope you learn from this. Second, it's a shame that our friendship had to end like this."

Fred remained quiet for some seconds, and Serge said, "I have to go to another meeting. Human Resources will send you some boxes to pack your personal belongings. Bye, Fred."

"Bye, Mr. Arden."

Fred walked back to his office. Serge took the back door and walked down the stairs to his vehicle. He had to run for his meeting with Alexander at Alliance.

Once Fred was at his door, he saw a security guard at the entrance.

"What's this guy doing here?" he asked his assistant.

"Sir, Human Resources sent him. They said it had been requested earlier by Mr. Arden."

"By Serge?"

"Yes, by Mr. Shultz."

Fred was bothered. He was being treated as a felon. Well, he was one, but that annoyed him to hell and made him furious. He asked his secretary to help him to fill the boxes with everything.

He went to his desk and sat. When he tried to open his computer, a message appeared on the screen.

"Your computer access is denied. Privileges revoked."

This irritated him even more. He grabbed the stapler and threw it at a table, breaking a white ceramic lamp and leaving a mark on the wall.

The security guard heard it and hurried in. Fred looked at him but remained silent. The guard left when his assistant called him. She came in, nervous, and started assembling the boxes.

"Where do you want me to start, Sir?"

"Wherever you want. You know what all my personal belongings are," he said while walking out of the office to the hall and stood for five minutes thinking and trying to calm himself.

***

The night before, Serge had agreed with the board members to temporarily appoint Carlos Penzo, the chief financial officer, as head of the bank. They had spoken earlier that day, and in coordination with the responsible of Human Resources, he had arranged some of that day's requirements. Serge had asked them to be at the bank at 8:00 a.m. They were the first to be informed of what was going on.

He helped Serge to get all the necessary information to understand the effect on the accounts and loans, at least a gross estimate due to the short notice. He was informed of his new position until someone had been assigned permanently, and if he wished, he could be a candidate. He accepted gladly. He hadn't had a good relationship with Fred. They had many discussions when Fred continuously tried to manipulate some numbers, but he didn't cooperate with him. He was pretty protected by two board committees and enjoyed some independence within the financial control unit.

When Fred was informed of who was replacing him, he grew exasperated again, and that was the last straw to his ego and equanimity. He didn't believe Serge was doing all this to him. By then, he was angrier with him than with Alexander.

CHAPTER 31

"Alex, I just received a call from the lobby. Mr. Arden is entering the building," Amanda said.

"Perfect. Let him in when he's up here."

"Are you receiving him here or at the conference room?"

"Here in my office, thank you."

His meeting with Mr. Sued had finished three minutes ago. He rushed to the bathroom and put his jacket on. He was ready to receive Serge, who arrived on time, famous not only for his punctuality, but especially for the decent man he was.

"Good afternoon, Alexander. Thank you for receiving me on such short notice. I appreciate it."

"Hello, Mr. Arden."

"Come on, Alexander. Call me Serge, or you'll make me feel older than I am. Please, just Serge."

"OK, Serge."

Amanda asked if they wanted coffee or something else to drink.

"Yes, please. Coffee and water for me. Thank you," Serge answered fast.

"Just coffee for me, Amanda. Thanks." Alexander went back to his visitor. "Serge, please come in. Let's sit down."

"Perfect. What a view you have here. I like it."

"Yes, it's nice. Thank you."

Since this morning, he was curious about Serge's request for a meeting. Amanda served them their coffees and left.

"Alexander, I'm glad you received me today, "Serge said. "It was important for me, and for my bank, but mainly for me. I need to have this conversation with you. I've been a banker for many years, and I've built many good relationships. I've been a strong competitor, but after all these years, I've achieved my main goal, and what I value most is having done everything, professional and in my personal life, with integrity."

"Yes. We all know that. You're well recognized for that."

"I have never, never, done anything improper to gain a business or for a personal benefit. That's the reason why I decided to visit you and to tell you in person what has happened recently at NDB."

"Yes," Alexander said, feeling so far, good with Serge's words.

"It's been brought to my attention that we haven't been applying the values and best practices at NDB. We have not been, how can I say it? Playing fair recently."

"What are you referring to, Serge?"

"I'm sure you know exactly what I'm talking about. I don't want to go into any details. That's not the purpose of my visit."

"What is the purpose?"

"I want to apologize personally, and on behalf of my bank, for what happened recently between our companies. From now on, I can assure you that our business practices will be maintained at the highest standards. We will compete, always, but it should always be a fair competition."

"I appreciate that you came here to tell me that. It's been some difficult weeks for us. I'm sure you know all the details."

"Yes, and I'm ashamed about that. I assure you that we've taken all necessary measures to make sure we'll conduct business by the highest standards in the future, or we won't make them."

"I hope so, Serge. Both companies can do business without killing each other."

"I'm sure of that, and I'll go even further. If we can do something together in the future, like joining efforts in any deal, Alliance will be considered."

Serge seemed to be honest and kind, and intelligent too. Alexander knew he didn't want to get compromised by saying anything that could make him or NDB liable. Also, he would avoid any retaliation from Alliance.

"Alexander, we've taken many measures. We cleaned up some areas, specifically in the sales unit. What I'm telling you now is something that will be known publicly later today. Please keep it confidential for now."

"Yes, of course."

Fred Shultz is no longer our chief executive officer. He's leaving the bank today and will be replaced temporarily by Carlos Penzo, chief financial officer."

"I didn't know."

"Yes, a change in leadership was necessary. Fred resigned, and he's leaving today. Please draw your conclusions. The fact is, we will do make everything we can to perform according to our values."

"Serge, I'm glad that you're telling me this, but why? Why take all this trouble with us?"

"First, because it's the decent thing to do after all the problems we caused. Also, as with other financial institutions, we could work together on many projects. There's no specific interest right now, but I'm sure that something could come up for both. We want competitors, or partners, not enemies."

"Serge, I appreciate you taking the time to come here and say all this to me. We have similar values, and we don't want to have enemies, same as you. But we will protect ourselves from any attack, especially when we haven't done anything to deserve it."

"I'm sure of that. And I'm sure we will grow both companies' relationship from now on. I've already requested Carlos to deepen the relationship with Alliance. We have services, and access to some products or securities, that your business might be interested in. And we can also use your funds to manage part of our liquidity."

They stayed in Alexander's office for about twenty minutes more, talking about things that they could do together and then about personal matters.

They realized they both liked to practice archery. In college, Serge had practiced it often.

As he walked Serge to the elevator, Alexander showed him some of their offices and introduced several team members.

"Alexander, I have to go. Thanks very much, and I hope we can have lunch soon, when the lockdown has been eased and everything is safer."

"Yes, Serge. Count on it. Stay safe."

"See you soon. Bye."

Serge stepped into the elevator and Alexander walked back to his office, feeling good and confident that the attacks would cease. It was ten minutes after one. He decided to go home and eat lunch there. Colonel Robles was waiting for him. Alexander grabbed his phone and walked back to the elevators. He saw a text from Antonio that came in during his meeting with Serge.

"Mr. Stern, can I come by your office later? Is 3:00 p.m. okay?"

"Sure. I'll see you later."

Alexander was curious about any news Antonio could offer, but now he felt relieved after his conversation with Serge. He wanted to go home.

After lunch with Gabrielle and Andrea, he stayed an hour with Gabrielle. He updated her on his meeting with Serge Arden.

"A decent man, Gabrielle. I trust he meant everything he said."

"Yes, that would help."

"If he does, we'll take a heavy weight off our backs, and Alliance can grow again. We're already seeing some results."

"How's that? Isn't it too soon for that?"

"Now that they've fired Fred's nephew and rates have been adjusted, some wealthy investors are coming back. Ryan told me about three investors who came back this morning."

"That's fast, but certainly good news."

"I'm just concerned about Fred," Alexander said. "What will he do now that he's been kicked out of NDB? It must be an unpleasant situation."

"Yes, it should be. But that's not our problem. He deserves that. It's a shame what he did."

"Anyway, we need to be careful about him for a while."

Colonel Robles drove him back to the office early in the afternoon. Once there, Alexander saw Antonio waiting for him on the couch outside his office.

They stepped into his office. Alexander sat at his desk and Antonio sat in front of him. He informed Alexander of the whole situation at Fred's bank.

"Mr. Stern, we don't know what had happened at that board meeting, but rumors are saying that Mr. Shultz is already out of the bank."

"I know that. Serge Arden was here earlier today and told me that."

"OK. But he's still at the bank. He may be leaving later, but other things have happened."

"Which?"

"A huge amount of money has come back to a local bank account which was used previously to send money out of the country to The Bahamas. And once there, it was sent back to Mr. Shultz's bank."

"What do you mean by huge?"

"Slightly less than two million dollars. The account was left with only a forty thousand balance. Somehow the board was able to make Mr. Shultz pay back an important part of his loot."

"That's a surprise. How were they able to make Fred send it back?"

"We don't know, Sir. It must be some kind of arrangement. Maybe to avoid going to jail. The two guys involved in the scam are out too. Another sales executive was also fired today. We're investigating this last one. It seems they just want to clean up that business unit."

"Serge told me that too. They want to cut all the rotten apples out of the bank."

Alexander remained concerned about Fred having to transfer the money back.

"Mr. Stern, my work here is done. We're cutting all our surveillance there. I hope you're satisfied with what we've done."

"Yes, Antonio, thank you."

"You're welcome. And remember, anything you need, just give me a call. I have instructions to take care of you whenever you need it."

"Thanks, but I don't expect to have any problem like this in the future."

"You never know," Antonio smiled. "You have important investors out there, and I have a mandate to protect their investments of anyone. Anyone includes you, Mr. Stern."

Alexander said nothing, and Antonio added, "I'm joking, Mr. Stern. They're your partners, and they chose everyone close to them very well. Take care now. I have to go. We'll be in touch."

Alexander stayed in his office and spent a minute thinking about Antonio's final words. He understood that the relationship with his US partners could turn dangerous, and he didn't have much influence on them. It was clear he had to find a way to gain leverage and have good cards to play in the future.

I'm glad to be recording all conversations and making a backup of all these guys' messages since days ago. I hope I don't have to use them, he thought.

CHAPTER 32

Fred sat alone at the restaurant's last table; one he often went to for lunch. He ordered an appetizer and a beer. He knew he had to stay calm. It was no time to do something stupid. He had to think. He'd been kicked out of his job and had experienced shameful moments earlier. He was not thinking properly and perhaps a moment of disconnection with NDB would help. He spent one hour there. After another beer, he returned to his office.

His assistant had been packing the boxes. All his personal belongings took up the five he'd received, two of them full of books. She had never liked Fred that much and was packing quickly. As soon as he left, she would feel better, but she was concerned that the new boss would hire another assistant. She had already worked twenty years there. Everyone knew she was extremely valuable, but that always worried her.

For many years she worked for Serge, and she helped him occasionally when he was at NDB. He wasn't there every day; his job as President didn't require it. He used to come in at least one day per week, in addition to the meetings he had to attend.

She hadn't been able to take lunch yet. After packing the last box, her meal consisted of an apple, a nutritional bar, and some water. She was eating the apple when Fred came back and opened the glass door separating her desk from the hall. As he entered, he watched the guard standing near his office. Once he came inside, his assistant walked to him.

'Mr. Shultz, I packed up everything. I didn't tape it up yet in case you want to check the boxes. If you prefer, I'll tape them now."

Fred opened three boxes to see what was in there and nodded.

"Ask someone to take them to my car."

"OK, Mr. Shultz."

She returned to her desk to call someone, then went back to his office to tape all the boxes. Ten minutes later, she was finished, just in time as a handyman came in with a dolly to take the boxes.

"Please take these boxes to Mr. Shultz's car. Put them in the trunk," she said.

The young man loaded them in less than two minutes and left through the back door to where the service elevator was. She walked with him to help him open it. Then she came back to Fred's desk. His office door was closed now. She heard him talking, but she didn't know whether he was with someone or on the phone.

At 2:30 p.m., Carlos came in and went directly to her desk. They said hello to each other warmly.

"Did you know Mr. Shultz is leaving the bank today, Carlos?" she asked.

"Yes, that's why I'm here."

"How's that?"

"I've being assigned to take care of his duties," he said.

"Wow, that's good news," she said with a smile.

"Thank you. It'll be just temporarily. But who knows?"

"Oh, so you'll be applying for the job?"

"Too soon to say. This was a surprise for everyone."

"Yes, it was."

"Is Fred inside?"

"Yes, is he expecting you?"

"He should be now," Carlos said.

Serge had requested Carlos to be ready until it was time to go to Fred's office. Five minutes earlier, Serge had called Fred to inform him about the decision. Then Serge called Carlos to go upstairs to take care of everything. He approached Fred's office door and knocked twice.

"Yes?" he said loud from inside.

Carlos opened the door and entered.

"Good afternoon, Fred."

"So, it's you who'll be taking care of my bank."

"Yes. Serge asked me to do it temporarily," he said politely but wanting to tell him it was not his bank, and that thankfully he didn't work there anymore.

"As you see, I'm just putting some personal belongings in my briefcase and moving out of here," Fred said.

"May I sit, Fred?"

He nodded and pulled up his shoulders.

Carlos sat in one of the chairs and asked, "Is there anything urgent I need to take care of, Fred?"

"Nothing," Fred said with a smile and thinking. Right, if there is something, I'm certainly not going to tell you. Fuck you.

"Perfect," Carlos said, not wanting to say more. He understood Fred would not take well his appointment. Their relationship had been complicated for the last two years.

Fred continued packing and blushed. He was uncomfortable with the situation.

"Do you want me to do anything for you, Fred?"

"My access permissions have been revoked. I need you to send me a file that says: 'Personal Fred' in 'Documents.' Would that be a problem?"

"Not at all. I'll send you a USB with them tomorrow."

"It might not fit in just one USB."

"We'll make any arrangements necessary, Fred."

Fred nodded and continued packing the remaining items on his desk. When he'd finished, he glanced around to see whether something else needed to be done. Nothing.

He put his jacket on, and now with everything in his leather portfolio with a long strap, he slung it on his shoulder and stepped out of the office, accompanied by Carlos.

"Are you driving me home?" Fred asked sarcastically.

"No. You need to give me your ID tag and your corporate credit card. That's all I need from you, Fred."

Fred's red face said it all; he felt humiliated. He gave both to Carlos.

"Do you also want my business cards and my pin?" he asked.

"No, you can keep them."

"Bye."

That was his last word to anyone at NDB. He stepped into his car, backed the car out, and drove ahead to the exit of the parking lot.

Once Fred was gone, Carlos called Serge.
"It's done, Serge. He's out of the building."
"Perfect, thank you, Carlos. I'll see you tomorrow."

On his way to his home, Fred stopped at a liquor store. He walked to the whiskey section in a notoriously lousy mood, chose two bottles, and then went to the cashier. Used to pay with his corporate credit card, even personal expenses, he tried, but realized he didn't have it anymore, so he gave the cashier another card from the bank, one of the three personal cards he had. Fred was surprised when it was denied and tried with another one and the third one, all denied. His humiliation was now deep within his bones. He took a card from another bank and finally was able to pay with it. He hurried out, thinking, I can't believe Serge did this to me. The hell with him. He'll pay for this.

He opened one bottle and drank a small amount of whiskey before driving away. He went out of the parking lot and drank more whiskey at the next corner while waiting for the red light. He did the same all the way home.

***

Alexander didn't have the stress to work as another sales executive at Alliance, fighting to retain clients and interviewing potential new ones. With clients' problems easing, he had time for other matters.

That afternoon he continued reviewing some policies and incentive plans for the company. Ryan entered his office at four and told him one new customer who had previously left for Fred´s bank had returned, and no more customers were requesting unusual redemptions.

"You mean Fred´s ex-bank," Alexander said.

"What do you mean? Isn't he there anymore?"

"No. By now, he should be out of there permanently."

"Excellent. That might help us."

"Sure, it will."

Alexander served himself a whiskey and sat down on the couch for some minutes. I´m glad this problem ended. Now we can move forward and work on growing our business, he thought.

His phone vibrated: a text from the Senator. He decided not to say anything to find out how much the Senator knew. He expected that Antonio had already told him everything.

"My boy, how are you?"

"Everything is fine, Sir."

"I heard that your problem with the other bank is solved."

"Yes, Sir, finally. Thank you for that."

"Don't say anything. We're partners, and friends of course."

"How are you doing there?"

"Many things are going on. Not easy."

"I hope everything is fine, Sir."

"Will be, my boy. We´ll speak soon. Take care."

Minutes later, Colonel Robles knocked on his door.

"I´m back, Mr. Stern."

He had driven Rachel to buy some groceries and the courier office to pick something up.

"Perfect, Colonel. We're leaving home soon."

Alexander called his mother after he recalled he hadn't done it regularly in the last two weeks. They spent the next ten minutes talking about the family, her health, and various topics about Santo Domingo and Mexico.

His mother was concerned about what she had heard on the news about COVID-19. Alexander urged her to stop her escapades to Mexico City and anywhere outside her apartment. He wanted to have her in Santo Domingo, but now with all flights banned, this was impossible.

He put his MAC inside his backpack and left his office. He was on time to get home well before five, but Colonel Robles had to get to his home before that hour too.

As a result, he arrived home earlier than any other day. With so many businesses closed and no schools, he could be at home in less than six minutes.

He was happy about the quick commute, but he worried about how many families would be affected by the lockdown. He would talk with Gabrielle about what they could do to help as many people as possible.

At his apartment, he followed the strict routine he'd agreed on with Gabrielle. Alexander's shower was his first activity after he arrived. The rest of the afternoon was dedicated to online work. He joked with a team member they could wear a nice shirt and jacket but boxers and sandals lower down—a new way of attending meetings.

***

Rachel worked sporadically on her macaroon business. That afternoon, Alexander made a quick stop in the kitchen, which would become a common practice in the following months and had a conversation with her. He was surprised at the sales level she had achieved in the last weeks. After the lockdown, there was no guarantee she could maintain them. Many events had been canceled, like companies' conferences and weddings, but so far, she had launched a generous business a year ago and by now had a well-recognized brand.

Once a financial executive, like Gabrielle, and now successful in her new business, was something he enjoyed, and had learned to accept. He recalled encouraging her to go back to work in a financial institution, but she didn't want that life anymore. Alexander thought of her coach's words when they hired him, thinking that Rachel was wrong. After four sessions, he came back with some recommendations.

"She's not wrong, just doing what she is passionate about, and she's having fun doing it. Rachel is clear about her business plan. Maybe the ones who need a coach to handle the situation are both of you. Let her do what she loves and support her. She'll surprise you."

CHAPTER 33

Fred made several stops before he arrived home. In all of them, he drank a considerable amount of whiskey. His maid had already left for the day. He would be alone. The gate opened slowly, and he drove in, making a sudden stop to avoid hitting the garage's front wall. He grabbed the portfolio from the front passenger seat and stepped out; he didn't mess with removing the boxes in the trunk. He opened the door typed the four-digit code in the white security panel to deactivate the alarm. Then to the kitchen. He poured whiskey from the bottle, now one-third consumed, in a glass half-filled with ice.

He took the glass, the bottle, and walked to the living room, placing them on the coffee table in front of the couch. Thinking on his last minutes at the bank, he kicked a side table, sending it and the objects on it flying. He hated to be embarrassed in such a way. He was usually tough, but after some drinks, he turned aggressive. His ego had been hurt, and he'd been affected financially. He was thinking on whom to blame for the day's events. The guilty ones in his disturbed mind were Serge Arden and Alexander Stern.

After the second glass of whiskey, he thought about what the board member had told him earlier by phone. His recommendation about leaving the country spun inside his head.

What if the Banks Commission or an auditor talked about it, and everything was discovered? It would be a mess for everyone, and I would be in jail, he thought.

That last anxious thought gave him a surge of adrenaline, and he evaluated his options. He left the glass on the table. He hesitated, but he was convinced he had to leave the country: too much risk, too many variables to maintain control. Chances were high something would go wrong at some point, and everything would come to light. No one could control all the mess he had created, not even Serge Arden.

That made him regain some clarity. He decided to escape the country. Better to a country that he would not be liable, but first he would make a stop in The Bahamas to retire the remaining forty thousand dollars still in his account. He didn't want to wire transfer the money and risk getting it blocked by someone. And anyway, he liked its capital, Nassau, as a place to stay for a while.

He recalled suddenly that all flights were canceled. He had to plan something else around it. Major airlines would not fly out of the country, but Jack Dowell could help him with the short-range airplane he used for travel to nearby islands. Maybe Fred would have to bribe someone at the airport in Santo Domingo and at his destination, but he didn't care about that.

He needed that money to live until he could sell his house and vehicle. Before leaving the bank, he had instructed his broker to sell his investments despite the eight percent loss due to the market conditions. He would have the money early the next day.

Fred took his glass and phone and went upstairs. He called Jack and explained the situation. He asked to lend or lease him the airplane he owned. Jack was OK with it if Fred paid for the fuel and other expenses. It would be ready the next day any time after noon. Fred was not running any risk. At least, that's what he thought.

Traveling with a suitcase, a carry-on, and a backpack was part of his plan. He spent the rest of the afternoon packing. He put all he expected to need on his bed: two suits, four shirts, and four ties. Everything else was casual clothes and personal accessories.

Inside his carry-on, he packed sets of casual clothes. Just in case he had to abandon his suitcase. His backpack was filled with personal documents, family photographs, electronic devices, and his passport. He would also put in it all the cash he had and his gun, that lay inside a small digital vault inside his walk-in closet. He wasn't flying with his gun, but he had some plans for it before leaving. After an hour and two more glasses of whiskey, he finished packing.

He called a real estate broker, one of his friends from college. He needed to sell his house fast. Depending on how fast, he would need to reduce the price, his friend explained. Fred didn't have a mortgage on it, which would speed up the sale. They agreed on the price, and depending on the sale amount and time, the commission would be adjusted. Any offer would be texted to him immediately. He prepared a Power of Attorney for his sister. She would be able to sign everything and send the proceeds to him, wherever he was. She was the only person he could trust in addition to his mother, but she was too old to handle such matters anymore. He would call his sister later to tell her about it.

He went down to the kitchen. All the whiskey and the light lunch had had an effect on him. He handled it easily, with a ham and cheese sandwich and barbecue chips. Not his usual dinner but he was not thinking of preparing anything else. He sat again on the couch, and after one more glass of whiskey, he went up to take a shower. It was time to freshen up and to plan the following day. All his moves had to be well analyzed. No chance for any mistake, or he would end in jail.

The hot water helped to slightly mitigate the whiskey's effect on his body, as did the food he ate. At nine, he was done for the day. He lay down and slept in seconds.

***

The research into Jack Dowell had gone nowhere. His lover was found, but this was not a big deal. Antonio decided to stop all investigations of him.

Meanwhile, Jack was trying to find a way to regain the valuable piece of land owned by Mr. Ramos and his family. He called and texted him back again and again, offering a larger sum, but the preliminary numbers of Alexander and his partners were much better, and Mr. Ramos had already signed an agreement. He pushed back several times but received the same answer every time. Mr. Ramos stopped taking his calls.

Jack decided to move forward, but he would closely monitor Alexander's actions in the real estate sector. He decided to compete hard against him.

***

Fred opened his eyes at six the next morning and held his head with both hands. It was earlier than his usual wake-up time, but he had gone to bed earlier too. The previous night's food and the hot shower helped, but he had an intense headache from the liberal whiskey consumption. He tried to sleep more, but he couldn't.

After some minutes of turning, he went to the kitchen and prepared coffee. He walked to the living room, saw the side table, and recalled his reaction. He placed the table back where it was. The maid would fix that disorder when she arrived. He went out to the garden and sat on a wooden reclining chair. After various sips of his black coffee, he thought of his plan again. He felt depressed initially, but minutes later, he became troubled again. After he'd gone over in his mind what had happened on Tuesday at the bank, he instantly felt angry again.

All this was Serge Arden's and Alexander Stern's fault, he thought.

Fred agreed to meet with his sister that morning at eight at her home. He went upstairs, feeling better with the large cup of coffee he'd drunk and a pill he'd taken to reduce the effect of the hangover. He went over all his arrangements. First, with his sister to deliver the house keys and Attorney's Power of Attorney, someone from his friend's firm would pick up. Then back home to make some final arrangements. Finally, to wait until it was time to complete one last task before leaving for the airport without stopping anywhere.

He had second thoughts for some minutes about completing his plan, but he remembered some of his previous night's thoughts.

What if the Banks Commission or an auditor talked about it, and everything was discovered? ... I would be in jail for sure.

He convinced himself again he was not taking any risk. That morning, even during that week, he hadn't expected any complications, but now, anything could go wrong, and his chances of ending up in jail would increase every day. He wanted a beer, but he had to keep a clear head. Anything could go wrong with even a minimal mistake.

He recalled he had not made a hotel reservation. He reserved three nights at a hotel in Nassau. Once there, he would decide where to live next. He would have to find a reasonable option because now he had to pay for it, not his bank. His anger increased minute by minute when he realized all he had to arrange. His life had changed, and he didn't like it one bit.

Fred dressed in jeans and a shirt. At the entrance, he pushed aside the portfolio he'd left on the floor the night before, grabbed his car keys from the hanger beside the door, and left the house. Walking to his car, he saw the maid coming in by the street entrance.

"Hello, Mr. Shultz."

"Hi. I have to go now, but I'm coming back in an hour."

"Yes, Sir," she said.

He drove to his sister's home. After talking casually, she offered him breakfast.

"Thank you, sister," he said. "Look, I have to leave the country today. I don't know when I'll be coming back."

His sister just laughed, thinking he was joking.

"What are you talking about, Fred?"

"Don't worry. I have to leave today, but I'll call you soon to tell you everything. Please don't worry, and please don't say anything to Mom."

"Fred, what's going on?"

"Please pay attention. These are my house keys. A broker will come to get them. He'll show the house to potential buyers. It's on sale now. Also, here is an envelope for my lawyer. He'll send someone to pick it up. You need to sign the document inside.

"OK, Fred, but please tell me what's going on?"

"Don't worry. I'll come back in a few days. I'll call you tomorrow to explain everything in detail. I have to go now."

He gave her a kiss and a strong hug. He ran out of her house and got in his car. A few seconds later, he was out of sight. She came back in wondering what was going on, concerned whether he had any kind of problem.

Back home, Fred stayed there the rest of the morning. He took a shower and packed the carry-on with his items. Ten minutes before noon, he went down with all his luggage and put the backpack in the front passenger seat. When he opened the trunk, he had to take out the five carton boxes. He carried them into the garage. The maid was there.

"Are you traveling today, Mr. Shultz?"

"Yes, for a few days. My sister will call you to arrange something with you."

"OK, Mr. Shultz. Have a safe flight."

He didn't say anything else to her. His sister would have to handle that. He would give her instructions later.

Fred stopped and looked in the rearview at his house before turning left. After a couple of seconds, sadness on his face, he rolled up the window and dropped away.

He drove more slowly than usual. He appreciated the surroundings. He had accepted his situation, but he was willing not to leave without doing something that would give him some satisfaction. He had lost his life as he knew it. He was calm, but now he was sure to complete his plan.

After driving for twenty-five minutes, he arrived at the place he had to be before 1:00 p.m. He went into the underground parking and saw the vehicle he was looking for. He parked in available space to the left of the entrance door.

He had a perfect view of the door and the vehicle. He would stay there until he was able to see him. He turned off the car and the interior lights, too, and stayed calm and vigilant. A security guard was approaching, so he pushed down his backseat to avoid been seen. Once the guard passed, he put the seat back up again and continued patiently waiting for him to come out the door. He would have to wait for no more than twenty minutes.

He grabbed his backpack and placed it between both seats. He held the right side of the front pocket with his left hand and opened the zipper. When it was open, he pulled out his gun and stiffened for some seconds, checking to see that no one was nearby. Then he thought, what am I doing? After some minutes, thinking about what had all happened to him, he evaluated the scene in front of him and thought, what the hell, it must be done.

He pulled his gun from the holster. He removed the magazine, checked it out, and pushed it back inside. Then he cocked it with his left hand. The lock was still on, so he unlocked it and watched a small red circle appear. Now he was fully prepared.

This would be his last stop before getting on an airplane to fly out of the country to the Bahamas—his final stop of a plan he'd devised in the last twenty hours.

CHAPTER 34

That morning, Alexander went again to the park. After shooting the usual sets of arrows, Colonel Robles took him back home. Half an hour later, they were on their way to Alliance.

The weather was nice, but colder in a month that generally was warm. He thought that, after all, maybe the lockdown measures were helping to reduce global warming.

Rumors about Fred being ousted flew everywhere in Santo Domingo. When he arrived at the office, two team members told him about it. Ryan addressed him with that too, before giving a brief on the clients' status. No more clients were coming back, but one executive spoke with one who had requested an update on rates—neither new redemptions of investments from the famous list. So far, things were improving.

Alexander attended various conference calls. Then he called Susan to request a status on the new change in shareholders ownership, but nothing had been received. She doubted that the regulators had reviewed it. Many of the employees were sent home, as happened at many other companies.

Susan was working from home as much as she was able to, but now that many government offices were semi-paralyzed, she wasn't able to advance on many fronts. They would have to wait for some weeks to continue the process.

Watching the news, Alexander was surprised, specifically with interviews in supermarkets. All were crowded. Many people wanted to replenish their stocks at home. The stores were making a handsome profit in this situation.

Colonel Robles was driving Gabrielle to her mother's home. She wouldn't be able to see her for some days. After the increase in COVID-19 cases, the family agreed that her mother would stay with Gabrielle's sister. She delivered some groceries to her and some medicines.

After leaving Gabrielle at home, Colonel Robles drove to Alliance. When he arrived, he showed himself through the door of Alexander's office.

"Hi Colonel, we are leaving in half an hour."

"Yes, Sir," he said.

After reviewing some documents, Alexander prepared to go home, closed the door, and walked to the elevators. He was starving, thinking of the roast chicken Gabrielle had prepared for lunch, one of his favorites.

***

Serge arranged to meet with Carlos that morning at ten. Once Carlos got to the bank, he went directly to his office. He hadn't moved to Fred's office yet, and he wouldn't do it. He wanted to wait until a final decision was made on who would replace Fred. In the meantime, he would spend half a day at his office and in the meeting room on the afternoons, in case it was needed.

Serge had planned to be at the bank almost daily the following weeks. He would be supporting him in all decisions related to the issue they had to fix, interviews with candidates, and a review of all the established controls in many areas, especially among the business units. What had happened in the past had to be stopped effectively.

He briefed Serge about his encounter with Fred.

"How did he take it?"

"Not that bad, Serge, but he was irritated."

"He must be. I made a huge mistake with him."

"It's not your fault. Who would have imagined?"

"I know, but I appointed him. He was my responsibility."

Serge felt ashamed for what had all happened. He'd promoted Fred for many years, but no one could blame him. Everyone well knew Serge Arden's character and principles.

They discussed in detail the plan to reimburse clients with the money sent back by Fred, and to cancel the loans. They agreed it had to be done expedite. Only one officer was assigned to manage all these registers in the accounting books and would be approved directly by Carlos. Everything had been planned since the night before by Serge. A formal memo would be signed, detailing the "operational mistake" of sending the money of those accounts to another bank. If detected, the clients would have their money back already.

The loans were already written off. The only alternative was to apply recoveries and adjust any remaining amount.

The plan was finalized. If successfully implemented, they would avoid all sanctions from the regulators, clients' money would be back in their reactivated accounts, and the loans' losses would be recovered. The only weakness in the plan was if someone talked about this. Just a few people knew it, and others who could say something would go to jail—a strong incentive for not doing so.

Serge personally calmed Fred's assistant. She was concerned, and he noticed it. Despite not saying anything, he knew her well. He guaranteed she would have a job at the bank until her retirement.

At one, they had to leave. Serge arranged a meeting with the Superintendent of Banks to inform him of the recent change due to Fred's resignation. They were lucky to be received by him on such short notice. They put on their jackets and went down to the underground parking. They took the elevator in the back of the building.

***

Fred saw him through the glass door coming out of the elevator. With his gun ready, he was prepared to open fire. Someone was beside him when a folder felt from his hands and several papers lay spread on the ground. He made a sign to the other man with his arm, seemingly to tell him to continue walking. After a couple of seconds, he did so. He went out, look to both sides, and walked to the right side of the entrance.

A perfect time for Fred to take action. He got out of his car, left the door half-open, and walked to the entrance. The glass doors opened when he approached closely enough to be detected by the infrared sensor. He raised his right arm and shouted to him.

"Hey! Now you're gonna pay for everything."

Alexander was picking up the papers when he heard someone shouting. He stood up and the papers fell again. His backpack hung on one side in front of him. He tried to see who it was, steps away, but he couldn't as he was wearing a cap and sunglasses. A deafening noise made him close his eyes. He felt a warm pinch in the left side of his waist and realized he had been shot. Then another shot hit his backpack, knocking him off balance and throwing him against a plate glass window behind him, and then a third shot that he felt below his left shoulder. The window behind him broke, and he fell to the ground.

He heard another two shots farther than earlier ones, but he didn't feel anything else. He was either too ill or too dead to feel them. He lost sight and closed his eyes, and only sensed cold cement on his back, colder every second.

Fred felt the first shot in the center of his neck. The bullet entered on the right side and went out on the left. He felt a sharp pain. A second later, another bullet hit his head, and he went down. He was dead before he hit the ground.

Colonel Robles went cautiously forward. He looked all around him to make sure no other person was out there. No one was. He approached Fred, and when he saw where his shot had hit, he didn't need to check if he was dead. He rushed to the broken glass window where Alexander lay on the floor. After a glance to assure no one was there, he knelt down.

"Mr. Stern, hold on. Help, please help!" he shouted.

"Mr. Stern, stay with me."

Alexander barely heard what was going on. He was not able to think clearly. He felt a sharp pain in his waist and near his heart. The blood marks on the floor slowly spread. A person approached and Colonel Robles pointed at him. He was an unarmed security guard assigned to the underground parking. He put down his gun and shouted at him, "Call an ambulance! Fast!"

The guard took his radio and called for help. When Colonel Robles saw the blood mark on the floor, he was clear about what to do.

"We don't have time. Help me carry him to the vehicle."

The guard didn't move until Colonel Robles shouted again, "Help me! We don't have time!"

The guard reacted and they held Alexander up. They walked to the SUV, one on each side. Alexander's backpack still hung on his shoulder. Once they got to the vehicle, they put Alexander in the front passenger seat and reclined it. They closed the door and got in on the left side. The guard stepped into the rear seat, almost over Alexander, pressing hard where the blood had stained Alexander's clothes. Colonel Robles started the SUV, backed out of the parking space, and sped to the exit. Once there, he accelerated out through the ramp, breaking the plastic barrier ahead of the cashier's booth.

"Use your radio! Tell someone to call CEDIMAT! They need to be prepared to receive him."

The guard managed to grab the radio with his right hand, pressing the other against Alexander's shoulder. He got someone and tensely explained Colonel Robles' instructions.

"Do you understand?" the guard asked.

"Yes, man shot, CEDIMAT, they need to be prepared, you're taking him there. Copied," someone answered.

Colonel Robles drove through streets without stopping, but he had to wait some seconds to move forward on an avenue. After continuous use of the SUV horn, the two vehicles ahead moved, and he was able to turn left on Tiradentes Avenue.

"Stay with us, Sir. Stay with us," he shouted.

Two minutes later, they arrived at the hospital and parked at the emergency entrance, steps away from the door. A doctor and two nurses holding a wheeled stretcher were waiting for them. The doctor opened the door and held Alexander. Colonel Robles was already there to help and they laid Alexander on the stretcher. Colonel Robles was coming in with them when a guard at the door stopped him.

"Sir, you need to wait here."

"But I need to go inside with him."

"Wait here, Sir. He's in good hands. We'll give you some news as soon as possible," the guard said.

Colonel Robles halted. He was trying to see inside, but the doors were closed now and had a tainted frame that didn't allow him to see anything. He stayed there, holding his head with both hands and looking down to the floor.

The building's security guard leaned over the vehicle, holding his body with his left arm straight. He heard his radio; someone was calling. He grabbed it from the rear seat and heard part of the conversation.

"… respond. Inform your situation."

"Copy. Already at the hospital. He's with the doctor now in the emergency."

"Copy that," someone answered.

He felt somewhat relieved but was still notably nervous. Colonel Robles was more disturbed. He sat on the SUV's rear bumper. Two persons waiting out there approached him.

"Sir, do you need help with something?"

He shook his head and put both hands on his face.

Colonel Robles knew well these cases. With all the blood Alexander had lost, chances were not on his side.

CHAPTER 35

He seemed to be unconscious in the emergency unit. Alexander showed a minor reaction with his eyes practically closed before the doors closed. A thin intermittent trail of blood ran from the vehicle to the entrance. The mark of blood on the street, right where he was taken from the vehicle and still receiving drops, shocked people standing nearby.

Extremely worried, Colonel Robles realized he had not called Gabrielle yet. It would be difficult to give her that message, and he didn't want to relay it by phone. She would take her vehicle immediately and come alone. He went to the right side of the vehicle, where the guard stood and closed both doors.
"I need to bring Mr. Stern's wife. I'll need you to stay here in case they say something. I'll be back soon."
"No problem. I'll be here."
Colonel Robles left the hospital and drove to Alexander's apartment. He waited four minutes to call Gabrielle until he was closer to the building. He thought of changing vehicles; he didn't want her to see all the blood inside Alexander's SUV. That would be even more shocking. He called Alexander's assistant to inform her of the situation. Alarmed, Amanda told him she would inform Ryan and Susan. William was out of the city, but she would try to reach him.

Almost arriving at the building, he made the difficult call to Gabrielle.
"Mrs. Stern, I need to tell you something. I left Mr. Stern at the hospital."
"What? What happened?"
"Mrs. Stern, it's better that you come down. Please bring your car key. I'm at the underground parking."
"What's wrong, Colonel? What happened to him?"

"I'm already here, Mrs. Stern. Please come down. We need to go to the hospital."

Gabrielle hung up and ran to the door, put her shoes on, grabbed her purse and car key, and ran down the stairs four floors down. Colonel Robles had parked the vehicle when she exited from the stairs and ran to her vehicle.

"What happened, Colonel?"

"The key, Mrs. Stern. I'll tell you in the car."

She gave him the key. He started the car and began driving.

"Tell me, what happened?"

"Mr. Stern was attacked at the office, at the underground parking. I had to take him to the hospital."

"What? How is he?"

"He's in good hands, at the emergency."

"But how is he? What happened?"

"He's being examined by the doctors now, Mrs. Stern."

"Colonel, tell me exactly what happened. Now."

"Mrs. Stern, he was shot. I killed the attacker. We took Mr. Stern to the hospital immediately. An ambulance would have taken too much time."

Then, a moment of silence. Gabrielle pinched her eyes, and tears fell down her face.

They arrived at the hospital. Gabrielle expected the worst.

***

Amanda called Ryan and Susan. Both were shocked, wondering who could want to do something like that. They tried to contact William, but they weren't able to find him. Susan left him a voice message and several texts.

A minute later, once he'd spoken to Susan, Ryan took the lead in managing the emergency. He sent a text to Alexander's staff in a group chat they used for business purposes. He informed them what had happened and asked for full discretion. He promised to update everyone as soon as he'd more information. He also asked them to pray for Alexander, his valued friend and leader. They were impressed.

Ryan also called Susan, who cried but managed to control herself. He asked her to contact an attorney. They would need to address any legal implications that could arise. Ryan was sure the police would soon visit Colonel Robles. He had shot a man and would be held in custody until all inquiries had been completed.

After some calls, a recognized legal firm that worked on many matters with Alliance assigned an attorney. He would drive to the hospital to manage the situation.

***

They stopped at the main entrance of the hospital.

"Mrs. Stern, do you want me to call someone?" Colonel Robles asked before she stepped out.

She remained silent for some seconds.

"My sisters. Tell them we're here, nothing else. Tell them not to say anything to my mother or Alexander's family."

"Yes, Mrs. Stern."

"Where is he?" she asked.

"They told me to wait outside the Intensive Care Unit, and someone would come out to give the family an update."

She went down and hurried to the information booth. A hospital employee gave her directions. She took the stairs up to the third floor. When she got to the ICU waiting room, it was empty. She knocked on a door, and seconds later, a nurse came out.

"Hello, can I help you?"

"My husband is here. May I see him?"

"Alright, what's his name?"

"Alexander Stern."

"Let me check. I'll be back in a minute."

The nurse went in and closed the door. Gabrielle, tears still in her eyes, stayed nearby, waiting for the nurse to come back.

Colonel Robles entered the hospital after parking the vehicle and saw the security guard.

"Hi. Thank you for staying. Is there any news of his condition?"

"Nothing. I believe they'll only inform it to his relatives."

"OK. His wife is already here."

"Good."

"I have to go with her. If you want to leave, it's fine. We'll take it from here. Do you need a ride back?"

"Don't worry. I'll handle it."

The security guard told him where the ICU was, and he went left the hospital lobby. Colonel Robles walked up the stairs, got outside the ICU, and saw Gabrielle standing by the main door.

"Any news, Mrs. Stern?"

"Nothing."

"Do you need anything?"

She shook her head.

He stepped back and found a place where he could watch her and the elevator, the stairs, and the aisle.

The attorney arrived at the hospital half an hour later. When the elevator door opened, he saw Colonel Robles guarding the main entrance. He noticed his white shirt and part of his jacket showed spots of what seemed to be blood.

"Hello, Sir. Are you Colonel Robles?"

"Yes. And you are?"

"I'm an attorney assigned to Alliance, Colonel. I'm here to support you in anything you need. We need to discuss what happened as soon as possible."

"OK."

Amanda had texted Colonel Robles about the attorney minutes ago.

"Is Mrs. Stern the woman standing right there?
"Yes."
"Alright. Let me talk to her, and I'll come back in a minute."

He walked a few steps towards Gabrielle.

"Mrs. Stern, I hope everything goes well with your husband. Anything you need, just let me know. I've been assigned by Alliance to take care of any legal matters that may come up."

"Thank you."

"Mrs. Stern, I have to talk to Colonel Robles. Please excuse me."

Gabrielle nodded and started pacing back and forth.

Colonel Robles told the attorney precisely what had happened since they'd left Alliance. The attorney told him he would manage everything, but he would be asked to make a declaration soon, and it would be better to present themselves proactively.

"We'll need to arrange something for that," Colonel Robles said. "I can't leave this place without anyone to guard."

"I'll arrange that, Colonel; let me talk to Mr. Stern's assistant to work on it."

After a long wait, Gabrielle saw the same nurse coming out, followed by a doctor. The doctor addressed her while Colonel Robles and the attorney stood three steps away to hear.

"Hello," the doctor said. "Are you Mr. Stern's wife?"

"Yes, I'm his wife. How is he?"

"Mrs. Stern, let's have a seat."

They sat on an oversized couch opposite each other while the nurse stood in front of them.

"Mrs. Stern. I need to inform you that your husband is in surgery. He has two bullet wounds, one in his right waist and another below his left shoulder. The one in his upper body went out after impact. The bullet in his waist is still there. He's lost a lot of blood. He arrived here semiconscious.

"Is he going to be alright?" Gabrielle asked.

"It's too soon to confirm that, Mrs. Stern. He just entered surgery. We'll have to wait before we can give you more information."

"How long will the surgery take, doctor?"

"I can't say, exactly. Once the surgeons examine him and determine what's been damaged, we can estimate. It could take several hours, Mrs. Stern."

Gabrielle started crying again.

"Mrs. Stern, your husband is in good hands. We're doing all we can for him."

"Please save him," Gabrielle said, in tears.

"We're doing all we can, Mrs. Stern. Please excuse me, I have to go now, but we'll keep you informed."

Gabrielle nodded, unable to say a word.

The doctor and nurse left, and Gabrielle remained seated, crying and praying for Alexander. Seconds later, her sisters and brother-in-law came into the ICU waiting room. Andrea arrived minutes later. Gabrielle told them what the doctor had said.

Colonel Robles was back in the corner where he was before with the attorney. He looked pale and anxious. He felt guilty.

Some friends and family members would be arriving to stay a few minutes. Alexander's staff agreed that Ryan and Susan went there to avoid getting the place crowded.

Ten minutes before three, the third driver Alexander had interviewed arrived. Amanda had arranged everything with the security company.

He had a ten-minute conversation with the attorney and Colonel Robles, who told him how they would alternate at the hospital. Instead of waiting for investigators of the Policía Nacional or any other authority, they would make a declaration proactively.

Legal recourse with a high-ranking contact and someone from the prosecutor's office was prepared, allowing Colonel Robles to declare and let him out, avoiding the legal custody required by law, under the joint responsibility of Alliance and the attorney's firm.

***

The same doctor came out of the ICU at four. When he saw the number of people, he asked Gabrielle to come into a small office inside. Andrea was allowed to accompany her.

"Mrs. Stern, I'll give you an update on your husband."

"Please, tell me, doctor."

"He's been in surgery for two hours. The surgeons were able to remove the bullet in his waist, but some fragments spread nearby. They removed them and they're checking all organs. The bullet in his shoulder went out but damaged some muscles and other parts. It's going to take more hours before the surgery is done."

"But is he going to be fine, doctor?"

"Mrs. Stern. I'll be honest with you. The amount of blood your husband lost brought some complications during the surgery. The bullet fragments are complicating surgery as well. He's in critical condition right now. We were able to stabilize him, but I don't have any more information at this moment."

Gabrielle remained silent and closed her eyes, while Andrea held her. After several seconds, the doctor held her arm.

"Mrs. Stern, your husband is strong. And he's fighting. We're praying for him."

"Thank you, doctor," Andrea said.

"The nurse will accompany you outside with your family. As soon as we're able to give you an update, we'll come to you immediately."

Gabrielle and Andrea went out. Both were crying. Everyone there went quiet. Gabrielle told her sisters that

Alexander's situation was very delicate, and he was still in surgery.

Alexander's mother didn't know yet. Andrea spoke earlier with Matt, Alexander's brother, and they agreed not to tell anyone until they had more information. Then they would decide how to inform everyone in Mexico, including Rachel.

Colonel Robles had been at the Policía Nacional for almost two hours. The attorney stayed with him all that time. Alexander's assistant arranged with the building administration to send them copies of security videos. Once the investigators watched them, they were asked to sign a document and left the station.

Colonel Robles was taken back to the hospital, but he wore new clothes instead of his jacket and shirt bloodstained.

Ryan and Susan arrived at four. So did Amanda, and she took control of all administrative issues with the hospital and the insurance company. Ryan confirmed that Gabrielle didn't need anything before they left, fifteen minutes before the lockdown at five. He would come back the next day. Almost everyone had gone. Just Andrea and Gabrielle's older sister stayed to spend the night with them in the waiting room.

A doctor who had been in the surgery stepped into the waiting room around six.

"Mrs. Stern?"

"Yes, doctor," Gabrielle said.

"Mrs. Stern, I'm doctor Franklin. I was in charge of your husband's surgery. We finished ten minutes ago. Right now, your husband is in stable condition. We removed all the bullet fragments. He lost a lot of blood. We can't determine if the lack of blood flow affected anything else, including his brain."

Gabrielle started crying and strove to retain her composure.

"Mrs. Stern, the following hours are extremely critical for your husband. We're keeping him in the ICU. A surgeon will be checking on him, and he'll stay for the night in case anything goes wrong, and we have to intervene again."

"What can go wrong, doctor?"

"Right now, he's stable, but these cases can generate many complications. Maybe not in his case, but it's too soon to discount anything. We're prepared to address anything that might come up. He's delicate, but he's fighting."

"Thank you, doctor."

"I hope he gets better, Mrs. Stern. I have to go back, but we'll keep you informed."

Colonel Robles switched with the other driver at six. He would come the next day at five in the morning. Gabrielle's sister had brought something to eat earlier from the cafeteria, but she just had a coffee and some water.

At 9:30 that evening, a doctor came back with a quick update. Alexander's situation hadn't changed; he remained stable. The following hours would be critical for him. He was fighting, but as the doctor had said, many complications could occur.

CHAPTER 36

When Gabrielle opened her eyes, she looked around, anxious. She woke up by the conversation between Colonel Robles and the new driver, who informed him of the night events and Alexander's status. She looked at her phone: 4:55 a.m. The other driver got up and nodded to her as he left.

"Good morning, Mrs. Stern," Colonel Robles said while seated in a chair.

"Hello."

She continued watching the room. Andrea and her sister were still sleeping. Her sister on a sofa and Andrea nearby, her head on Gabrielle's leg and her feet dangling slightly on the couch.

The last update by the doctor in charge of the ICU came minutes after two. Alexander was still stable.

Gabrielle rose, leaving Andrea's head softly on the couch. After a stretch, she walked to the corner where Colonel Robles was sitting. He stood up and Gabrielle posed the question she'd wanted to ask him since yesterday afternoon.

"Colonel, what happened yesterday? But this time, give me all the details."

"Alright, Mrs. Stern."

He looked down a second, thinking of where to start, then told her everything.

"We were coming down from the office and took the elevator. Once we got to the underground parking where Mr. Stern's assigned space is, we stepped out of the elevator and walked outside to the small lobby."

"Before the glass doors?"

"Yes."

"And then?"

"Mr. Stern had a red folder with some papers. It dropped, and all the papers fell to the floor. I was beside him and leaned over to help him, when he said, I've got them, get the SUV, Colonel. I continued picking up some of the papers, but he waved his arm and insisted I get the vehicle."

"What happened next?"

"I followed his instructions. I went out of the glass doors, checked both sides, no one was there, then I walked to where the vehicle was parked nearby."

He stopped to take a quick breath while Gabrielle kept looking at him and continued.

"I was opening the vehicle when I heard someone shouting. I didn't understand it well. I turned around and saw someone standing and pointing a gun at the lobby, where Mr. Stern was picking up the papers."

"And then?"

"I took out my gun, but he'd already fired three times when I shot him, twice. The first bullet hit his neck and the second one his head. He went down instantly."

Gabrielle covered her mouth.

"I ran to the lobby. When I saw that the man had been neutralized, I checked around to see whether anyone else was there, then I hurried where Mr. Stern was. He lay on the other side of the lobby. The window on that side was broken. I made sure no one was there and leaned over to check on Mr. Stern."

"Continue, Colonel."

"A security officer who usually makes rounds came to us. I asked him to call an ambulance, but when I saw the blood mark spreading on the ground, I knew we didn't have time to wait for an ambulance. I asked the guard to help me get Mr. Stern into the vehicle. We got him in and hurried out of the underground parking. I asked the guard to call someone in the building to ask the hospital to be prepared for when we arrived."

"Why this particular hospital?"

"I heard Mr. Stern saying to you once that in case of a real emergency, our first option was this hospital."

"Right, I remember. And then you went to our apartment?"

"Yes. We left Mr. Stern in the emergency unit and I went to pick you up. I asked the security guard to stay here. Considering the situation, I didn't want you to come alone in your vehicle. I also called Mr. Stern's assistant. You already know the rest of the story."

"And who shot Alexander?"

"I didn't know at that moment, but when I went to the Policía Nacional yesterday, they told me it was someone called Fred Shultz."

"Fred Shultz shot Alexander?"

"That's what they said, and the attorney confirmed it.

The nurse came in, and Gabrielle rushed to her.

"Mrs. Stern, there's been no change in your husband's status. He's stable and there are no complications so far. I'll let you know later how's he doing, or Dr. Franklin. He should be here at eight."

"Thank you."

"Mrs. Stern, the longer your husband is stable and without complications, the better it is."

"Thank you. I hope so."

***

William was at the beach for the week with his family. He checked his phone for messages that morning. Unable to reach him since yesterday, Amanda had recorded a message for him the fourth time she called. When he heard it, he called her immediately before Gabrielle.

She explained everything to him and the last status report they've received. He was speechless. He told his wife about it a minute later. Then, he called Gabrielle. She didn't answer, as she hadn't done with any other call or text message. He called Ryan, who gave him the same status report he had received from Amanda, and an update on Alliance regarding this situation.

***

Doctor Franklin walked fast in front of them. He didn't stop for any greetings, just nodded to Gabrielle while stepping into the ICU. Her other sister arrived minutes later.

No one had come out to give them an update on Alexander. Gabrielle was becoming nervous; it had been a long time since the previous briefing around five. At nine, the first doctor she had spoken to yesterday came out of the ICU.

"Mrs. Stern, I need to speak with you. Please have a seat."

Gabrielle worried something might have happened.

"Mrs. Stern, there's been a complication."

Gabrielle felt her heart pounding. She held her breath a couple of seconds and remained silent. Andrea held her hand while the doctor continued.

"Your husband has been taken back into surgery. He's experiencing internal bleeding. The surgeons are preparing right now to intervene."

"What happened, doctor? What's caused the bleeding?"

"That's all the information I have right now, Mrs. Stern. Excuse me, I have to go. I'll come back later as soon as I have more news."

Gabrielle put both hands to her face, but she managed not to cry. She had a bad feeling. Her sister came closer and tried to calm her.

"He must be suffering," Gabrielle said, her voice faltering. Everyone remained silent.

The following hours were difficult for all. Gabrielle thought of Rachel and became even more anxious. She still didn't know about Alexander's condition. Matt had called Andrea an hour earlier to get the last update, and Gabrielle had spoken to him. Her mother didn't know about it either. They agreed to keep it confidential for the following hours.

Family members constantly called for an update on Alexander's condition. Amanda came to see whether Gabrielle or their family needed anything. She knew they hadn't eaten much since last night and brought some croissants, juice, and coffee for everyone. She gave Ryan an update as soon as she was back at Alliance.

At eleven, Dr. Franklin came out and Gabrielle approached him.

"How's my husband, doctor?" Gabrielle asked.

"Mrs. Stern, please have a seat."

"I'm fine, doctor. Please tell me."

"Mrs. Stern, we detected internal bleeding earlier in the left side of his waist, where the bullet was. We were able to control the bleeding. He lost some more blood, but he's stable, and still in a delicate condition."

"Is he going to be fine?"

"We need to wait. He's fighting, and we're doing all we can. Now, please excuse me, I have to go back and check on him and other patients. I'll see you later."

***

Ryan arrived at Alliance and sent an email to everyone at the company, informing them of Alexander's situation. The news was spread around. He scheduled a meeting with the sales executives, updated them, and reviewed a client's script in case someone called. He wanted clients to remain calm. Later that day, some of them did.

He and Susan were the most senior ones at Alliance, and partners now. Both agreed that Susan would call the shareholders to update them on Alexander's and Alliance's status.

The Superintendent called that morning. He had been informed of Alexander's situation. Susan explained what had happened and gave him the last update. He told her that if Alliance needed anything from them, she just had to call immediately. He gave her his phone number.

Rumors were spreading. Everyone had expected that. It was uncommon for the two top executives of two financial institutions to be involved in the same case. Now, one was dead, and the other was fighting for his life at the hospital. No one knew the exact details and, what was worse, many false stories surged rapidly. Ryan decided to call Alexander's closest clients and the wealthiest investors to calm them. The marketing head prepared something for publication if necessary.

***

Dr. Franklin briefed her around three.
"Mrs. Stern, based on the latest examination of your husband, we're positive the surgery we performed will have a good outcome. Alexander's condition is still delicate, but he's stable, and his vital signs and blood tests are showing improvement. We still can't ensure anything, but so far, these are encouraging news."
"Can I see him, doctor?"
"We need to wait, Mrs. Stern. Anyway, he's not awake. Depending on his progress, I'll let you know later."
"Thank you, doctor."
"I'll come back in a few hours with another update. I'll see you later."

For the first time, everyone felt relieved. Dr. Franklin's report was encouraging indeed. Gabrielle would wait by the minute for the next update. She called Matt and Paula immediately. As things were improving, Alexander would probably be able to speak with them later or the next day, as well as with Rachel and his mother.

Gabrielle decided to go down with Andrea to eat something at the cafeteria. They took the stairs instead of the elevator. They spoke more than they had in the last twenty-four hours while they shared a cheese sandwich and water. Neither of them wanted to be far from the ICU, so they ate and went back.

When Gabrielle finally took out her phone from her purse, she saw all the messages waiting to be answered. She hadn't been checking on them. Several longtime friends arrived and were surprised at what had happened, hoping Alexander would get better.

She saw various messages from William and texted him back with Dr. Franklin's latest update. He told Gabrielle he would be at the hospital tomorrow.

The following hours were long as they wait for more news about Alexander. Gabrielle was about to knock on the door when a nurse came out.

"Mrs. Stern, Dr. Franklin will be here in a minute."

She hadn't finished when Dr. Franklin opened the door and asked Gabrielle to come near it.

"Mrs. Stern, Alexander is still delicate, but stable and showing continuous improvement. He's awake now. If you want, I can take you to him, but only for a few minutes."

"Yes, doctor," she said, excited.

"Just one thing, Mrs. Stern. Please don't be alarmed. He's covered with many bandages, and he is intubated. We had to do this earlier, but if everything goes well, we'll remove it soon."

Gabrielle felt anxious already, and she hadn't even seen him. She said nothing but nodded and followed the doctor.

She walked down the hall to Alexander's room. She was alarmed when she saw him, but the doctor's warning had prepared her. More than being shocked by the tube, she felt overwhelmed by all the medical equipment around him.

She stopped at the right side of his bed. She took his hand, and he opened his eyes slightly. When he saw her, a tear rolled down his face. Some tears fell from her face too. A nurse passed her a tissue, then Gabrielle wiped Alexander's eyes and both sides of his face.

"Alex, my love. You're going to get well."

He closed his eyes and opened them again. Then the doctor intervened. "Mrs. Stern, you may give him a kiss if you'd like."

She leaned over him and kissed his front head carefully. Then Dr. Franklin said, "We need to go now, Mrs. Stern."

"So soon, doctor?"

"Yes, hospital rules. Actually, I'm breaking them right now."

She turned to Alexander and gave him another kiss.

"Alex, we're all outside. Please get well. I love you so much. I'll see you soon."

She held his hand again, then stepped back and walked out of the ICU escorted by the nurse.

Her sister and Andrea rushed toward her, and she anticipated their questions.

"Look, he's tubed. We couldn't talk. But I was able to see him awake and he's conscious. Just that. It was very quick."

Andrea asked, "But how is he? What did the doctor say?"

"Not much. Alex is awake now and he recognized me, and that's a good sign. But we still need to wait."

***

On Friday morning, after his first round of checking on patients, Dr. Franklin came out to speak with Gabrielle. He showed her a discreet smile.

"Good morning, Mrs. Stern."

"Hi, doctor. How's Alexander today?"

"He's wearing a mask to give him oxygen. All his vital signs are better, and the blood tests that we received this morning are showing significant improvement."

"Thank God."

"He wants to see you, Mrs. Stern. He told the nurse that he would come out if you didn't come in. He's been pretty persistent, so I'll let you see him again, and please help me calm him down."

"Yes, doctor, I will," Gabrielle said, a smile on her face.

"I believe we may have some problems restraining him, but at least that means he's getting better."

When they arrived at Alexander's room, the doctor walked out and left Gabrielle with a nurse.

"Mrs. Stern, you can stay for five minutes. Please don't make him talk too much," the nurse said.

"Yes, thank you."

The nurse turned around to take notes while watching some monitors.

"Alex, the doctor says you're getting better."

He moved his head slightly forward.

"Thank God, Alex. We were terrified. But you're getting better."

He lifted his arm and moved the mask from his face with some effort.

"Love you. Andrea? Rachel?" he said quietly.

The nurse turned and said, "Please, Mr. Stern, don't remove your mask. Soon you will not have to use it. Please be patient."

"Andrea is in the waiting room," Gabrielle said. "Rachel doesn't know yet, just Matt and Paula. Your sister tried to reserve a flight, but they're all banned, even for these exceptional cases. Your mother doesn't know yet, too. We all agreed to tell them when you're able to speak with them. That will calm them down.

Alexander nodded and smiled at her.

"Do you want us to tell them?" she asked.

He shook his head, no.

"We better wait for you to talk to them, right?"

He nodded.

"OK. I'll talk to Matt and Paula later and tell them everything."

The doctor came in again and told her it was time to let Alexander rest. Another nurse was preparing to draw some blood for more tests. Gabrielle gave him another kiss and walked out. In the waiting room, she told everyone that Alexander looked better than the last time, but he seemed tired.

Gabrielle called Paula first, and then Matt. She asked them not to call her mother and Rachel yet; Alexander wanted to do it when he could talk with them. She told them that he was improving. At least he was until that moment.

CHAPTER 37

On Monday morning, Dr. Franklin permitted Alexander to be moved to his room, a suite on the fourth floor. He had improved the previous days steadily. He would be more comfortable there, which would be essential for his emotional condition.

He had already spoken to her mother and Rachel. They agreed to say he'd an accident, but everything was fine. Alexander talked to them every day and downgraded the event's seriousness. Later, he would tell them the truth.

At noon, Alexander was in his room. He still experienced some pain, but less due to the potent cocktail the nurses injected into him every day.

Gabrielle asked Andrea to bring some groceries such as bread, cheese, and juice from home after lunch.

When things were settled, Alexander made a video call with his mother and Rachel. This time they were able to see each other. He lay in bed, almost seated, and Gabrielle had fixed his hair. He was careful to show his face only, avoiding his immobilized left arm, hoping to transmit a degree of tranquility. So far, it had worked. He talked to Matt and Paula, too.

His colleagues wanted to see him, especially his new partners. Flowers and fruit baskets were delivered to his room. They served to decorate it nicely. Despite it being a lovely suite, it still was felt like a cold hospital room. Ryan dropped in that afternoon at Alexander's request. Gabrielle didn't want him to, but Alexander insisted. He wanted to find out about everything at Alliance. Since starting to work back there, he'd struggled to transform Alliance into a great company, and hated not receiving news about how it was moving forward.

His upper left side had been practically immobilized. The bullet had not affected any vital organs, especially his heart, but some muscles had been damaged. The best remedy was to avoid all movement for some weeks. The doctor explained to him in detail what the bullet had done and emphasized that a few inches lower would have been fatal. The other bullet also didn't affect any vital organ but had caused the internal bleeding that fortunately had been detected and controlled. All fragments were removed, despite the task had been for the surgeons.

Gabrielle sat on the couch beside Alexander's bed, resting her head back. He was checking his messages but wasn't able to do so efficiently with just one hand, despite using his right one. Twenty minutes later, he became desperate and put down the phone. Instead, he would call anyone he needed to speak to.

Colonel Robles stood outside the room. Gabrielle wanted to talk with Alexander about him, but she hadn't found the right moment. Now they were alone for some minutes, and she was not going to wait any longer to talk with him about what was deeply bothering her.

"Alex, I spoke last week with Colonel Robles. He told me all about what happened last Tuesday. Something is bothering me; I can't take it out of my mind. Why Colonel Robles walked out to the SUV instead of staying by your side? He told me you asked him to do it."

"That's right, Gabrielle. I asked him to get the SUV. He didn't want to, but I insisted; a stupid request is what I thought yesterday while reconstructing everything in my mind. But after thinking about it further, I came to another conclusion. If he'd been by my side, maybe both of us would be dead now."

"Why do you say that? If he'd been there, he would have been able to protect you."

"Fred walked to me deliberately to shoot me. When I looked at him, the gun was already in his hand, and he was pointing it at me. He was very close, just steps away. Colonel Robles wouldn't have been able to take out his gun before receiving one or two shots himself. And then I would have received more than the two bullets I was hit with, for sure."

"Okay. I hadn't thought it that way. It just seemed strange to me that he wasn't by your side, especially that day and precisely at that moment."

"At first, I thought just like you. I even thought that he could have been colluding with Fred, but then yesterday, with a fresh mind, I thought If he hadn't been where he was standing, he would haven't been able to shoot Fred, before him shooting me more. If everything had happened that way, I'm convinced I'd be dead."

"I think you may be right," Gabrielle said.

"And remember something else. I insisted Colonel Robles get the SUV, but he didn't want to leave me."

"You're right, Alex. I guess you were both fortunate that everything went the way it did."

"I'm sure, Gabrielle. I owe my life to him, and maybe to some good luck too."

Gabrielle felt better after their conversation. Then she recalled she and Colonel Robles hadn't finished their conversation. The nurse had called her when they were speaking the other day. Now, she had to talk to him.

Andrea arrived ten minutes later with the groceries. After putting some in the minibar and some on the small table in the annex, she went inside the room to talk with Alexander. She kissed him and sat on the couch where Gabrielle was seated and started talking.

Gabrielle told them she would come back in a minute. She left the room and called Colonel Robles into the annex. She invited him to sit, but he preferred not to.

"Colonel, we didn't finish our conversation the other day. Sorry, I just remembered it."

"No problem, Mrs. Stern."

"I just wanted to thank you, Colonel. You're the main reason Alexander is alive today. We owe his life to you."

"Mrs. Stern, you owe me nothing. I feel ashamed about what occurred last week. It shouldn't be like that. I shouldn't have left him alone. Mr. Stern insisted I get the vehicle, but I should have stayed with him."

"I'm sure that saved you both, Colonel. Think about it. I hate that this happened, but now I'm sure things went like this for a reason. If you hadn't been standing by the SUV, both of you would be dead now."

"Maybe you're right, Mrs. Stern."

"I'm sure of it, Colonel. Thank you so much." She hugged him when she heard Alexander calling her.

"Excuse me, Colonel."

She turned and walked to Alexander's bed.

That afternoon, another bouquet was delivered. Alexander hadn't seen the cards that had come with each one. He was curious about who had sent them all. He asked Gabrielle for each basket card. She didn't know who had sent the last one. When Alexander saw it, the handwriting looked familiar. He read it silently.

Alex, we hate to hear what happened. We wish you a speedy and full recovery. Anything you need, just let us know. We'll see you very soon. Take care.

BC-CM-AB

He knew exactly who was sending it. He told Gabrielle it was from their US shareholders.

"Why they didn't write their full names, Alex?"

"You know how these guys are or everything related to discretion. They're rather special, mainly the Senator."

Some friends and relatives visited Alexander that Monday. Only a quick stop to check on him; everybody knew it was his first day after being at the ICU for almost a week. And as the doctor had recommended, he had to rest as much as possible, except for some short walks in the room and later on through the hall. Additionally, he wanted to limit visits due to COVID-19. Getting infected just after the surgery would be extremely risky for him.

Ryan arrived at four. He had just half an hour to brief Alexander on Alliance. Everything seemed to be moving well. All the funds were growing. Alexander was mainly concerned about the wealthier clients, but he explained what he had done to manage it. He was glad about all the actions taken. Alexander thanked him especially for his dedication and commitment in the previous days and weeks.

William arrived at the hospital as Ryan was leaving. He had only five minutes before leaving for home, and assured Alexander he would be there to support him whenever necessary. He offered to stay on as a board member for the next two months until Alexander had fully recovered and was back at Alliance.

"Perfect, William, thank you. Maybe after those two months I can convince you to stay permanently."

They laughed, but William already had plans in the future that Alexander would have to accept.

Gabrielle stayed with him that night. They watched TV together for an hour, and then he slept. He woke up around ten, and after a short conversation, they sleep until early the next day.

The other driver arrived to guard all night, until Colonel Robles came the next morning back. Everyone was optimistic about his recovery and Alexander hoped to go home as soon as possible.

CHAPTER 38

Alliance was doing great. Alexander was entirely in charge again but working from home. That Wednesday, he had already conducted three conference calls online.

Four weeks had passed since his encounter with Fred Shultz and death. Thankfully, it was Fred's death and not his own. At least I just had to use this walking cane temporarily, he thought, while remembering that day.

The Adagio project was advancing slowly. Mr. Ramos had been extremely cooperative, and now that Alexander was getting involved again things had started to gain some traction, at least the tasks that could be done with COVID-19 restrictions and with many government institutions not working as usual.

The lockdown had been extended. George and Axel finally agreed with the new plan, which had been postponed for some weeks, but they were willing to support Alexander in their new business entrepreneurship.

Gabrielle paused her business activities that day to prepare lunch. Alexander looked forward to eating the great tomato soup she'd cooked for him. It was one of his preferred choices, of many old and new ones she had integrated into her menu.

After eating lunch in the kitchen, Alexander went slowly to the studio. He moved faster every day, but his left arm was still immobilized until he recovered completely.

"Alex, do you want some coffee now or later?" Gabrielle asked when he was halfway to the studio.

"Later, thanks."

Once he sat down at his desk, he opened the first drawer on the right side. Some papers were still waiting to be archived, digitalized, or thrown into the garbage. He saw and organized the cards from the hospital. Then the envelopes were almost all thrown away immediately, mainly invitations.

He saw the handwritten card from Antonio with the Senator's message and the threat left on his SUV. When he saw both, he noticed some similarities in the handwriting. Suddenly, he was distracted by the intercom. Someone in the lobby was calling his apartment. He heard Gabrielle answering it, then she shouted.

"Alex, are you waiting for someone?"

"No. Who is it?"

Gabrielle didn't answer. She appeared at the studio, surprised.

"Alex, I'm not sure, but apparently, the three US shareholders of Alliance are down in the lobby."

"What? They can't be. Are you sure?"

"That's what the guard said."

At the same time, Alexander's phone received a text message from the Senator.

"My boy, please call down the lobby. Allow us to go up to your apartment."

"It's the Senator, Gabrielle. What is he doing here? Please call the lobby and ask the guard to let them come up."

"OK."

Alexander texted back to the Senator, "Yes, Sir. Right away, I'm calling now."

Gabrielle returned to the studio. They were surprised.

"Where do you want to receive them, Alex?"

"Here in the studio, I guess."

Alexander waited for them at the main door. A minute later, they stepped out of the elevator. The first to appear was someone he didn't know; he seemed to be a security guard. After him, Senator Brian Cox, Christopher Mattis, and Adam Branning came out.

"Gentlemen, what a surprise," Alexander said.

"I hope it's a nice one, my boy. May we come in?" the Senator asked.

"Yes, please."

After shaking hands with all, he closed the door.

"Gentlemen, please pass to the studio," Alexander said, pointing to it with his walking cane.

Alexander invited them to sit on the couches, and then he sat on a leather chair.

"This is a nice surprise," Alexander said again. "How did you get here? There's a ban on flights from everywhere right now."

"Oh, yes, my boy," the Senator said. "That was a challenge, but our friend Antonio helped with that and Chris with the jet. My boy, we just came to see you for a few minutes. We're on our way to another country, but Christopher recommended we visit you."

"Alex," Christopher said. "About what happened with the banker a month ago, we feel rather guilty. We just wanted to help."

"Don't be. It wasn't your fault. This guy was sick."

"We hope you're feeling better now. I'm glad you came out of this difficult situation much better than Fred Shultz."

"I did. Thanks, Christopher. I'm feeling much better now too. Sorry, gentlemen, would you like something to drink?"

"No, thank you, Alex. We need to hurry. The jet is waiting for us. We need to be there soon," Adam said.

"The next time you come, do so with more time."

"Sure, my boy. We'll do that," the Senator said.

They stood up and walked out of the studio to the door. After they'd shaken hands, Adam opened the door. The security guard called for the elevator and it opened immediately. They walked in, and the Senator remembered something.

"Uh, my boy. Did you receive our flowers? I asked Antonio to write a message from us on the card."

"Yes, Sir, thank you."

"See you soon, my boy. Bye."
"Bye, gentlemen."

After Alexander closed the door, he instantly recalled the card and was shocked.

What? It couldn't be true. It couldn't be the same, he thought. He closed the door and came back to the studio. He picked up the threat note, the business card Antonio had given him at the airport, and the card from the flowers delivered at the hospital. He lined them up in front of him.

It couldn't be. Was this possible? They all seemed to be written by the same person.

EXCERPT FROM BLOODY GROWTH, CHAPTER 1

It was time to evolve. Alexander's business was outperforming, but he had to prepare for the next stage. He knew from all his life experiences that he had to. The north breeze pushing his yacht and his crew at some point either had to ease or halt. They had to find a new awe-inspiring wave to ride, and sustainable energy was the one with enough power to lift them to levels they expected until many years ahead. Notwithstanding the personal risks that would come with it, for his business, and his life.

It was the right initiative in all aspects. New technologies were getting cheaper and more accessible. And fuel costs were increasing again. Everyone was investing in the clean energy sector or hoping to. Brands were benefiting from it; good public relations were always productive for those betting on them. Besides any favorable factor, he was driven by the idea of changing the world for the better, and financing these types of projects was his way to contribute.

Alexander Stern spent countless hours in the last four months researching solar panels and batteries, wind turbines, biomass burning, tidal and hydro energy, electric vehicles, and other information on the topic. But of them all, solar and Eolic solutions grabbed his interest the most.

...

ABOUT THE AUTHOR

Vincent J. Wallace has lived in Mexico, the United States, and the Dominican Republic, and has visited many cities around the world. This international background and his 27-year career in the financial sector have given him many experiences that will become material for financial-crime thrillers ... because some stories, including ones about criminals, have to be told!

Vincent started writing many years ago, but it wasn't until 2020 that he decided to take his hobby to the next level. Now he alternates his role as an active securities market executive with his new career as a writer of novels. He is an Associate Member of the International Thriller Writers organization.

Deadly Wealth is his first novel in the Alexander Stern series. He is busy writing a sequel, titled Bloody Growth.

Follow him and join his email list and social media links at:

www.vincentjwallace.com

Your review of this book is kindly appreciated:

https://www.amazon.com/dp/B08WJTZD46

https://www.goodreads.com/book/photo/57062579-deadly-wealth

Printed in Great Britain
by Amazon